FATAL, FAMILY, ALBUM

BOOK #13 IN THE KIKI LOWENSTEIN MYSTERY SERIES

JOANNA CAMPBELL SLAN

spot on publishing

OUR FREE GIFT FOR YOU

Kiki and I have a Free Bonus Gift for you. It's a digital book with craft ideas and recipes. Just go to https://dl.bookfunnel.com/fsu24mc5qi

All best from your friend,

Joanna

THE KIKI LOWENSTEIN MYSTERY SERIES

BY JOANNA CAMPBELL SLAN

Every scrapbook tells a story. Memories of friends, family and ... murder? You'll want to read the Kiki Lowenstein books in order:

*Claim your copy of *Bad, Memory, Album* by going to: https://dl.bookfunnel.com/jwu6iipeɪg.

PROLOGUE

The death of any member diminishes an entire community. But the death of a woman like Nancy Owens causes a collective gasp of surprise.

Nancy was not the type of woman you'd expect to die in a random shooting. She was white, upper-middle class, plump, and wholesome. A stepmother and wife in her forties, Nancy had never been a leader, always a follower, except when it came to her love for her Hungarian heritage. There were rumors that she was the one who encouraged the mayor of St. Louis to connect with his Hungarian counterpart, so that our town and Budapest could become Sister Cities. Beyond that, Nancy never distinguished herself, although many considered her the ultimate volunteer. A real worker bee. She had been involved in the Young Women Leaders, Zoo Keepers, and the vestry at St. John's Catholic Church. In photos, her face could barely be picked out in the back row.

Surely you know someone like Nancy. She's the person who tries to bow out of the group photo, forcing someone to search for her and making everyone wait until she's found. She's the type who insists in standing where no one can see her. Nancy was colorless, odorless, and easy to forget. She had no kids from her first marriage. The divorce from husband #1 seemed amicable. No one was surprised to hear her husband had gotten bored with her. Most people doubted she would ever marry again. When Bert Owens asked her to be his wife, people asked each other, "I wonder what he sees in her?" After all, Bert was an attractive guy and a successful businessman, whereas Nancy Pirva Smith was a wee bit on the dumpy side and without any particular accomplishments to her credit.

Although Nancy had shopped at my store. I didn't know her as well as I knew most of my customers. I'd been nice to her, of course, because I make it a point to be nice to everyone. We did have one brief moment when we connected. We'd attended a lecture on blended families. After the presentation, Nancy and I bumped into each other. We got to talking, and she asked if I had time for a coffee. Sensing she needed a friend, I made the time. I'd been right: she needed a shoulder to cry on. I heard all about the problems she was having with her stepdaughter.

After we parted, as I was driving home, I counted my lucky stars that my second marriage hadn't turned out like Nancy's. My little blended family was doing just fine, whereas hers sounded like one of the levels of hell.

So when I heard that Nancy Owens had been murdered—shot in the head—while sitting in her car in a parking lot in Ferguson, I thought there'd been some mistake.

"She was shot? You're sure?" I challenged Clancy Whitehead, my good friend and co-worker. "We're talking about the same Nancy Owens? The Nancy Owens who occasionally shopped here? You're positive that's the same person they found shot to death in Ferguson?"

"Yes, indeed." Clancy nodded, causing her auburn pageboy to swing along her jawline. "It's all over the news. I even turned on my computer and caught it on the news feed."

"Wow. Shot in the head?" I was so shocked that I dropped my mechanical pencil. Okay, maybe it was just being a klutz, or maybe I was simply beat. I'd been doing paperwork all morning, trying to finish up for our end-of-the-year accounting. This is the one part of running a business that I hated.

"Shot in the head." Clancy retrieved my pencil from the floor. She's been worried about me returning to work so quickly after the birth of my son, so she's taken to babying me. I kind of like it. It's nice to be taken care of once in a while.

Handing me the pencil, Clancy continued, "Can you believe it? They are saying that Nancy was sitting in her white Mercedes in a parking space in front of a strip center. Minding her own business. Engine running. Some creep walked up, poked the muzzle of a gun through the open window, and shot her in the head. For no apparent reason!"

"The window was rolled down? You have to be kidding. Who drives to Ferguson and sits in a parking space with her window down when it's ten degrees outside?"

"Apparently, the answer to that question is...ding, ding, ding...Nancy Owens." Clancy's arched eyebrow added a touch of sarcasm that wasn't lost on me.

"Was it a robbery?"

"Not so far as anyone knows. The creep didn't even take the car—and get this—the doors were unlocked."

"I don't mean to sound cruel, but that's just plain dumb on Nancy's part."

Clancy sank into the chair across from mine. Propping her chin on her hand, she sighed. "We all do dumb things from time to time, but I have to agree with you. It does sound really, really stupid. There must be more to the story."

And, of course, there *was* more to the story. Soon enough I found myself smack dab in the middle of it.

1

The day before Nancy Owens died

"I CAN NEVER THANK YOU ENOUGH." Over the phone, Bonnie Gossage's voice was husky with emotion. "I wouldn't have gotten my son back if it hadn't been for you, Kiki. Thank you, thank you, thank you."

"You're holding him now?"

"Yes. The pediatrician just left. He says my baby's fine but a little dehydrated. He lost an ounce or two. They're going to give him intravenous fluids. They wanted to keep him overnight, but as you can imagine—"

"That was a non-starter." I chuckled. Bonnie's infant son had been stolen from the maternity ward of Southeast Hospital. Not surprisingly, Bonnie was so upset and grief-stricken that she totally shut down. The authorities couldn't get any details from her. Because Bonnie and I are friends, I was tasked with getting Bonnie to talk. I was successful. Armed with that information and my own observations, I poked around a bit. One thing led to another, and then I had a hunch that proved correct. Two hours ago, my husband, Detective Chad Detweiler, and his partner, Detective Stan Hadcho, arrested the abductor and recovered Bonnie's little boy.

With that assurance from Bonnie that all was well, I ended the call. My husband, Hadcho, and my friend Clancy Whitehead were all beaming with happiness as we sat around my kitchen table. We knew what a near miss we'd witnessed.

"This could have gone really, really wrong." Hadcho shook his head, changing it to a nod of thanks as Brawny, our nanny, poured him a fresh cup of coffee. "What if our kidnapper had panicked? That whack-job could have decided to dump the kid. What if she had left the baby on a doorstep? In these subzero temperatures, that poor newborn wouldn't have stood a chance at surviving."

"But the abductor didn't panic, she didn't know we were on to her, and Baby Gossage is fine." My husband leaned forward in his chair and put a reassuring arm around my shoulders. "Thanks to Kiki."

"Thanks to Kiki." Hadcho raised his mug of coffee to me. Clancy did the same. Detweiler pulled me closer so he could plant a kiss on my lips. I loved the affection and the accolades, but I couldn't shake my misgivings.

"You don't look happy." Clancy observed. She knows me too well. Now that the child was back in his mother's arms, I should have been relaxed, but a bone-deep fear had crept into my body. All children are vulnerable, in one way or another. You can *never* let down your guard. Oddly enough, once you have a child, you're immediately scared for your *own* life, because you realize how dependent that baby is on you. The plight of Bonnie's kidnapped infant had cranked up the volume on my natural fears...big time. All my nerves were raw as a peeled onion.

"This whole thing has been too close for comfort." My eyes filled with tears. "It could have been Ty. My son. My baby."

"But it wasn't." Detweiler grabbed my shoulders and turned me a quarter-turn to the right. He let go of me to point at a sweet bundle in a portable crib. "See? Look at him. Sound asleep. That's our son, and he's fine."

"Yes." I got up and walked over to the portable crib. Gracie, our harlequin Great Dane, was sleeping next to it. Instinctively she knew she needed to guard the youngest member of our family. She raised her blocky head to stare at me and cocked one of her uncropped ears in a way that suggested, "Should I be worried?" "It's all right, girl," I assured her, reaching down to stroke her silky muzzle. Even as I said the words, I was struck by how fragile my son was. I stood there, mesmerized, watching the soft spot in my baby's skull pulsate with each beat of his heart.

Detweiler came over to stand beside me. "Come on, sweetie. Let it go. You need to relax, Kiki." This time when he pulled me close, I rested my face against his chest, as I so often did. I willed myself to release the tension inside. I focused on the comfort my husband offered. How did that blessing for newlyweds go? *May your joys be multiplied and your sorrows divided.*

Detweiler gave me one last squeeze and returned to his chair. As the lingering warm of his touch faded, I lectured myself: He's right. We are celebrating tonight. All's well that ends well. All three of my children are safe and sound, under our roof, with two parents who love them. We're surrounded by friends. I couldn't possibly want or need anything more.

The buzzer on the oven startled me. Bronwyn "Brawny" Macavity, our Scottish nanny, had been in the family room, checking on our older two children as they watched *Frozen*. Now she bustled into the kitchen. When she opened the door to the oven, a heavenly fragrance filled the air. Wrinkling my nose, I picked out the individual scents: cinnamon, sugar, vanilla, butter, and a hint of nutmeg.

"What did you bake for me, Brawny?" Stan Hadcho hopped out of his chair and went over to supervise. Ever since he realized what a good cook Brawny is, Hadcho has become a fixture at our house. He's especially likely to show up at mealtimes.

"Yer getting skelped if you don't keep your hands off those cookies. Let them cool. Aye, and there's spice bread, too. Go sit down like a good laddie." She muscled Hadcho aside as she expertly balanced the hot baking pan on top of four cans of soup. The air flowing underneath would help the cookies cool.

"That spice bread needs more time. I can tell by looking at it. Who wants a cup of mulled cider?" Brawny slipped by Hadcho to reach into the refrigerator. After a chorus, of, "Yes, please," she poured the golden apple cider into a pot and added an apple studded with cloves. Next she tossed a pinch of spices into the mix.

"Cinnamon? Nutmeg?" I asked, following my nose.

"Aye. Perfect for the season, don't you think? In a tick, we'll have spice bread, mulled cider, snickerdoodles, and a batch of shortbread cookies I made yesterday."

"Any lemon curd?" Detweiler asked hopefully.

"Of course we have lemon curd. What would ye have me for? A heathen?" Brawny fisted her hands on her hips. Typically she wears a tartan skirt or black slacks with a starched white blouse. Today, she was dressed very casually in a pair of jeans and a sweatshirt from Washington University, a local college. In the seven months that she's been with us, she's slowly adapting to life in the heartland. For the most part, Midwesterners don't stand on formality, although areas of St. Louis could rival Boston with its preppy culture.

"Lemon curd, spice bread, cider? Good deal." Hadcho rubbed his hands together as he returned to his seat. "Sounds like enough to keep me going until dinner. What are we having?"

"Make yourself at home, Stan," Detweiler teased his friend.

"I intend to. How about if the four of us review everything we know about the abduction? I've got a Steno pad in my pocket. After dinner, I can go back to the police station and write up the report in a jiffy. I don't know about you, Detweiler, but I hate working in those stupid cubicles. I bet the ladies don't want to make a trip to downtown Clayton just to give their statements either."

"Agreed," Clancy said. I nodded, and Detweiler gave his friend a thumbs-up.

"We're having beef stew," Brawny said, stirring the cider. "With green beans almondine, crusty bread, and a garden salad."

"Count me in." Hadcho rubbed his hands together with glee.

The buzzer sounded a second time. The warm snickerdoodles were plated and set in the middle of the table. Each of us grabbed a small dish, a napkin, and a cookie. We'd just started work on the report when the doorbell rang insistently.

"I'll get it," thirteen-year-old Anya called out from the family room. She and five-year-old Erik were singing *Frozen's* theme song "Let It Go," a tune oddly incongruous given the news that Gossage baby's kidnapper would surely face a long stint behind bars.

Anya's soft-soled UGGS slapped their way to the foyer.

"Anya? You know the rules," Detweiler called out as he hopped up from the table. As Detweiler left the kitchen, Gracie got to her feet and trotted along behind him. Gracie rarely barks, as she relies on her size for intimidation. That usually works just fine.

"Anya, you know better," Detweiler warned, and his voice

drifted back to us. "You cannot open the door by yourself. It's not safe. We'll talk about this later."

Having a cop in the family is a constant reminder that bad things happen to good people, and life isn't fair. A little caution goes a long way toward crime prevention. Even so, I could imagine the pout on Anya's face.

A creaking of hinges and a rush of cold air suggested Detweiler had invited our guests into our home. A hushed murmur of men's voices could be heard, but I couldn't make out any specifics. We live in a house that was constructed more than 100 years ago. The wood for its frame was chosen piece by piece. The walls are thick and sturdy. I love this place with all my heart, and I feel safe here.

Brawny poured hot cider into our mugs and set a plate of sliced spice bread in the center of the table. She took shortbread cookies from a plastic container on the counter and put them in a tea towel-lined basket for us. Next to the cookies, she set a small jelly jar of lemon curd and a knife for spreading the tangy confection.

The murmur of men's voices in the foyer grew louder and louder.

"I bet that's the Center for Missing and Exploited Children's task force following up." Hadcho grabbed a slice of spice bread and went back to writing in his notepad.

"Could be a reporter who heard how you tracked down the kidnapper, Kiki. It's not every day that a craft store owner doubles as a successful crime-stopper." Clancy was teasing me. Her lipstick left a crimson kiss on her mug rim.

"Hmm. Right. Ha, ha." I bit into a shortbread cookie that I'd slathered with lemon curd.

Detweiler came back into the kitchen. The expression on his face was unreadable, the sort of blank mask he wears when he doesn't want to give his thoughts away. Behind him were two men in identical khaki trench coats. Their military bearing and short-cropped hair screamed law enforcement. The man in the front opened a leather wallet and flashed an FBI badge toward Hadcho, Clancy, and me. "I'm Special Agent in Charge Bret Sanders. This is Special Agent Phillip Montana. We're here to speak to Bruce Macavity."

"Bruce Macavity?" I repeated his request and glanced over at my husband. He was leaning against the doorjamb. Detweiler's strange expression confused me further. Why wasn't he correcting the agents?

"You must be misinformed," I went on to say. I pointed at Brawny. "This is our nanny, Bronwyn Macavity. Maybe she can help you find the person you're looking for."

Brawny stepped forward to face Agents Sanders and Montana. Squaring her shoulders, she wore a look I'd never seen before. It was as if she were being strangled by an invisible hand. Her voice trembled as she said, "I am—I was—Bruce Macavity."

2

"Corporal Bruce Macavity, we need to speak to you in private." Agent Sanders didn't ask; he demanded.

"Immediately," Agent Phillips added his two cents. Clearly, he was the second-in-command, and a real wannabe.

"We can use my office." Detweiler tilted his head toward the hallway.

"Sounds like a cue for me to leave." Clancy's eyes were huge, crowding her eyebrows off her forehead. "Thanks for everything. Kiki? My coat?"

"It's in the foyer closet." I waited for her to collect her purse and led the way.

"What in the world?" she whispered in my ear. I grabbed her coat from the hangers, positioning myself half-in and half-out of the closet proper.

"I have no idea!"

We stared at each other.

"You aren't keeping anything from me, are you?"

"Don't be silly. You're my closest friend. I'm telling you this is a shock to me, too."

"Did we hear it right? Brawny is, was, is, might have been...Bruce?"

"How should I know? Maybe it's a Scottish thing. Like here where girls get a family surname for a first name."

"Maybe."

Holding the jacket up for her, I watched as she wiggled into it. She whispered, "I'll expect a full report tomorrow at work, okay?"

"Of course."

I walked my friend to the front door, gave her a hug, told her to drive safely, and locked up behind her.

Muffled voices came from Detweiler's office. I tiptoed down the hall and closer to the door so I could eavesdrop. The "office" is actually a space intended as a formal living room. After moving in, we decided there was no reason to invest in fancy furnishings only to spend the next twenty years yelling at the kids to keep off of it. For the most part, our family liked to camp out in the family room and snuggle on its well-worn furniture. The pieces in that room were mismatched, so I redecorated them with cheap navy slipcovers and washable throw pillows. Lord above knew how often everything got washed. In fact, I'd finally invested in a second set of slipcovers because one was always in the dryer.

Of course originally, the formal living room was entered by walking through an open archway. That meant there'd been no privacy at all for anyone trying to get work done. One Saturday shortly after we moved in, Detweiler and his dad built out the wall and added a door that could be locked, giving Detweiler a real office. Thanks to this ingenuity, he could review files pertaining to investigations without fear of prying eyes. Later we added a combination safe and a gun safe.

All of us played a part in transforming the space into a cozy office. One Sunday, Detweiler and Anya put together a trio of cheap-o shelves from Target, and these lined the west wall.

"Power tools are so cool." Anya held up the electric drill for my inspection. Although I wonder whether it was really the drill or the fact she was bonding with Detweiler, doing a project that the two could stand back and admire.

Smack-dab in the center of the room an old desk floated like a proud island, anchored in place by a second-hand Oriental rug I'd picked up at a garage sale for $30. The office chair was a cast-off I'd found in a Goodwill store. Directly across from the bookshelves on the east side of the room were two leather club chairs we'd inherited from Leighton Haversham, our former landlord. Leighton had been the previous owner of this, his family home, and he had graciously left the club chairs behind for us to enjoy. Those seats flanked a short wooden file cabinet, a real treasure because the drawers could be locked with a key.

Even Erik got in on the action. Brawny helped him take photos of the Missouri landscape. These she developed and framed. They took pride of place on the wall.

Now all those efforts annoyed me, because it made the room a perfect place for a confab. From my place in the hall, I could hear the intensity of the discussion. I resisted the urge to press my ear against Detweiler's door only because I feared getting caught. If I stayed where I was, I could easily pretend I'd just come from the kitchen, the hall, or the family room. But as it stood, I wasn't close enough to hear the voices distinctly. Too bad you can't hit the "CC" or the "Closed Caption" option in real life!

I shook my head in confusion. Had Brawny lied about her gender so she could enter the British military service? If so, how had she pulled it off? Did she have a twin brother? Had they manufactured a switcheroo? Was her first name really Bruce? Was it a Scottish thing as Clancy had suggested? I mean, hello?

Clancy's real first name was Druscilla. Maybe Brawny's real first name was Bruce.

Then came a truly unsettling thought...was it possible Brawny wasn't really a girl? That she was a he? Or even more unlikely, was Brawny transgender like Caitlyn Jenner?

Nah. That was totally improbable. Impossible! She would have told us. *Wouldn't she?*

Brawny's former employer Lorraine Lauber would have told us. Surely she would have! Lorraine inherited Brawny after her brother, Van, died. Van had been Erik's stepfather. He'd been the one to originally hire Brawny.

Surely if something was amiss, Van would have told Lorraine, and she would have told us. Surely.

On the other hand, Lorraine had represented Erik as Detweiler's biological son, and he wasn't. Lorraine had also tricked Detweiler into bringing Brawny and Erik home with him from California. So, Lorraine was not above pulling a fast one when it suited her.

But did it follow that she lied to us about Brawny? Maybe lie was too strong of a word. Had Lorraine simply omitted this key detail of Brawny's past?

Was Brawny a complete sham? A totally fictitious human being? Was she even really a Scot? What exactly did we know about her for certain? We'd been told she was an accredited nanny, a graduate of a prestigious college for nannies, and a former member of the SAS, an elite military group. We knew—or rather thought—that she'd been born in Scotland. My head was spinning. It seemed like the universe was conspiring to make me crazier than a loon. First there was a baby's abduction and now this. I stood pressed against the wall at the end of the hall. My eyes never left Detweiler's office door. By golly, as long as it took, I was going to wait for him to come out. Hurry up,

Detweiler, I chided him mentally. What in the world is going on, buddy?

Hadcho must have been thinking the same thoughts. I'd totally forgotten about him after I got up to see Clancy to the door. Now he took a spot next to me at the end of the hall. The two of us stared wistfully at Detweiler's office door.

"What gives? Is Brawny really a guy?"

Although he'd spoken softly, his timing was unfortunate. Right around the corner came my daughter, Anya. She had been lured to the kitchen by the smell of food. But as I watched, she froze in place.

"Oh, no," I groaned.

Kids have this uncanny ability to ignore you when you want their attention, and to hear you very, very clearly when you'd rather they didn't. I could tell by the expression on Anya's face that she'd overheard what Hadcho had said. Every. Stinking. Word.

She went absolutely rigid. Then a slow red stain crept up her neck. That color change was the prelude to an explosion. I grabbed Anya by the elbow to hustle her into the kitchen. Fortunately, she was in such shock that she came along quietly.

I guided her into one of the kitchen chairs. "Shhh." I put a finger to my lips.

"Shhh? That's all you have to say? Shhh? Hadcho says Brawny is a guy and you want me to shush? Is it true? Is she? A he? A drag queen or whatever? Did you know that? Mom? Did you?" She spoke so fast and so angrily that I was left sputtering.

"Honey, I'm as surprised as you are. I don't know anything about Brawny for sure."

"But I heard what those men were saying. They called somebody Bruce, and then Brawny started talking. I know her voice, Mom. There's her accent, too. So Brawny is really a man?"

"I have no idea. I'll admit I was eavesdropping, too. How did you hear them?"

She rolled her eyes and threw up her hands in a "duh" sort of way. "Their voices came through the air vents."

"You can hear everything that happens in Detweiler's office?"

"Of course, I can. Geez. You didn't know that?"

I shook my head and blushed, remembering some racy fun I'd had with my husband and—

Anya interrupted. "Brawny's name used to be Bruce, and she was a he when she was in the service."

"Oh." I was dumbfounded. "That's news to me."

I felt like a total fool. Anya knew as much about our nanny as I did, and I was the adult in the room. I thought about chastising her for eavesdropping, but honestly, didn't we have a bigger problem here? Yes, we did. Who was that person who'd been living under our roof? The person I'd trusted with my children?

I could not go there. "Maybe you misunderstood. Maybe I did, too. Sweetie, let's not jump to conclusions. I'm sure there's some reasonable explanation."

"Are you nuts? Totally stupid?"

"Anya, keep a civil tongue in your head." I itched to reach out and shake her, but I'd never do something so violent.

"Right, I need to watch my attitude because, hey, Brawny is a man. News flash, my smart tongue is the least of your problems. We've been living with a guy, pretending to be a girl. She must be one of those people who dresses like the opposite sex just to fool people."

"We don't know—" I steered Anya into the kitchen.

"You don't know what? Who she is? What she is? Geez Louise, Mom. Your job is to protect me. All day long, you and Detweiler harp on being careful and staying safe. Then what, huh? You two bring into our house a man who's pretending to be a woman? Good job, Mom. Do you know how many times I've undressed in front of her? Him? How perverted is that? It's sick. That's what it is. Sick! Embarrassing and awful and..." Rather than continue, she burst into tears.

Before I could collect myself, she threw her arms around my neck and wailed loudly. "M-m-mom. I trusted her. I shared my secrets. Stuff like you only tell your diary. Personal girls-only stuff. And she listened and she never stopped me. She musta had a fun time, laughing inside. How disgusting it that?"

"Sh." I stroked her hair, looking over her shoulder at Hadcho, who had walked up behind my daughter. He was shaking his head in disgust. That jet-black hair of his, a link to his Native American heritage, was hanging down on his brow, a sign he was upset, too. Hadcho is a sort of poster boy for good grooming. His haircuts cost more than one week's groceries.

"Look, Anya, honey, calm down," I said. "We'll get to the bottom of this. We need more information, sweetie, and—

"Waaaahhhhhhh."

My sleeping baby was awake, alert, alive, and hungry.

"The call of the wild." Hadcho grinned.

Anya was still hanging around my neck like a noose.

"Mama Kiki? Where is Daddy? Where is Brawny? Can I have a cookie? I am hungry." Erik galloped in, looking adorable in a pair of pajamas printed with happy cowboys riding ponies. "That baby is crying."

Erik had a habit of calling Ty "that baby." He'd regressed a bit since Ty's birth. Clancy told me that all of this was normal.

Normal? Considering the conversation about my nanny, life seemed anything but normal.

"Yes, honey, I know Ty is crying."

"I smell cookies. Who had cookies? I want cookies." Erik pushed past me and climbed onto a chair. Before I could stop him, he had cookies in both hands.

Anya pushed me away. She threw her arms wide in a gesture of capitulation. "It's always something these days. The baby. Erik. Detweiler. The store. I miss the old days when it was just you and me."

With that, she flounced up the stairs. To her retreating back, I said, "Sometimes, I do too."

"You take care of the baby, and I'll tackle the Cookie Monster," Hadcho said, as he scooped Erik up. "Come here, little rascal."

"Thanks. You might see if the stew is ready. Bribe him with cookies as a chaser."

"Will do." For a single guy, Hacho's pretty good with my kids. Of course, he's not much use when Ty needs to nurse. Then nobody but Mom or her milk will do. I picked up my infant son and cradled him in one arm. Ty's eager lips puckered and searched for his dinner. "Hang on there, partner. Let me disrobe. Otherwise, you'll get a mouth full of cotton." But all the drama had done a number on me. I couldn't get my fingers to cooperate. My free hand fumbled with buttons on my blouse.

Ty made no secret of his frustration. He pulled a face and let out a healthy, "Waaaaahhhha!"

He was seriously ticked off.

Frankly, I wanted to cry like a baby myself.

3

After I buttoned myself back up, I burped Ty. Then I checked and discovered that his diaper was soaked. Although I wasn't supposed to carry him up the stairs, I did it anyway. While I was changing the baby, Erik shyly joined us.

"Did Uncle Hadcho get you some dinner?"

Erik nodded. "Stew and cookies."

Now that Ty had a full tummy and a clean diaper, he was having trouble keeping his eyes open. I sank down in the rocking chair. Erik came over and stood at my elbow, staring down at his brother.

"Why don't you get a book, sweetie, and I'll read it to you and Ty?"

His choice was *Lyle the Crocodile*, a story I can recite by heart. I shifted Ty around so that Erik could climb up on my lap. With one boy cradled in the crook of my arm and the other leaning against me, I read the silly story of a crocodile. Erik turned book pages for me.

By the time we got to "The End," Ty was sound asleep.

"Erik, sweetie, are you ready for your bath? How about if you take it in Ty's bathroom? Let me go put Ty in his crib."

"Where's Brawny?" Erik asked. She usually gave him his bath.

"She's talking to a couple of guests." I tried to sound nonchalant. "Would you like to play with Ty's rubber ducks? I don't think he'll mind. He's too little to use them yet."

This entailed a thorough discussion of whether ducks were faster than boats or not, with Erik pretty certain that since this particular yellow duck was bigger than his red boat, the duck could go faster. When I went to lift Erik out, he clung to me like a monkey. I was woefully unprepared for him to press his wet self against my dry surface. By the time I got him dried and dressed for bed, I was soaked, shivering, and tired.

Erik took advantage of the fact the household was in an uproar by asking me to rub his back. Luckily for me, he could only keep his eyes open for five minutes. Usually, I love spending time with the little guys, because their needs are so simple and straightforward.

Tonight, I was torn because I wanted to know what was going on with Brawny. That push-pull from trying to balance my needs took a lot of energy. After leaving Erik's room, I checked in on Ty again. He was fine. From there, I went to Anya's room. I had hoped to talk with her a little more, but her light was out and her bedroom door was locked.

Defeated, I went back downstairs only to find that Hadcho had left for the evening. Before going, he'd put all the dishes in the dishwasher and cleared the table. He'd scribbled THANKS! on the wipe board we keep in the kitchen. While I appreciated his thoughtfulness and good manners, I gnashed my teeth because I hadn't gotten the chance to ask him what he'd overheard. If he'd overheard anything. Gracie paced the hallway outside Detweiler's office and whimpered. She, too, knew things were in turmoil. Or maybe she wanted to know what the scoop was on Brawny. Who could say?

My default move in times of trouble is to bake a pan of brownies. I don't care how much shortbread and spice bread we have in the house. When tough times hit, a person needs a good dose of chocolate to survive, and I desperately needed a chocolate fix right now.

We only had one box of the mix left, but one box was enough to keep me busy. In short order, I mixed the ingredients and popped a pan into the oven. I was standing there, staring at the mostly empty bowl, and debating how far to stick my head inside so I could better lick the leftover batter, when I heard the door to Detweiler's office open. Low voices continued in the hallway. A metallic click of the deadbolt and yet another blast of frigid air suggested the front door had been opened. The tone of the voices had changed, and although the words were muffled, it was clear from the texture that everyone was saying goodbye.

Seconds later, Detweiler and Brawny joined me in the kitchen. She looked like ten miles of bad road, and Detweiler didn't look much better. As a matter of self-preservation, I kept a firm grip on the mixing bowl. With a spatula from the utensil drawer, I quickly cleaned up the last gooey streaks of liquid brownies. I did not offer to share. No way. They would need to wait until the timer went off and the brownies were out of the oven.

Besides seeming uninterested in the chocolate treats, neither Detweiler nor Brawny seemed eager to chat. I opened my mouth to demand an explanation, but their sullen postures tied my tongue. What on earth had happened? What had they been discussing in Detweiler's office? Was nobody talking because Detweiler needed to speak to me alone?

This was totally weird. At some point or another, it irritated me and aroused a streak of stubbornness. Okay, I thought. Be that way! Don't include me.

Yes, it was childish and petulant, but I was tired and badly in need of sugar.

The three of us puttered around doing chores much longer than strictly necessary. Once we'd washed, dried, and stowed every item that came to hand, we moved in a slow dance, circling each other, warily. Detweiler and Brawny both avoided my gaze. Somehow they kept an arm's length from each other, even though all three of us were occupying a comparatively small space.

Finally, the oven timer dinged. I took the brownies out of the oven and set them aside to cool. My ears were cocked and primed, listening for the sound of a stirring child or a whimpering baby or a chatty iPad that should have been turned off. Instead, nada. This night, of all nights, I would have been happy for an interruption. Any distraction to postpone the hard conversation ahead.

But none came.

Detweiler leaned against the counter, appreciatively sniffing the air that was now chocolatized. He swept his eyes over the unusually tidy kitchen, and then he turned to me with a quizzical look on his face. I shrugged and glanced away. My mind had busied itself with a number of imagined conversations, and not one of them had ended happily. Could it possibly be true that Brawny was a man? How could I forgive Brawny for lying to us? Or at the very least, misleading us?

Okay, you could parse the details. You could suggest she hadn't lied, and we'd assumed she was a woman, but geez, wasn't that splitting hairs? If it walks like a duck and it quacks like a duck and it looks like a duck, why wouldn't you put your faith on it being...a duck? Wasn't that what we'd done? We'd accepted her—him—as she presented herself to us. Bronwyn was a woman's name. The person we'd brought into our house as a nanny wore a skirt. Sure, you could call it a kilt. You could argue that the garb was gender neutral, but wasn't that beside the point? She looked like a woman. She used a woman's name. She never left the toilet seat up, and she always replaced empty toilet paper rolls with fresh ones. I'd overheard her ask for directions on more than one occasion. Short of asking her to drop her drawers, what were we to think except that she was, indeed, who she seemed to be?

And who was she, really? This woman I had trusted with my children? The woman who'd delivered my baby? The woman who'd driven my kids to school, who cooked our meals, who'd washed our clothes, who'd sat at my table, night after night, listening to me talk about my day and teaching me to crochet a granny square? Was she really any of those people? Or was she a complete phony? Was she really a man? Or had she been a man, and she was now a woman?

It boggled the mind.

As hard as I tried to tell myself, It doesn't matter, an equally authoritative voice came back with, Oh, yes, it does! If I didn't know that Brawny was a man, what else didn't I know about her/him? What other secrets was she/he holding? How could I even understand this person, if I couldn't find the correct way to label her/it? I remembered an anthropology lecture where the prof suggested that if we can't name a thing, that thing ceases to exist, because otherwise, we can't talk about it, catalog it, store it, or retrieve it.

So who was that person standing beside me and folding the dish towel with such precision? Who was the person staring at me with sad eyes and a searching expression? That human whom I'd accepted and welcomed and shared my home with, but who hadn't trusted me enough to give me the most basic of all information, the sort of facts I generally used as a foundation on which to build a house of friendship? Who was Bronwyn Macavity or was it possible that Bronwyn didn't really exist?

Worse yet...did this mean I'd spent thirty-three years, living as a fool who didn't have the slightest idea whom to trust?

All this angst roiled inside me, twisting my gut and pushing me to the verge of tears. Detweiler pulled me close. He slipped his arm around my waist, tilted my chin so he could kiss me, and then he said, "Honey, we need to talk."

4

The natural place for a candid discussion was the family room. That's where all of us felt the most at ease. Detweiler and I claimed our accustomed spots on the sofa. After tucking an afghan—one that Brawny had crocheted for us—around my feet and loading up a plate with warm brownies, I was comfy. However, Brawny remained standing.

"I'll be right back," she said before disappearing.

The sound of her footsteps suggested she'd climbed the stairs and gone to her room. She returned with a glass bottle that caught the light from the fire, causing the vessel to glow like an oversized version of one of those luminescent sticks so popular around Halloween. Setting it down on a side table, she went into the kitchen and brought out three short drink glasses. With a quick twist of the wrist, she opened the bottle. A heady alcoholic aroma filled the room.

At first I turned down Brawny's offer of a "wee nip of whisky." I could tell Detweiler was really upset although not showing it, because he accepted a short glass of the amber liquid without a second thought. As the odor of peat and oak filled the space, I realized that under any other set of circumstances, this would be a delightful evening. He and I were snuggling on the sofa, enjoying the warmth cast off by the dying logs in the fireplace while a friend sat nearby. Now and again, a rogue spark flew up from the glowing coals, like a firecracker shoots into the night sky, and then it would die, extinguished by the effort of its flight.

But it wasn't a happy evening. The quiet wasn't companionable. It was tortured. The brownies were sticking to the roof of my mouth.

Brawny glanced from me to the bottle. "The byproducts of alcohol don't pass into breast milk. 'Tis not to say there are no risks at all, but in truth, the bigger concern is that the mother will hurt the baby. Drop him or such. Are ye sure ye don't want a wee nip?"

There was no way I'd drop my baby. None. Ty was a sound sleeper, and at night I generally only lift him from the crib to the rocker. It's not like a parade around the block with him. And golly, didn't I need a stiff drink, considering what was to come?

I felt my head move as I nodded, "Yes."

Brawny moved the bottle closer to me. The motion sent the whisky sloshing. The rich smell of fields in Scotland came my way. The gold liquid seemed ancient and wise and mysterious. Not surprisingly, it promised a dulling of the senses. I took the glass and tried a small taste. One sip convinced me I'd made a good choice. In fact, I took the second even more quickly, hoping a soft buzz would envelop me quickly.

Brawny watched all this with serious eyes. After clearing her throat, she said, "I owe you both an apology. As often happens, the longer I waited to tell you about my past, the harder it became. One day melted into the rest, and I put the issue out of my head. 'Twas a stupid way to handle things, and I shall regret it to the day I die. I never meant to pull a fast one on ye. I regret this with all my heart. I canna say it often enough, but I am well and truly sorry."

"What should you have told us?" I stared at Brawny. She opened her mouth to explain, but I barreled on ahead. First I wanted to know that my family was safe. "Who were those men?"

"FBI agents," Detweiler said. "They needed Brawny's help."

"Are you in trouble?" I kept my gaze on the nanny, even though Detweiler had answered for her.

"I am not."

"Why did you all take so long in the office? Why was Detweiler involved?" The whisky had made me bold. Boy or girl, man or woman, I needed answers to those questions before I turned my attention to Brawny's more personal dilemma.

"Sweetheart, they want my help on a situation that will be happening here. Soon. They are part of an advance team. But I can't talk about it yet. Nor can Brawny. Let's get our own questions taken care of first. Then we can move ahead to business." With a gentle squeeze of my fingertips, my husband reassured me.

"Okay. Fair enough." I gathered my courage. "Who is Bruce Macavity?"

"I should have told you," Brawny answered. "It's not what it seems. Yes, I was born as Bruce Macavity, but no, I wasn't a male. Not entirely. I am not transgender. My situation is more confusing than that."

Detweiler stiffened at the word "transgender." It took all my willpower not to turn and look at him.

"Does or did Lorraine know?" I stared at Brawny.

"No. She didn't. At least not from me. Her brother, Van, might have told her."

Detweiler shifted his weight, acting uncomfortable. I needed to communicate with my husband in private. Usually we saved up our deepest fears, our most revealing concerns, for those relaxed moments when we lay side by side in bed. Thanks to Brawny's big reveal, tonight would be a marathon session.

Whether she noticed Detweiler's reaction or not, I can't say. Brawny took a gulp of her drink and continued, "I was born with a wee bit of this and a wee bit of that. Every baby is a miracle, is it not? When you think of everything that has to go absolutely right to make a healthy child, it boggles the mind. In my case, the best explanation is that I have a birth defect, a problem that started in my development in the womb. When the good doctor looked me over, he was stumped. Without an x-ray, he didn't know what the situation was internally. Externally, well, I was neither fish nor fowl. Not enough of either for the doctor to be sure who—what—I was. Aye, and since the doctor was my mother's second cousin once-removed, and he knew me da was keen to have a son, he pronounced me a boy-child."

"Wait a minute." I shook my head to clear it. "How could the doctor make a decision like that?"

Her laugh was dry and fragile. "Back then, it happened all the time. The doctor was considered the expert. Often he operated on the child to bring the child's bits and pieces into compliance. Rather like treating a hare lip or a tied tongue."

"How could he just do that? He didn't do an x-ray?" This confused me. "How could a so-called expert be so confused?"

"I was born at home. A midwife delivered me. A doctor came after. He expected to pronounce me fine, and then to sit and down fine whisky with my da. He never expected to see a problem. Such training didn't exist back then. He told himself I was different, but that I might grow into conformity."

"Surely your parents noticed?" Detweiler raised a curious eyebrow.

"Aye, my ma did, but my da never changed a nappy in his life. Ma relied on what her cousin had told her. To tell the truth,

I think Ma was a wee bit ashamed, thinking she'd done something to cause my...deformity. Of course, she didn't know what was or wasn't there inside of me."

I tried to put myself in Mrs. Macavity's place. I, too, had relied on doctors to tell me that Anya was perfectly fine and healthy, so why wouldn't any new mother do the same?

"I've been told that the doctor told Ma that a surgery might be necessary, but that there was nothing to be done until I grew to be a man. At that time, an informed decision could be made."

"Sounds like what we call 'kicking the can' down the road," said Detweiler.

"Aye," she agreed.

We were engrossed in Brawny's saga; the three of us thinking our individual thoughts. I put myself in the place of Brawny's mother, trying to imagine the fear and shame and guilt, because every mother carries a heaping helping of guilt for the role she plays in her children's lives. How could we not? They were born of us.

A small log crackled, split, and dropped onto the hearth. The noise sounded fearful, but in truth, nothing much had happened. More of a surprise than anything else. With sudden clarity, I realized the activity inside the fireplace had summed up our position entirely. There was a lot of noise, the breaking of hearts, and a loud thump as our relationship hit rock bottom, hard. To all outward indications, nothing dangerous had happened. And yet, the balance of our world had shifted. That person we'd grown dependent on, the one we thought of as indestructible, had crumbled to dust.

The whisky wrapped my brain in a gauzy fog. Whereas once I'd felt uncharitable, now I focused on the person seated across from me. Her pain was undeniable.

Turning away from us as she sat on the ottoman, Brawny's cheeks flushed red. Was it heat, booze, or embarrassment?

"I grew up as a boy-child. My parents dressed me as a boy. Of course, I knew I was different because I had eyes. My ma did her best. She told my da I was a little different 'down there,' but he didn't ask anything else. I kept to myself. My school was naught much more than a one-roomed house, and that made part of my life easier. But I couldn't use the facilities. It was a rule, you see, one my da and ma came up with, a rule that I could never break or I'd be sent away. Aye, you can guess how hard that was for a little tyke, being forced to wait until I got home. Once I even wet my britches rather than break that rule. My da praised me for making a good choice.

"I spent most of my youth hiding. The secrecy and the shame worked on me. I became determined to be the best man I could. Since I worshipped my da, I wanted to make him happy. I knew I was different. I could see that, but I kept myself to myself. I figured that one day, I'd undergo surgery and everything would be put right. But in the meantime, I had to struggle, because the parts inside me were growing too, and so my very being was at war with itself."

Closing my eyes, I tried to imagine our own child, Erik, in a similar circumstance. I couldn't, and that brought a new layer of sadness. Potty-training is a rite of passage, a step toward independence. Certainly, it can create a sense of shame if not handled correctly. To be a child and not be able to go to the restroom when you needed to seemed incredibly cruel. It takes kids a while to develop the ability to hold out, and another span of time to realize their limitations. Waiting is hard for all of us, but for a kid? Nearly impossible.

"Don't ye get the wrong idea about my parents," Brawny said as she seemed to read my mind. "I don't blame them. Not one bit. They were good people, through and through, but they didna know what to think, or how to handle a changling such as myself. My da was a proud man. As I said earlier, he'd made no secret of the fact he wanted a son. After I was born, the neighbors opened their best bottles of whisky and toasted my da for his good fortune. How could he look those same good people in the eyes and tell them his boy was something other? A thing they'd never seen, a monster of sorts? And my ma? She loved my da with all her heart. A good woman, that she was—still is—but not much education. At first she blamed herself and told my da she musta done something wrong. The doc promised her that she hadn't. But guilt, it clings to us like lint from the dryer, eh? She couldna work out what to think of me. How to square it in her head. When I was young, she believed it would sort itself as I grew. When my classmates' bodies changed, and mine didn't look as it should, she took me to a specialist in Edinburgh. What he told her was horrifying.

"I remember her keening as if someone died. I suppose in a way, someone did. She lost her son and gained a monster. I didn't know what to think, except that I was 'wrong' in one way or another. I felt frightened. Sick at heart. I had questions, but they were private ones. I couldna ask them in front of my ma. Aye, no one else coulda gotten a word in. Ma was so upset that she jabbered on and on. Rather than leave after the consultation, she pestered the doc, begging him to 'fix' me proper. To her way of thinking, it was a small bother, not much more than a cleft palate or ears that stuck out like wings. She was that sure I could be brought into line if he'd only use his knife on me."

That sent a shiver up my spine.

After topping up Detweiler's drink, Brawny poured herself another glass. I considered asking for another round, too. But I wanted to be clear-thinking while she talked. After all, this was important. At the end of her recitation, my husband and I would have to decide what to do next. Would she stay or would she go?

Through all of Brawny's explanation, Detweiler had not spoken a word. I wasn't surprised. Not really. He once told me that he'd worked hard to master the art of staying silent. His philosophy was that most of us talk too much. We're too eager to share our opinions when we should be listening and paying attention. His discipline served him well at work; now he would test its limits in our private lives.

"What about after puberty? How did you cope then?" I wondered out loud.

"Ma took me straight from the doctor to her sister, Alva, who lived in Edinburgh proper, just a short walk from the high street. While I sat there red-faced, she told Alva what she'd learned. No one knew exactly how my body would change. I'd been careful, but how would I participate in sport?"

I nodded, thinking how odd it is that she called "sports" by the singular "sport" and "math" by the plural "maths." What was it that Clancy quipped? Two countries divided by a common language? It was true.

"Alva suggested the Roman Catholic school on the other side of the high street. She knew the nuns were very careful about nudity. The headmistress was an old friend who'd known Alva for years. I could live with my aunt and my uncle. They had a spare bedroom so I'd have my privacy."

"Was Alva kind to you?" I asked.

"Aye. She was a wonder. If it hadn't been for her, I don't know..." and Brawny's voice tapered to silence. "As ye might imagine, my body and my mind was every bit as confused as my folks were. Was I a girl? No, it couldn't be. I was not dainty like my sisters. I had this stocky build even when I was a youngster. My oldest sister, Bridget, used to say I was built like a wooden block person. And so I was. Was I a boy? They told me I was, and they presented me as such. I could run and wrestle and scrabble about with the best of them. We decided, the three of us, that I'd continue on as a boy."

"How did you get past the service? Surely they examined you." Detweiler sounded like he was ticked off.

"That's true enough, but to them I was a sad excuse for a man. I said I'd been in an accident as a child. That's all. Short of asking for my DNA, there wasn't much they could do. And then, wouldn't I have a case against them? Besides, by that point in my short life, I'd made it my goal to be the best man standing. At my new school, I threw myself into sport. I passed the physical handily. I was determined to out-man every man in her Majesty's Service. That burning desire gave me an extra edge over my mates. They had nothing to prove. I had everything to lose. If I wasn't a man, what was I? A monster. *Aye,* I see the confusion in your eyes, but consider my position carefully. If you're not a man or a woman, if your bits don't look like normal bits, where does that leave ye?"

She had a point. The late Congresswoman Shirley Chisholm had said she'd been more discriminated against as a woman than as a black. From the moment of our first encounter with a new person, we attempted to size the other up, to quantify, to categorize. What was Brawny? A mistake. A blot on the face of God's green earth.

"But I undressed in front of you!" The words blurted out of my mouth.

"Think back, please. I would always turn away, eh? I never undressed in front of ye."

"Anya." One word. One name. That was all Detweiler needed to share.

"The same with her. I've been very careful to turn away when young miss is changing. Oft times, I've stepped out of the room, feigning an errand or a call from her brothers. Beyond all that, ye must remember I am trained as a medic. Seeing you in your birthday suit matters naught to me."

"Huh." It came out a bit more snarky than I'd intended. "It

matters naught to you, but it means a great deal to me. You've invaded my privacy!"

"I did a job I was hired to do. If I'd been a man, and if you'd known it, would you feel differently? I think not. You have a male gynecologist, right? You'd have found your level of comfort with me if you thought I was a man. That's what I robbed ye of, that level of comfort. I shoulda been honest from the beginning, and I'll live to regret my mistake until the day I die."

She stopped talking. We all sat there quietly, digesting what we'd learned. After what seemed like an unending silence, Brawny added, "Just so we are clear, I am not a pedophile. I love children, aye, but I have no sexual desire for them. In fact, I have very little sexual drive at all. 'Tis to be expected, I guess."

Another crackle from the fireplace reminded me that the hour was late. Although I'd followed everything that Brawny had said, I was dog-tired. Concentrating was growing more difficult by the minute.

"I'll need a while to think this over, but in the meantime, who were those two goons in the matching trench coats?" I asked.

Detweiler stared down into his empty glass. His overt silence suggested he was waiting for Brawny to answer.

Instead, she sighed deeply. "As ye saw from their identification badges, they work for your government. They're FBI agents."

"Okay, and? There has to be more to the story. Why did they show up here on our doorstep?"

Detweiler still said nothing. This, more than anything, more than all the other problems we were facing, started to honk me off. I'd accepted the fact that as a cop's wife there would be times – many times – when he couldn't share details about what he was working on. *Right.* That came with the territory. But this was a new twist, an extra layer of irritation on top of an already stressful situation. Why had two government agents boldly knocked on my front door and demanded to speak to my husband and my *nanny* in private? Not only had they turned our lives upside down, but they hadn't had the decency to include me in their conversation with not one, but two, members of my family. I'd been given no more consideration than they might have shown the check-in clerk at a Holiday Inn. Scratch that, less consideration because the clerk could have demanded a look at their drivers' licenses.

The silence was suspiciously pregnant with possibilities as I waited to hear what the two agents had wanted.

"Detweiler? Brawny? I deserve an answer. Who were they and what did they want? Why did they come here? To my house? And why wasn't Hadcho invited to hear what they said? If it was a crime they were investigating, wouldn't he be privy to their information, too?"

Detweiler swallowed. Slowly, he raised his eyes and stared at Brawny. She gave a tiny sigh of surrender. "Your husband canna tell you. Nor can I. Not yet. It was but an exploratory meeting. The goal was to discuss certain possibilities. But they are contingent."

"Contingent on what?"

"On whether ye decide to keep me in your employ or not."

We hadn't voiced our decision, but after she said it, I realized she was right. This wasn't just about being shocked or disappointed. The question was, "Could we regain our trust in Brawny?" Its partner raised its ugly head, "Can you live with another person who's not...normal?"

Even as these fuzzy thoughts became clear, I felt sick. Who was I to judge another human being? I, who had been judged over and over and found wanting? But wasn't this my responsibility? To make judgments about what was best for our children's lives? Wasn't that what adulthood, and more specifically parenthood, was all about?

Detweiler reached for my hand. "Honey, it wouldn't be fair to tell you why they visited. Not yet. First we need to talk about Brawny and this new, um, information. Otherwise, you might make a decision for the wrong reasons."

"That's about as clear as mud. I really, really don't like the fact the two of you are colluding to keep me in the dark."

"I promise you on my honor as a Scot that I will tell you everything just as soon as I'm at liberty to do so."

"On your honor as a Scot? Excuse me, but right now that lacks a certain amount of credibility, don't you think? Given the circumstances?"

"Aye," she said with a sad shake of her head. "I can certainly see why you might think that way."

Detweiler was the first to get to his feet. I followed. Brawny stayed where she was.

Looking up at us, she said in a husky voice. "One last thought before you go. Whatever you decide, I shall comply with it. These are your children, and you know what's best for your family. As you consider what to do, please remember this: I love them. All three of them. Anya, Erik, and Ty. I would gladly give my life for any of them. Never doubt my love."

5

Later I snuggled up in my accustomed spot under my husband's arm. Putting my head right against his chest, I listened to the soft *lub-lub* of his heart. We'd been awkward with each other while getting ready for bed. Not prickly or angry, but withdrawn and isolated. Detweiler usually fell asleep almost as soon as his head touched the pillow. However, tonight he squirmed and struggled to get comfortable. I suspected that he was working everything through in his head, as I was trying to do in mine.

I also suspected that he hadn't come to a conclusion.

I hadn't either, and I also felt slighted because I still didn't know why we'd been visited by two FBI agents.

Mentally, I'd lined up arguments. On the con side, I wanted to fire Brawny because she hadn't been honest with us from the start. I wanted to march over right now, at half past eleven, and bang on the door of the cottage that Lorraine Lauber shared with Leighton Gage, even though they weren't home. They'd flown to Hawaii for a long vacation, taking Lorraine's dog Paolo with them. But they were planning to come back, and when they did, I could imagine myself jabbing a finger into Lorraine's chest while I gave her an earful for foisting Brawny on us. I wanted to scold Lorraine for not doing a thorough investigation of this essential part of our nanny's background. At the very least, her brother had to know. From all I'd heard, Van and Lorraine were extremely close. Who would neglect to mention a detail like, "I just hired a person of indeterminate gender"?

I burned with fury. Lorraine had tricked us into adding Brawny to our household. Tricked Detweiler, actually, by setting him up at the airport. She'd known that Erik would cry for his nanny. That was to be expected. But she'd also encouraged Brawny to pack her bags so she'd be ready to join Detweiler and Erik on their flight to St. Louis. Then she told Detweiler she was happy to pay Brawny's wages. As a final salvo, she said, "Your wife will need all the help she can get with a new baby on the way, a child adjusting to the death of his mother, and a teen struggling to find her way. All that on top of her working full-time. Brawny will grant you both breathing space."

Later we had learned that Brawny's presence was a necessity for other reasons. Reasons that Lorraine hadn't shared with us at the start. Both she and Brawny had worried about Erik's safety. As Van Lauber's heir, the little boy stood between certain greedy people and a fortune they'd love to claim. Brawny and Lorraine knew these forces were desperate to see Erik smudged out.

Okay, I needed to settle down or I'd never get any rest.

I tried counting my blessings, a nightly ritual that has always sustained me. I was thankful that Lorraine had seen to the boy's safety. True, we'd benefited enormously by having Brawny work for us on Lorraine's tab. Honestly, I had no idea how I'd manage running a store while parenting three kids. Or how I'd manage to glue together our chopped and blended family. In fact, I wasn't sure I could keep all those spinning plates in the air. But Lorraine had taken away my power of choice, and we all know that being able to choose is vitally important. Furthermore, she'd taken advantage of our trust.

Or had she?

My counting ceased and my fretting began. How would I explain Brawny's gender to the kids? What should I call her? A he or a she? Our conversation hadn't even taken us that far.

Was she the boy she'd been designated as at birth?

Or the girl she'd slowly become?

I needed answers. Although I waited for them patiently, none came.

DETWEILER ALWAYS WOKE up before I did but not this morning. I'd been awake most of the night. When the first rays of sun slipped between the slats of the blinds, I crawled out of bed and padded downstairs. Along the way, I gripped the handrails firmly because I felt light-headed.

Not surprisingly, Brawny was already up. She sat at the kitchen table, drinking coffee and writing in a journal. At least, I assumed it was a journal. I'd seen ones like it at Walmart.

Hearing me approach, she closed the book on the pen. Her face turned to me with an expectant look and a coiled sort of energy that suggested she might run away at any minute. Her eyes were ringed in red, and her nose was pink as a peony.

"Good morning," I said, determined to be cheerful and civil. However, I could feel a headache waiting for the chance to take over. Wincing I put one hand to my head. Brawny saw the movement. She jumped out of her chair, grabbed a glass, and poured me eight ounces of water.

"Good morning," she answered. "You might be suffering a wee bit from the whisky. Water will help. May I make you a cuppa tea? Or a mug of decaf?"

I hesitated. It seemed morally wrong to ask her to resume her responsibilities when we weren't sure whether we wanted to keep her. I dithered before deciding the best course of action was to carry on as if nothing had changed.

"Yes, please. Decaf. I think I'll have a slice of spice bread, too."

"*Aye*, and there's fruit salad I made fresh. I ran to the market earlier."

"You couldn't sleep." It was a statement, not a question.

"Not a wink. And you? Typically Detweiler is up before you." It wasn't an accusation, just an observation.

"I couldn't sleep." I didn't add that I felt a bit dizzy. I hoped that would pass.

"Ah."

She set the mug down in front of me, before going back to the refrigerator for the spice bread and the fruit.

"Tell me about your time in the service," I asked. I was still trying to figuratively get my arms around the trajectory of how Bruce became Brawny.

"I joined up early. I figured that if I was to be a man, I should do what all the men in my family had always done and serve the Crown. Surprisingly, I breezed through the physical, using the excuse that I'd been the victim of an accident on the farm. I said I'd been caught with my trousers down in front of an angry cow."

That almost caused me to laugh as I tried to visualize such a thing.

"Aye, 'tis funny what explanations are acceptable and what are not. I was determined to make myself into a man in every way that I could. The basic training was not very hard for me. That I went through without a hiccup because I was committed to not being sent home. Sure, I was teased, but by then, I was accustomed to having to fight for my life. After a while, the others let me be. Then I decided to really put myself to the test. I wanted to be a member of SAS. You might have read about your Navy SEALS? We're the UK equivalent. It takes an inhuman amount of willpower. They try to break your spirit, to push you past your physical endurance, but it felt cleansing in an odd sort of way. I put all my hurts and fears into it. The program is designed to winnow down the masses and carve out the elite. But by then, I'd found solace in exercise. By the grace of God Almighty, I made it through. Soon I was stationed in Afghanistan."

I tried to imagine this strange person, hiding herself and subjecting herself to ridicule and pain, and for what? To prove she had a right to exist. I could relate to that. I thanked her as she slid a plate of spice bread and a bowl of fruit my way.

"In Afghanistan I concluded that I couldn't pretend any longer. I spent weeks watching other servicemen die and I promised to give their loved ones a last message. Hearing those final words..." She stopped and wiped her eyes with the back of one hand. "It forced me to accept reality. Life is short. Any deceptions I'd carefully nurtured fell by the wayside. Those sacrifices peeled away the false mask I'd taken such care to construct. Each and every person who died from our squad chipped away at my fake identity."

I shivered, thinking of my own struggles with post-partum depression. I understood what she had gone through. The food in front of me sat untouched. The lump in my throat was too raw to allow me to swallow.

"My whole life was a lie. There was no one walking this earth who really knew me, who'd been allowed to get close. I'd kept them all away. I'd held them at arms' length, and now if I died, I'd vanish because I'd never had the chance to just be myself. Just plain me. My mourners would regret the passing of a cardboard figure, a murky presence who kept to himself and never trusted enough to let anyone into his heart. Without that protective veneer, my emotions overwhelmed me. I suppose you could call it a breakdown. I crawled into a bed and turned my face to the wall and retreated inside myself. They tell me I quit eating, drinking, and waited for my body to shut down."

"Wow. Kind of a bad time and place to have a breakdown. I can't imagine that your leaders had much sympathy for you."

A smile flickered and went out. One strong hand reached out to capture her journal and set it on her lap, under the table, almost as if she was worried it would tell her secrets. "Nay, they dinna. The last thing they needed was an emotional person handling a personal crisis in the midst of a war zone. My fellow officers whispered among themselves. They worried that I'd fall apart out on the battlefield. They sent me back to Edinburgh for a psychiatric evaluation."

"That was when I got lucky. I met a doctor with knowledge of my condition. Or more precisely, a doctor who had some experience with what others do when confronted with gender confusion." With trembling hands, she scrubbed at her face. "What is worse? To die or to die knowing that no one had seen your real self? That you'd been a fake your entire life? With Dr. Carnegie's help, I realized how stupid I'd been. How I'd focused on keeping a secret rather than living, because isn't that the purpose? For us to battle our way past obstacles, to stumble, to fall, to persevere, all for the chance to find out who we really are? And as I realized all this, there was this keening, a wail that bubbled up inside, that screamed and demanded attention. How dare I die without living? As I thought about those other brave men and women, I thought, At least someone who knew them will hold them like a keepsake to their hearts. I faced the knowledge that when I died, I would leave no void, just a husk. An empty shell. They'd be left to bury a carcass as empty of humanity as it had been while I still drew breath."

6

I thanked Brawny for the decaf and the food. A glance at the kitchen clock told me I might be able to sneak in another thirty minutes of rest, if not sleep, before the children got up. She realized what I was thinking. "Go on back to bed. I'll take care of the children as normal while you..."

"Yes," I said, cutting her short. I didn't want her to say, "Decide whether to kick me out of your house." That's exactly what we had to decide.

I climbed the stairs and crawled back under the covers. Somehow I slept until Detweiler woke up. Through half-opened eyes, I watched Detweiler lace up his gym shoes.

"Are you still going to exercise with her? Given what you know now? Even though we haven't come to a concrete decision?"

"Yes," he said. "Is that a problem for you?"

"No. I think we should go on as usual until we come to a decision, don't you?"

"I think so, too. Otherwise, we are making a decision by ostracizing her."

"That wouldn't be fair. She deserves better."

"I agree." He stood up, went into the bathroom, and shut the door behind him.

The routine they'd invented had saved his life. Thanks to Brawny's tutelage, my husband was stronger, faster, and more agile than ever. She'd been the best personal coach we could have asked for. In addition to monitoring his exercise routine, Brawny had taught Detweiler hand-to-hand combat moves she'd picked up from the SAS. At least once that I was aware of, this special training had helped him bring down a creep who'd been intent on doing Detweiler harm. I also knew she'd been teaching him how to throw a knife with deadly accuracy. Her skill at knife-tossing had brought down a man who'd crashed our wedding for the purpose of...

It didn't bear thinking. Detweiler stepped out of the bathroom and planted a kiss on my forehead.

"Good," I said at last. "I'm glad you're still exercising with her. It's been beneficial for you, so I'm happy that you're keeping it up."

"I've been thinking." He stretched out on his side of the bed. His fingers sought one of my curls, and he twisted it the way a baby grabs a lock of her mother's hair. "But I would like to know what you're thinking first."

"Why? Whatever decision we come to, it has to be unanimous."

"Absolutely. That said, I don't want my ideas to color yours."

"Chicken." I punched his bicep lightly. "You're willing to let me climb out there on a very shaky limb."

"Not alone. We're in this together. Have you given more thought to Anya? And her reaction. I'm happy for us to let things go on as usual until we decide, but she was pretty hacked off. I'm wondering how she's going to deal with this news about Brawny."

"I woke up twice during the night, thinking about what she'd said." I didn't add that I'd pushed those concerns aside as I grappled with my own worries.

"She was pretty angry. I don't know that I've ever seen her like that. I tell myself it was her first reaction, right? A knee-jerk response."

I blew out a long sigh. "Yeah, but you are right. She was really upset. I mean she was livid. I think I know why, too. I have reason to believe that Anya had shared her deep, dark secrets with our nanny. And she'd disrobed in front of Brawny."

"Got it." Detweiler had grown up with two sisters. He knew the depth of a young woman's insecurities. He'd seen firsthand how embarrassing it could be when your period suddenly started and you weren't prepared. These were all life events that Anya was navigating for the first time.

"Sometimes I think that Anya's easy acceptance of her role as a big sister was only possible because..."

"Because Brawny had her back?"

"Yup. When Erik gets on her nerves, Brawny swoops in to distract him. When Ty's crying gets annoying, it's Brawny who whisks him away to give us all a chance to recoup. Lately, Anya's been wondering about boys. I overheard her asking Emily if she'd ever been kissed."

"Emily? My niece?" Detweiler looked alarmed. His head was resting on his hand, which was propped up by his forearm as he faced me.

"That's normal, honey. They're that age. I overheard them talking on the phone. I was eavesdropping. From Anya's side of the conversation, I realized she has her sights on a particular guy, Mason, but she's not sure about how to win his affection. I broached the subject, and she told me to back off in no uncertain terms."

"You're thinking she's discussed this with Brawny?"

I used my fingertip to draw a lazy circle on the white tee shirt that covered my husband's chiseled chest. "I'd lay money on it. Before Brawny came along, Anya would talk to Laurel, but Laurel's been scarce since she and Joe got engaged. She'd sometimes talk to Rebekkah, but Rebekkah has gotten busy with school and Horace's health problems. By default, Brawny became her 'go to' surrogate older sister."

Detweiler's sigh was longer and louder than mine had been. "Taken to its logical conclusion, that means Anya not only lost a confidant, she's probably feeling tricked as well."

Rubbing my temples with my fingertips, I did my best to cope with the warning twinges that signaled a headache on the way. "Yes," I said. "Tricked, betrayed, lied to, and taken advantage of. You pick two. Anya is taking this particularly hard."

"Then your vote is to get rid of Brawny, ASAP."

I did my best to focus. The right words were important, especially when picking my way through a minefield like this one. "No. Actually I think we should ask Brawny to stay. At least that's what I'm leaning toward."

"Explain."

"I've never seen Hadcho without his pants on. Or Clancy for that matter. Nor do I care to. Or need to. I know their hearts. I know they love me and my family. I know they'd do anything for us. It seems to me that Brawny's in that same elite club. You know and I know that she'd lay down her life for us and our kids. If this gender situation hadn't come to light, it would never have been an issue, would it? Her physiology has nothing to do with her relationship to us. Once I teased that out from the rest of this mess, I realized I was angry because Brawny didn't trust us. So I was mad at her for doing exactly what I was doing now. Does that make sense?"

"Sort of."

"She didn't give us the benefit of the doubt. She figured we'd get all weird about her gender issues, and we did, but not for the reasons she predicted. I hate that she told us a lie of omission."

"Can we live with that? Can we forgive her?" he wondered out loud. As he did, he moved his arm so that he was lying flat on the bed, staring up at the ceiling. We looked at that stupid ceiling all the time when we were talking. I felt like I should grab a Sharpie marker, pull up a ladder, and write, "The answers are not up here!" on the surface.

"That's what I have to grapple with." A wave of honesty swept over me, and I added, "Okay, I hate to admit it, but I am not totally sure how I feel about having a he-she nanny. It's an ugly part of me, and I don't like it, but I have to be honest with you."

Raising up on one elbow again, he leaned in for a kiss. "We're in agreement. Totally. I am ticked as all get-out that they withheld this information, but I've been working hard to separate that sense of unfairness from the big question, Is Brawny good for our family or not? Can I accept her as she is? Can we accept her as a family? And that answer is crystal clear. We're better off with her than without. I have tried to imagine our lives without Brawny. It's not just childcare and housekeeping. She's my workout buddy and coach. She protects our kids. She makes our lives easier. She's been a good friend, stepping up and taking our part when there's a problem."

"She helps out at my store. She worked some sort of hypnotism magic on my mother to make her manageable."

"If we could hire a replacement to take over those services, would you want to?" he asked as I admired the manly bulge of his bicep.

"Maybe," I said. "Maybe this is just a personnel issue. A hiring decision."

That shut us both up. We knew how hard it could be to find the right person. I added, "Even if we found a person who could do all that and do it at a price we could afford, we'd also have to find someone whose personality meshed nicely with ours."

"It's more complicated than that. This is like finding the right roommate in college, because that person would live under the same roof and have to share our values."

"One hundred percent."

"And we'd have to break that new person in. Teaching her or him what the kids like, what we need, what our schedule is."

"To recap," he said, "on one side we've got dealing with our hurt feelings and Anya's rightful anger. On the other, we've got replacing someone who gets along with us and who does a terrific job helping us keep our show on the road."

"Hmmm." I closed my eyes, blocking out everything but my gut reactions. The pain in my head was threatening to mushroom out of proportion. If I could muster up the energy, I needed to go downstairs and drink another eight ounces of water before the pain had me at its mercy. But first, we needed to bring this conversation to a conclusion. "At the risk of mixing metaphors, there's an elephant in the room. Brawny's identity and sexuality. We can't just pretend she isn't who she is. Although, nobody needs to know, do they? This isn't anyone's business but ours."

"Ours and the kids." Detweiler rubbed his eyes, almost as if his body was sympathetic to the pain in mine.

"Are we confusing tolerance with convenience? Are we using her because she's helpful, rather than accepting her for who she is?"

"Maybe." His voice was soft but full of conviction.

"What would we do if she wasn't our nanny? If she was only a friend or a next-door neighbor? How would we feel about her? Are we willing to put up with this just because she's a labor-saving device?" The words echoed in my head: Put up with this. Really? I thought I was a better person than that. I wasn't "putting up" with anything. Brawny wasn't hurting me. She wasn't asking me to change my life, my standards, or my morality. She'd been born into a horrible situation, and bless her, she'd made the best of it. Who was I to label it "putting up with" as though she posed an ongoing problem in my life?

Detweiler had taken note of my verbal misstep. His long fingers rubbed his neck as he worked to sort his thoughts. His silence suggested he was wrestling with the same issues that I was.

"I can't believe I used the term 'putting up with,'" I said. "That's not like me. That's not the person I want to be. She doesn't inflict any problems on my life. No one needs to know about her, do they?"

"I don't see why they should. It's our business, and hers, but no one else's." He laced his fingers through mine. "If she wasn't our nanny, I'd like her as a friend. Not just because she's such a big help. I like being around her. She's smart, well-read, and curious. She has an incredible work ethic. She's loyal to a fault. I admire her. I like her sense of humor. It warms my heart to see her with Erik."

"And with Ty," I added. "She looks at him as if he was the most important person in the world, even when she's changing a poopy diaper. Until this happened, she was Anya's rock, wasn't she? Anya's been leaning on Brawny more and more since Sheila's been away in rehab."

"Anya can find her way through this. She's a good kid." Detweiler stretched out his arms, sliding one beneath me, so he could hug me.

"I agree, but she is still a kid. As much as I'd like to take the high ground here, we have to be practical. If Anya can't find a way to accept Brawny, we have a real problem on our hands. I don't have the energy to referee their relationship. If we could have discussed this in advance, things might be different. Unfortunately now we're stuck dealing with Anya feeling that she's been tricked."

"We all have," he said.

Once again I felt a slow burn of anger at Lorraine. How much did she know about Brawny and how much had she kept from us?

Detweiler summed things up nicely. "It comes down to this: Either Anya can forgive Brawny or she can't. If she can't, we might have no choice but to let Brawny go."

7

Brawny was very understanding when we told her we needed a while to think things through. She'd acknowledged our desire not to make a decision right away with a brisk nod of her head and, "Aye. Ye take all the time you need. I'll continue on as before, unless ye say otherwise."

"All that aside, we have to be practical. You're okay with giving us time," Detweiler said, "but the British government and the FBI need a quick response. Brawny and you and I need to get Kiki up to speed. Especially since we need to consider your situation."

"She needs to know everything." Brawny's expression changed from emotional to coolly professional.

"Can it wait? I don't think I can handle more intrigue this morning," I said, even though I was burning to know why the two feds had visited. My curiosity was tempted by the ache in my head. "The kids will be up any minute. We have to get them dressed, fed, and ready for school, and then I've got to get to the store."

"It can keep for 24 hours, but not much longer. Unfortunately, there are a lot of moving parts, and most of this is out of our hands." Detweiler sighed.

"Out of our hands?" That didn't make sense to me. My minor headache was causing a major disruption in my ability to think clearly. "Come again."

"Our hands, as in yours and mine and our family's. But we're not the primary stakeholders here. First and foremost, the American government has to make a decision. Visiting Brawny and me was part of that decision. It's an operational thing."

I tried to nod as a way of signaling my understanding. Evidently Detweiler and Brawny had been dragged into something because they were well-respected in the local law enforcement community and could advise the Feds. After getting involved with Detweiler, I'd learned a lot about how law enforcement worked in our country. At any time, one agency or another would reach out to consult with locals under the assumption that the folks in the area knew more about their own turf. So the Feds' visit hadn't been a big deal. At least, that's what I told myself. A glance at the time suggested anything more intriguing would have to wait.

That's how we back-burnered a discussion that would have been front and center under normal circumstances. By mutual agreement, we went on with our daily routines. I took two Advil and a glass of water, before going upstairs to shower and get dressed. Detweiler left to run his usual eight miles. Brawny woke up Erik and knocked on Anya's door.

The hot water and the drugs helped my headache, but now my stomach was tied into a knot. I couldn't help but think about Brawny's parents, and the difficulties they'd faced. How tough this must have been on them. Every child represents a dream. Long before the baby is born, you have fantasies about who he or she will be, and what your relationship will be like. The most fundamental question is, *Are you having a boy or a girl?* What would it be like to live with that being up in the air? The poor Macavity family! Poor Brawny! She never asked for this birth defect. And the doctor? He must have been at a loss, too. And then all the adults colluded to make what they considered the best choice possible...only it was the wrong choice.

I ran my hands down my body and considered how lucky I was to have all the right pieces in the right places. Being raised the wrong gender must feel a lot like wearing the wrong size shoes, day in and day out. I winced thinking of how it might chafe.

Feeling much more charitable toward everyone concerned, I dressed in a nice pair of dark green pants, a simple white blouse, a floral cardigan that picked up the green of the pants, and went downstairs.

Erik was seated on his booster chair. Usually he alternates between spooning out his cereal and picking it up with his fingers. Today he only nibbled on a Cheerio while delicately holding it in his fingertips. Because he is biracial, his skin is the color of a vanilla latte from Starbucks. My Anya, on the other hand, is a true-to-life version of Snow White, but with platinum blond hair. Sitting side-by-side, they seem like two sides of a coin, because both are beautiful children.

However Anya's expression was anything but pleasant. She was one iota away from scowling. I decided to ignore it for the time being.

"Erik, please eat your breakfast," Brawny said. She jiggled Ty on one hip while she watched bread in the toaster. My little guy whimpered sadly as I lifted him out of the nanny's arms.

"Ty is not a happy bunny," Brawny said. "Erik isn't either. The sun isn't shining today. Not yet."

This was her code for Anya being in a bad mood.

I nodded to Brawny.

The back door opened, and Detweiler huffed in, hot and sweaty from his run. "Good morning!" he sang out as he moved through the kitchen and raced upstairs to take his shower. Gracie trotted upstairs behind him.

"Right." I grunted as I cuddled Ty and carried him over to a kitchen chair. My youngest was becoming quite the butterball. Mindful of the need to be modest, I grabbed a dishtowel to cover his mouth and myself, and then I sat down. I'd only gotten him settled and latched on, when Brawny handed me a plate of toast, crispy bacon, and apple slices. "Tea comes next," she said.

What would we do without her? The thought popped into my head and crowded out everything else. Meanwhile, Ty fussed around. He couldn't seem to get comfortable. Usually he attaches to me like a vacuum cleaner, but not today.

"How are you this morning, Anya?" I asked.

"Fine."

"What do you have going on today at school?"

Before she could answer, Erik explained that they were adding big numbers today and learning to read real books. He was very excited about being able to read to himself, and he chattered happily about the Bob's books and the new words he was learning.

"Bob's books?" Brawny asked.

"Actually that's *Bob's Books* with two capital B's. They were introduced here in the US thirty-five years ago," I explained. I knew about them because Erik's teacher, Maggie Earhart and I were friends. "They do a wonderful job of moving kids into reading."

"I can weed," Erik affirmed.

"The word is 'read,'" Anya corrected him.

"That's what I sayed."

Anya leaned closer so that Erik could hear her more clearly and see her mouth form the letter "r." "R-r-r-r-read."

"Weed."

"Whatever." Anya shrugged.

I noticed she'd poured herself a cup of coffee. Usually I don't allow that. I knew Brawny didn't serve coffee to my daughter. This was Anya's none-too-subtle way of saying, "I'm a grownup."

But she wasn't. Not at thirteen. I thought about saying something and decided to keep my mouth shut.

A minute later, when Brawny asked her whether she'd prefer Grape-Nuts or granola, Anya pretended not to hear the question. I opened my mouth to correct my daughter's behavior, but Brawny lightly grabbed my forearm.

"Nay." She spoke in a whisper. "Leave her be. Please."

Maybe she was right. I cradled Ty against my chest and noticed how warm he felt. My baby nursed weakly. When he unlatched, I grabbed the dishtowel off of him with one hand and moved him to an upright position. Lifting him higher, I moved Ty so that his face rested against my collarbone. Once he was balanced, I kissed the nape of his neck. It was scalding hot.

"Brawny, I think Ty has a temperature."

I'd no sooner gotten the words out when Ty gurgled. Hot vomit squirted inside my collar and down the back of my blouse. I gasped but kept my grip on the baby.

"He pooked!" Erik pointed a spoon my way. "Eoooo. Yuck! It smells!"

Ty cried weakly. Drool and puke continued to dribble onto my blouse.

"I'll get ye a big bath towel and some wipes." Brawny raced out of the kitchen.

I used the dishtowel to wipe off Ty's mouth. I was doing my best to calm the startled baby, when I heard a loud *harrumph-ah-harrumph-ah* sound, the precursor to puking.

I looked away from Ty in time to see that Erik was heaving. I watched in horror as his stomach spasmed. Hoping to intercede,

I hopped to my feet, but not gracefully because Ty's weight proved cumbersome. I tried to grab Erik's cereal bowl and hold it under his mouth like a basin. Reflexively, he turned his head away from me. With the force of a firehose, Erik spewed milk and cereal all over the table top.

"*Ew*, gross," Anya said. Holding her nose, she walked out from the kitchen.

A part of me wanted to reprimand her. Another part was relieved she was gone. Anya has a notoriously touchy tummy. I didn't need her getting sick, too.

"Hang on while I grab a towel!" Brawny called from the laundry room. Erik burst into noisy sobs. He heaved once more. This time he vomited all over my leg. The force of it scared him because he couldn't breathe while it lasted.

"It's okay. It's okay, sweetie."

I had one boy sobbing in my right ear, and the other crying in my left. I smelled awful, and my headache started up again. I wanted to plop down onto a kitchen chair and cry, too, but I couldn't because right then, Gracie wandered over to see what was happening and to help with cleaning up. "No, Gracie, don't!"

Brawny stepped out of the laundry room into the hall to see what the dog was doing.

With Ty in one arm, I was grabbing at Gracie's collar, trying to pull her away from the mess when Detweiler came galloping down the stairs. He was fresh from his shower and feeling fine. His attention was on the act of buttoning the cuffs on his shirt, so he wasn't watching his feet. As I watched in horror, he stepped squarely into the puddle of milk and cereal.

I watched it play out in slo-mo. Like a cartoon character, his legs went up, up, up into the air. Both his feet flew out from under him. Gracie scuttled to one side, like a cow dodging a man with a branding iron. Detweiler seemed to be suspended there, above the mess. His arms windmilled. His unbuttoned cuffs flapped. But gravity can only be denied for so long. It always wins. Detweiler came down hard on his butt right in the middle of the mess.

All I could think to say as I stared down at him, was, "Is anything broken?"

8

The rest of the pre-work and pre-school scramble went about as well as could be expected, which is to say, it was a cross between a living nightmare and a Keystone Cop routine. Detweiler got up off the floor. I locked Gracie in a bathroom. I cleaned up Ty. Brawny cleaned up Erik. Detweiler mopped up the mess, and somehow we both got ourselves clean and dressed in fresh clothes. I gave my nice green pants one last look before I put them in the laundry bin. Shoot. I really liked those pants. Nothing much fit me these days. Fortunately, I hadn't given away my maternity clothes. From my dresser, I pulled a tired pair of black maternity pants. A red, black, and white smock-top covered the two buttons that strained at my waistband. Not as nice looking as my original outfit, but I was presentable.

While Brawny took the little ones to the pediatrician just in case it was more than a tummy bug, I put Gracie in my old BMW and drove Anya to school. At the drop-off lane, she flounced out of the car but hesitated with one hand on the passenger side door. With a dramatic pause, she delivered her *coup de grâce*: "I'm officially running away from home. I can't live in that environment. Don't bother trying to pick me up. I'm going to live with Nicci Moore. *Forever."*

As I struggled to wrap my head around what Anya was saying, she added, "And I have Mrs. Moore's permission."

Of course I would have argued with Anya, but there was a line of cars behind me. That little minx of mine had chosen her moment carefully. As I struggled to decide what to do, the teacher on duty waved me forward. I had no choice but to pull through the drop-off lane and keep going.

I drove to the store in a blur of tears. If Gracie hadn't been so accustomed to our routine, and therefore, eager to get out of the car and water a shrub, I might have sat there and sobbed. Instead, I had to take care of my dog.

There was no time to mope about Anya. Once Gracie had emptied her tank, we hustled out of the cold and into the warm back room of Time in a Bottle, the area's finest scrapbook and crafts store. I put on a pot of coffee for Clancy and made a cup of decaf for me. Then I sat down at the break table to tackle a stack of invoices. Because we were approaching the end of our fiscal year, I had to get these finished. When they'd been double-checked and our inventory had been taken, Margit Eichen would close out the books. Only then would we know exactly where we stood financially.

Margit and I make a good team. I hold the majority of Time in a Bottle shares; she is a minority shareholder. I am the creative director and a big-picture person; she is a stickler for processes and details. Doing math is a struggle for me, but it suits her down to the ground, which makes her the right person for balancing the books.

I hoped diving into the paperwork would take my mind off my family problems. I'd lost track of time when the back door opened. Clancy blew in on a stiff breeze of cold air. The wind gave me the shivers. I stood up and went over to the counter to turn on the electric kettle and make myself a cup of hot decaf Earl Grey.

"Good morning." Clancy unwound her maroon woolen scarf and shook the snow out of her hair before unbuttoning her Burberry coat. Giving me an up-and-down look, she paused when she got to my shoes. "At least I think it is. You have on two different shoes. Was that intentional?"

I'd noticed my gait seemed a little off.

"I'm lucky to be dressed at all. It was one ugly morning at the Detweiler house."

"Yes, well, at least you lived to tell about it."

That's when Clancy told me about Nancy Owens.

"She was shot? When?"

"They found her body this morning. She must have been shot yesterday.

"You're sure? We're talking about the same Nancy Owens? The Nancy Owens who occasionally shopped here? You're positive that's the same person they found shot to death in Ferguson?"

"Yes, indeed." Clancy nodded and pulled off her gloves. "It's all over the news. I even saw it on television this morning when I stopped at a gas station to fill up my car."

"Wow. Shot in the head."

"Shot. In. The. Head." Clancy retrieved my pencil from the floor and continued, "Can you believe it? They are saying that Nancy was sitting in her white Mercedes in a parking space in front of a strip center. Minding her own business. Engine running. Some creep walked up, poked the muzzle of a gun through the open window, and shot her in the head. For no apparent reason!"

"The window was rolled down? You have to be kidding. Who drives to Ferguson and sits in a parking space with her window down when it's ten degrees outside?"

"Apparently, the answer to that question is...ding, ding, ding...Nancy Owens," Clancy said as she poured herself a cup of coffee.

"Was it a robbery?"

"Not so far as anyone knows. The creep didn't even take the Mercedes—and get this—Nancy's car doors were unlocked."

"I don't mean to sound cruel, but that's just plain dumb on Nancy's part."

Clancy sank into the chair across from mine and sipped her coffee. Propping her chin on her hand, she sighed. "We all do dumb things from time to time, but I have to agree with you. It does sound really, really stupid. There must be more to the story."

But we didn't get the chance to speculate because the phone rang. Clancy was closest to the handset so she walked over and answered it. I went back to the stack of inventories, a pile that seemed to be growing bigger instead of smaller.

"Margit won't be here," Clancy said as she returned the handset to the base. "She's at the nursing home going through her mother's things. Now that her mother is dead, they want to rent out her room. Someone else needs it. As you might guess, space there is at a premium. Margit doesn't want to keep paying rent."

Margit, Clancy, and I have all tried to be good daughters to our aging mothers. Margit is ten years older than Clancy. Clancy is ten years older than I am. Each of us sees a preview of coming events as the other cares for a parent in declining health. When Margit's mother died on the day before Christmas, I thought Margit would be despondent. Instead, she described being in the midst of a bittersweet tug-of-war, pulling her from relief to grief and back again.

"*Mutter* was lost to me years ago," Margit had said as we cleared the table after our holiday meal. "The one who died is not the woman who raised me from a child. Then she was my best friend and my rock. I have tried to be that to her, but it was hard. I am glad she is at peace."

Clancy slapped the tabletop. "All righty then. Moving right along, we need to get busy taking inventory. You can finish that paperwork up later. Who's coming in to help?"

I'd been dreading this moment. Delivering bad news is never fun, and delivering it to Clancy gives me heartburn. She's a methodical person who keeps a daily planner with entries made in ink. In front of customers, she acts calm, cool, and collected when a problem crops up. But one-on-one, when the unexpected occurs, she can get cranky.

"I'm not sure who's coming. Laurel should be here any minute."

Laurel Wilkins was as dependable as the sun in the sky, so it was strange she hadn't arrived already.

A ding on my phone signaled an incoming text message from Brawny: *Kids have tummy bug. Heading home to keep them hydrated. Will stay with them.*

Great, I thought. Just ducky.

I texted Laurel. I read her reply out loud: *Sorry for late notice. I have some sort of a bug. Been up all night. Sick at my stomach. Don't want to share it! I need to stay home. Sorry!*

Clancy poured herself a cup of coffee and settled into the chair across from mine. "Who else did you schedule to help us take inventory?"

"Nobody, and I'm not joking." I worked to sound neutral, but there was an edge of desperation. Gripping the handle of my mug, I went down the list of folks who would not be available to help us with inventory. "Brawny was going to come and count. Erik would be at school. Ty could sit in his bouncy chair. But she can't bring the kids here because they both are running a fever. They're contagious. You know about Laurel and Margit."

"How about Rebekkah?"

Rebekkah Goldfader is the daughter of the late Dodie Gold-fader, my mentor and the founder of Time in a Bottle.

I called her and she answered on the third ring.

"Wish I could help, but *Abba* isn't feeling well," she explained, using the Jewish term for father. "In fact, we're on our way to a doc-in-the-box."

"Oh, no!" This put a scare into me. I had promised Dodie that I'd look after Horace, and with my own drama unfurling, I hadn't spoken to him for days.

"I think he might have walking pneumonia," she added in a low voice."

"Please let me know what you learn," and after saying good-bye, I hung up.

"That stinks," Clancy said. "Who can we call? Someone we can rely on? Someone honest and mature?"

"Not that I can think of. Most of our customers are hunkered down, staying out of the cold."

"There must be someone!" Clancy threw her hands in the air. "I know this is last minute, but if we don't get help, we'll be here all day and all night. Without that inventory, you can't verify how much you've got tied up in stock."

Mentally, I ran down the list of possible helpers one more time and came up dry. Counting stock is no fun. None. Because Time in a Bottle has a wide variety of crafting items, there's a lot to count. Clancy was right. We needed help and we needed it ASAP. Searching a mental Rolodex, I came up with a name, someone already in my phone contact listing under the letter "A" for Alderton.

Lee Alderton is a dear friend, one of those people you instantly gravitate to. Probably because she's always in a good mood, she looks for the good in every situation, and she's kind to the bone. I hated asking her for help. Hated it. But my back was up against the wall.

First I called Lee's cell phone number but that went directly to voice mail. Fortunately, I also had the Aldertons' landline at home. I dialed that.

"Lee?" I spoke hesitantly into my iPhone when she answered. "Are you busy today? I need help."

Bless her heart, Lee quickly picked up on the panic in my voice. "Give me thirty minutes. Do you mind if Jeff comes too?"

Of course I didn't mind. I was delighted her husband could join us. I got off the phone, relayed the good news to Clancy, and put the CLOSED FOR INVENTORY sign on the door. It felt odd to lock the front door during the day, but we couldn't handle customers and inventory at the same time.

9

While we waited for Lee and Jeff to come to our rescue, Clancy grabbed her Dell tablet computer, and then we turned on the little television in the office. Dodie had purchased the second-hand set expressly for following the news. Sure enough, we caught a couple of local reporters talking about Nancy Owens. We learned that nothing seemed to have been stolen from the car. Not Nancy's diamond. Not her purse. The authorities thought it might have been a random shooting. Or a case of mistaken identity. Or even a targeted shooting that was wildly inaccurate.

But those last two theories didn't make much sense. How could you mistake someone's identity at close range? You'd have to be blind. A stray bullet shot through an open car window? Not likely.

"Of course, all this begs the question: What was Nancy doing in Ferguson?" Turning off the TV, I got up, walked to the counter, and started the kettle so I could make another cup of tea.

Clancy took a chair at the break table. She tapped the keyboard on her tablet. "Hmmm. At the gas station, the reporter said that all this happened after Nancy attended a meeting of Zoo Keepers. Have you heard of them?"

"They're a group that supports the St. Louis Zoological Park's efforts to replenish exotic animals that are endangered or near extinction. That's all I know."

"That's about the extent of it for me, too. I had a neighbor who used to be on the board. Back then they met in an office building in Olivette. I can't imagine them meeting up in Ferguson."

"Then Nancy had another reason for being there." I shrugged. "Who knows what or why? More and more I feel like a victim of the fickle finger of fate, you know?"

"I bet you do. That reminds me. What happened with the Federal agents and Bruce Macavity? Is that Brawny's real first name? What gives? With all the news about Nancy Owens, everything else flew out of my head. So, dish. Is your nanny a cross-dresser? Let me guess. The FBI guys just happened to be in the neighborhood and thought they'd drop a bombshell, like, 'Guess what? Your nanny is a manny?'"

"Ha, ha, ha." Usually I have a terrific sense of humor, but her baldly dismissive tone irked me. "Easy for you to laugh." To my surprise, I burst into tears.

"Come on." She patted me awkwardly on the shoulder. That's about as warm and fuzzy as Clancy gets.

"Yes, there's a situation with Brawny," I blubbered.

"But who is Brawny? Is she really Bruce? And is she in trouble? Is that why the Feds came?"

"She was born as Bruce. She's not in trouble. The Feds just came to talk. The FBI agents wanted Detweiler and Brawny's input on a situation that they've got."

"Probably the visit from the young royals," Clancy said.

"Probably." I hadn't thought of that, but she had to be right. The whole state was aflutter with the news that Prince

William and his beautiful wife, Kate Middleton, were coming to St. Louis. I agreed that it was cool, but I didn't expect to get within a country mile of the dazzling couple so my enthusiasm was seriously curbed. However, Anya had been bitten early by the Anglophile bug. It was an interest she shared with her grandmother, Sheila Lowenstein Holmes. For weeks I'd heard nothing but a steady stream of speculations about Will and Kate.

"You're right, Clancy. That has to be what they were talking about. It's the only reason I can think of for them to ask specifically to talk with Brawny. That's all I can come up with ...so far." A tear leaked from my eyes and ran down my face and over my chin.

Gracie heard the tremolo in my voice. She lifted her blocky head to stare. Clancy grabbed a paper napkin from the dispenser on the counter and handed it to me.

"So you aren't worried about the Feds. You're upset about Brawny being Bruce?"

I shoved the stack of papers to one side. "Wouldn't you be? She lied to us! She was born a he!" The force behind my words shocked me. After talking it over with Detweiler, I thought I'd calmed down regarding Brawny and her gender issues, but here it had come out of me like that ugly toad that jumps out the mouth of a princess in a fairytale I'd once read.

"Really? She really, truly lied to you?"

"Kinda, sorta." I rambled along, explaining what we'd learned about Brawny's unusual condition.

"Gender dysphoria," Clancy said after I sputtered to a stop.

"What?"

"It's called gender dysphoria, and she was lucky."

"How so?"

"Typically the doctor gives the infant a cursory examination, and then he tells the parents that the child needs surgery, and

that it's a standard procedure. It's called infant gender assignment. Especially if there's a urologist involved. Then the parents
are warned that there will be long-term negative consequences
if they wait on surgery. Of course, that's a load of hooey. There's
so much involved in gender, and a quick peek under the diaper
is not nearly enough for anyone to make an informed decision."

"That sounds like what happened to Brawny. Except they
didn't do surgery. They just kept her condition a secret."

"Can you imagine the confusion and the shame that
produced in her? That's why the suicide rate for people like
Brawny is nine times that of the average population."

"You sound so informed." I got up and grabbed a Diet Dr
Pepper out of the refrigerator. My self-imposed caffeine limit
was one can per day. I needed the extra zip, and I needed it
badly.

"Not that informed. Okay, maybe more than most." Clancy
cocked her head as she considered what I'd said. "As a high
school teacher, I needed to be informed. I had students who
shared their sexual orientation with me, but whose parents had
no idea what was happening. It was my job to protect my kids. I
understood that school had to be a safe place for them. They
needed a universe where they could be the gender that felt most
comfortable. Sometimes, their parents were totally unaware of
what was happening."

"You kept it a secret? That doesn't sound fair to the parents. I
would want to know!"

Clancy chuckled. "The parents 'knew' but they didn't really
'know.' I suspect that all of them knew their kids were different.
They knew something was up, but they didn't have the whole
story. Kids are fluid in high school. It was my job to build a
bubble around them until they found their true identities. I had
to wait until they were ready to share what they learned with
their parents and the world writ large."

"Writ large?"

"In this case, it means 'in the bigger world.'" She sighed. "Hey, so Brawny started life as a he. Big deal. I used to have boy babysitters all the time while my kids were small. They're much more attentive than girls. You never come home and find your kids have gone berserk using crayons on your walls while the sitter was doing her nails."

"But Brawny didn't tell us about her past! She pulled the wool over our eyes."

Clancy smirked. "More like she pulled a Shetland sweater over your eyes."

"It's n-n-n-n-not funny!" I stuttered. I took a quick breath and added, "Anya is so upset that she ran away from home."

"What? How could she do that? How far could she run in this weather? She doesn't have a driver's license or a car."

There were times when I really hated how cool and logical Clancy could be. This was one of them. I wanted to lash out at her and the way she was minimizing the problems in my life. "Of course she doesn't have a car! I drove Anya to school. Instead of kissing me goodbye, she announced that I shouldn't bother to pick her up. She wouldn't be coming home ever. She was moving in with Nicci Moore, and Jennifer had given her permission."

"Did you call Jennifer? What does she have to say about all this?"

"Of course I called! It went to voice mail."

"Then you are getting your panties in a bunch for no good reason. Jennifer will back you up. You know that."

She was right. Jennifer would take my side. But just the thought of my daughter telling me that she was "gone, baby, gone" hurt me terribly. The pain was like a knife wound in my gut.

Clancy stared at me for a sec before saying, "You realize that

Anya knows exactly how to push your buttons, right? All kids do. They own our hearts, and they know it. After everything you've gone through to keep custody of Anya, saying she was moving out would have to hurt you terribly. That's exactly why she did it. She intended to get maximum mileage."

Yes, Clancy was right. That was exactly why Anya had said she was moving out. Her intent had been to hurt me, and she had succeeded. I couldn't decide what hurt most: the fact that she'd intentionally hurt me or the fact that I was so dumb I hadn't seen her manipulation coming.

Clancy leaned close to me. "Kiki? Can you hear yourself? Honestly. Get a grip. This doesn't sound like you at all. You know Anya is a thirteen-year-old who has been through a lot in the past three years. She's hormonal and emotional. Her grandmother, her dear friend, has married and is out west at a rehab clinic. Imagine getting not one but two brothers in less than six months. And a new father. Your family just moved from a small house into a bigger one, and everyone knows how stressful moving is, even when it's for the best. The news about Brawny was a breaking point for Anya. That poor kid has been coping with overload for a long time. She's just come to the end of her rope. Give her time to come around."

I sniffled and mopped my face with a clean paper napkin.

"Why do I think something else is going on? Did you have any alcohol last night?"

"Yes. Why? I'm an adult."

Clancy rolled her eyes. She never used to roll her eyes, but after spending time with me, she'd adopted the habit. "Yes, you are an adult. As your friend, I've noticed that the day after you've had something to drink, you're usually just a tad depressed. Not surprising. Alcoholism runs in your family. You're sensitive to sugar. It's part of your chemistry." With that, she got up to rinse out her coffee cup.

Not surprisingly, I felt defensive. "Maybe it's not the whisky I had. Have you thought about that? Huh? I told you that I had a bad morning. A really, really bad morning. That's why I'm so down!" I proceeded to tell her about the puke-fest in my kitchen.

Clancy laughed so hard that she had to grab the refrigerator handle to keep from crumpling onto the floor or falling face first into the sink. "That's the funniest story I've ever heard. You are full of it, Kiki. What a hoot! You've been watching entirely too much reality show TV."

Her raucous amusement was totally at odds with the sleek, sophisticated style that Clancy projects. People often remark that she's a dead-ringer for the late Jackie Kennedy. Although she would never admit it, Clancy cultivates that image. From her carefully colored auburn pageboy to her classic wardrobe, she mimics the iconic former First Lady. That sense of style is compounded by her demeanor. Clancy is borderline OCD, well educated, cultured and restrained.

"I can just imagine Detweiler slipping in that mess and Gracie trying to...oh...yuck!" Clancy does not erupt in giggles. She does not laugh so hard she wets her pants. Nor does she dissolve into belly-laughs that weaken her knees.

Until today.

Today she raced into the bathroom rather than tinkle on the floor.

When she staggered out of the john, I said, "Glad to know that one of us is capable of laughing."

This time she actually threw her arms around my neck. I stiffened with surprise, just for a second. Her affection overwhelmed me, and after the shock wore off, I relaxed and leaned against her. She held onto me and patted my back. "Someday you'll laugh about it, too. In the meantime, I'm here for you. We'll talk more about this later. Why don't you give Jennifer Moore another call?"

This time I got her, but Jennifer couldn't talk. "It'll be okay. I'll come by at noon and bring you lunch," she said, in a voice made breathless because she was hurrying to get somewhere. Her goodbye was simple: "Later."

"Thanks. See you later," I echoed.

"Enough lollygagging," Clancy said. "We have to get the store organized."

10

For the next twenty minutes, Clancy and I kicked it into high gear to prepare the place for inventory. We organized the shelves, returning supplies to their designated places. We were sorting stray sheets of paper when the ringing of the doorbell in the back sent Clancy racing to greet our guests.

"Hello," Lee sang out.

"Ta-dah!" Jeff shouted as he waved to me. "Let's get this party started."

As always, Jeff was dressed to the nines. He could have walked directly off the pages of GQ. I had no idea which designer made his sweater, but I could bet it was someone famous. His slacks held a neat crease, and his shoes looked like soft leather.

And Lee? Her sparkling blue eyes drew you in. She also wore a lovely cashmere sweater and nice slacks, but those eyes were the showstoppers.

"Jeff brought supplies." Lee's eyes sparkled with mischief. "He's volunteered to be a celebrity bartender at a fundraiser for War Dogs."

"You couldn't have caught us at a better time." He pulled bottles of liquor out of the bag he'd been carrying. "I need to practice my skills making cocktails, and there's nothing like a live audience."

"No drinking on the job." Clancy shook a finger at Jeff. His mega-watt smile faltered.

"Don't mind her. She's not a teetotaler, but Clancy can be a bit uptight," I said. "She's worried because I'm worried about getting all of this done in time to finish updating my profit and loss statements."

"Why didn't you say so?" Jeff's impish grin came back. "Let me call in reinforcements."

"What do you suppose he meant by that? Reinforcements?" Clancy whispered as we used bright blue masking tape to section off the store. Otherwise, it would be too easy to do the same areas twice.

"Beats me. I'm thrilled we've got help. As for the booze, sounds like a plan to me. I could use a stiff drink."

Lee knew the store, and she was a big help in dividing the place into manageable sections, while Jeff disappeared into the back.

"Are we ready?" Clancy asked as she handed out clipboards. Attached were sheets we would use to document our counts. At the top of each sheet was the general category of merchandise and a map of the store with each category marked in colors. Lee, Clancy, and I divided the areas to be covered and began the laborious act of physically counting stock.

Jeff rejoined us, working next to me to take counts. "Thanks for calling us."

"Huh?" I looked up from the torn container of tiny brads that I held in my fingers. Each of us had a bucket for spoils, for merchandise that was damaged or defective. I grabbed tape from my bucket, sealed the brad container, and tossed it into the bucket. "Did I hear you right, Jeff? You're thanking me? I asked you to come do manual labor and you're grateful?"

"Lee needed to get her mind off of Nancy Owens' death. She's been really upset. In fact, they'd been to the same Zoo Keepers' board meeting yesterday. It must have been right before Nancy drove to Ferguson." Jeff marked the counted items with a yellow sticky note.

"I'm so sorry! I didn't realize that Lee was on the board of Zoo Keepers or that Nancy and Lee were friends."

Jeff tilted his head thoughtfully. He said, "I wouldn't call Nancy and Lee friends exactly. In fact, Nancy was one of the few people that Lee doesn't get along with."

With that, I dropped another open container of brads. This time the pieces scattered all over the floor.

"Come again? I can't imagine Lee not getting along with somebody."

Jeff smiled as we both dropped to our knees to pick up the tiny brads. "It is pretty hard to believe, isn't it? Lee gets along with everybody. She even got along with Nancy until recently."

"What happened?"

Holding up a tiny red brad, Jeff studied it. "Zoo Keepers fiscal year starts each January 1. There was an election. Nancy went from being the treasurer to the vice-president. Lee was voted in as the new treasurer and believe me, she was really excited about being a part of the board. Can you keep a secret?"

I crossed my heart.

"You know how the media has been buzzing about the upcoming visit of Prince William and his wife Kate Middleton? Well, as you've heard, he's coming here to talk about his efforts to save the rhinos from extinction. Here's the surprise: Zoo Keepers will be handing him a check for one million dollars. That's money they've raised in support of his cause."

"A million dollars?"

"Right. They've been working really hard to get that much, but last month they hit their goal. Lee's thrilled."

I could see why. "What a terrific time to be elected to the board!"

"So, the election happens. The officers are sworn in, and Nancy took her sweet time getting Lee the books. Finally, she handed them off to Lee right before their board meeting. Typically the Zoo Keepers' board meetings take place an hour before their general meetings. When Lee got home after the general meeting she had her first chance to look over what Nancy had given her. That's when Lee discovered a missing check. One that couldn't be accounted for, written on their money market account."

"Is that a big deal? I void checks all the time."

"Yes and no. Like a lot of charitable organizations, Zoo Keepers keeps the bulk of their money in reserve, separate from ongoing operating funds. Usually if there's a voided check, you write that down in the register. It just needed to be accounted for. That's all."

"Okay, that doesn't sound like a big deal. Not to me, at least." I didn't add that I once lost a paycheck and had to dig around in the dumpster behind the store for it. Of all people, I was the most likely to lose a voided check and to forget to write down what had happened.

"Lee didn't want to make a big deal out of it, but she did want to act responsibly. So she called Nancy at home and asked where the check was."

"How did Nancy react?"

He chuckled. "At first, she didn't believe Lee. Nancy was adamant that Lee was mistaken. Lee offered to show her the checkbook. After sputtering around, Nancy swore the check had been there when she handed the checkbook over, but Lee knew it hadn't been. I was in the same room when Lee made the call, and I could hear the escalating tension. Nancy became defensive. She told Lee that she must have voided a check and forgotten to write it down. That's perfectly reasonable, but why hadn't Nancy said so in the first place? Why had she insisted the check wasn't missing? Lee decided to end the conversation rather than push the matter."

"Sounds ugly."

"It was. When Lee got off the phone with Nancy, she called Fareed Farkada, Zoo Keepers' president. He told Lee that he and Nancy were meeting soon to get the cashier's check for a million dollars, and he'd discuss the missing money market check with her face-to-face."

"Why were they both going to meet at the bank?"

"In most non-profits, it takes two signatories to write a check over a certain amount."

"Oh. So he didn't think it was a big deal? He wasn't worried about the missing check?"

"Fareed has known Nancy for decades, and he assured Lee he'd get to the bottom of the situation. Lee was careful to say that she didn't want to make trouble. She wasn't accusing Nancy of any malfeasance. She just wanted Fareed to know about the missing check in case any questions arose in the future."

I gestured with my head toward the rack of ribbons that we'd count next. Jeff nodded. As I watched him flip the page, I couldn't help but think that Lee had handled the missing check as graciously as she possibly could under the circumstances.

I counted the packages of ribbon, gave Jeff the number, and moved to the rolls of ribbon. "So Fareed handled it, and that was that, right?"

Jeff frowned. "Not exactly. Fareed called Lee back. He said he and Nancy had gone to the bank and gotten the cashier's check to give Prince William. He told Lee that he'd discussed the matter of the missing money market check with Nancy, and he was satisfied with her answer. In no uncertain terms, he told Lee it was handled. Done. End of story."

Jeff shook his head. "Things got even stranger. At the board meeting yesterday, everyone was supposed to sign this big card that would be handed to the prince along with the cashier's check. The mood should have been celebratory, but Nancy was acting very strange. She kept glancing at her cell phone. Lee said she was jumpy."

"Jumpy?"

"That's right. You know Lee. She's pretty unflappable. The meeting ends. Everyone leaves the building, but Nancy and Fareed. They hang back in the meeting room and talk. Lee decides to use the ladies room. When she comes out of the stall, Nancy is standing at the sink, waiting for her. Lee decides it's a good time to mend fences. She says to Nancy, 'I'm sorry if you took it the wrong way when I asked about the money market check.' And then Nancy explodes! She gets right up in Lee's face and warns her to let it go or else!"

"Nobody overheard this, did they?" I was busy re-winding a roll of stickers. I hate stickers. Probably because they often come on these big rolls that easily unwind, ruining stickers and making a mess.

"Fareed was nowhere around. Lee assumes he'd left. The only other person in the building besides Nancy and Lee is the janitor. He was standing in the hall, waiting for them to leave. They head out the door. He locks it behind them. Lee keeps trying to apologize, and Nancy keeps on screaming. She actually follows Lee into the parking lot. Then Nancy notices two board members scraping ice off their windshields. They're staring at her because she's acting like a crazy person. Only then does Nancy quit yelling. Lee was shaking when she got into the car."

"And now Nancy is dead." I shook my head, thinking how awful the situation must have been. I could imagine being screamed at, because that's happened more times than I want to count. But to get screamed at and then have that person die the same day? That would be awful. Just terrible. I would hate the fact that my last memory of that person was such a negative one. But then, that's just me, I guess.

However, Jeff seemed to have read my mind. "Yes, and Lee feels terrible that they parted on such bad terms. As you said, Lee likes everybody, and she gets along with everybody. Lee was trying to act responsibly when she brought up the check, and she was trying to be a good sport by apologizing to Nancy."

"Wow. What a mess." I craned my neck around the shelf unit so I could see Lee and Clancy discussing whether to move all of our glitter off the shelves or count the bottles in place. "Jeff, is it okay that Lee's here? I mean, if she's upset about Nancy—"

Jeff smiled at me. "Are you kidding? Like I said, I was glad you called. This was the perfect opportunity for Lee to shake off the whole nasty business with Nancy. Honestly. You might think we're doing you a favor, but you're actually doing one for us."

I reached over and gave him a hug. It was nice to know I'd done the right thing. As we went back to counting, I realized the conversation needed closure. "Okay, let me make sure I've got the timing of this right. Nancy screamed at Lee in the parking lot. Both women got in their cars. Lee came home, and Nancy drove to Ferguson where she was shot in the head. Ugh. That's ending a board meeting with a bang."

He looked at me. I realized what I said and added, "Oops. My bad." We both smothered the kind of nervous laughs you get when you're feeling guilty.

"Yes," Jeff said with a sigh. "Despite all that, Lee really admired Nancy. That woman was really devoted to animals. I once heard Nancy say that because she didn't have kids, her legacy would be the sister city program and the zoo's breeding program. It's a real shame that she died before she could see the prince receive that check. Nancy cared so much about the zoo and was looking forward to hearing the prince speak."

He was interrupted by a knock at the front door. The sound puzzled me because the sign I'd taped up had made it clear that we weren't open for business.

"I'll get it," Jeff shouted and he scurried off. He came back with six young people.

"Reinforcements from Wash U's School of Business," Jeff explained. Leaning closer to speak quietly, he added, "My interns. I'm always looking for real world ways to get them involved. This is about as real world as it gets."

I panicked. "Jeff, I don't have the money in the budget to pay them."

"You don't need to. This is great experience for them. It'll give them a better idea of how a real business requires hands-on attention. Now that we have reinforcements, I need to practice my bartending skills."

"Bartending skills?" I had no idea what he was on about. "You aren't going to make drinks for the interns, are you?"

"Certainly not. But I do plan to practice my drink-concocting skills on you, Lee, and Clancy. I need to polish my pour."

He winked at me and disappeared into the back room.

A part of me wanted to ask questions. What exactly would he be mixing for us? Would the drinks all be alcoholic? Was it rude to drink in front of the interns? The practical part of me suggested that I accept my good fortune and move on down the highway. If I didn't have to pay for the help, and if warm bodies were here who could make the grunt work go faster, all good, right?

Time to tackle the embroidery flosses. A job I couldn't delegate. A total pain in the backside. And a section that Margit or Brawny typically counted because both of them knew the threads and colors better than I. I started with the neutrals, white, off-white, grays, and blacks.

After I finished those, I moved on to the browns. My head was spinning with thoughts about Nancy Owens, vanishing rhinos, gender identities gone amuck, and my AWOL daughter. When I fingered a denim blue, the same shade as Anya's eyes, a lump crowded my throat. How was I going to get my daughter back? How could we help her get over her feelings about Brawny? Would she ever come home, short of getting Jennifer to kick her out?

I kept counting packages of embroidery floss while the uber-organized Clancy settled our new helpers into specific areas of the store.

Jeff presented me with a frosty martini glass. "Would you prefer a lemon drop martini or a Cosmos?"

"Lemon drop martini?" It came out as a question, not a request, but Jeff raced away and came back with a silver decanter that he shook to a marimba beat. "Cha-cha-cha," he sang while moving his hips to a Latin beat. "Behold, my first lemon drop martini. Try it, won't you? Tell me if it's too tart or too sweet?"

"I haven't had much booze. Just glasses of wine at Shabbat since Ty was born," I said, "and a little whisky last night at Brawny's insistence." I hoped that didn't make me sound like a lush.

"A year without spirits makes one weak," quipped Jeff.

"You aren't breastfeeding are you?" Clancy asked.

"Yes, I am, but I'm also expressing milk. He's happy with me or his bottle, although he prefers me. Ty is a regular chow hound. Detweiler keeps threatening to feed him pizza. But Brawny told me that alcohol does not get into your milk, and she would know. She's studied such things." I sniffed the drink in my hand. The color was a delicious pastel yellow. The fragrance reminded me of summer, and on this cold day, that alone boosted my mood. The sugar around the rim sparkled like diamonds, leaving the single slice of lemon to stand out like a jewel in a necklace. One taste and I was hooked.

"This tastes terrific!" I leaned against the wall space between the racks of paper. The alcohol took all the pent up tension in my body and released it.

Lee giggled. "Lucky for you, he has to practice making a lot of these and making them fast, to keep up with the demand."

"That's an easy cocktail. Wait until you see the fancy-schmancy drink I'll be making next. Prepare to be dazzled." Jeff reached into the reusable grocery bag and withdrew a Tupperware container full of lemon peel cut into strips. Next, he pulled out a cigarette lighter. Holding the peel, he warmed it by waving the flame up and down the piece. With a deft gesture, he squeezed the peel. A burst of oil shot out – and like a fire eater in a circus, the liquid ignited with a dramatic *whoosh.*

"Good show!" Clancy applauded.

Jeff rubbed the peel around the rim of a glass and mixed another drink. Clancy reached for it and after taking a sip, pronounced it, "Excellent. I've never seen that trick with the oil. Pretty flashy. May I try it?"

"Sure." Jeff took her through the steps. When the oil ignited, Clancy crowed with delight.

"You try it," Jeff urged me.

"I'm not into tricky moves." Backing away, I put up two hands to emphasize my reluctance.

"Come on, Kiki." Clancy had finished her drink. "I want another of these. Help Jeff out."

"How can you ignore a plea like that?" Jeff handed me the peel. Holding one end in my fingertips, I warmed the skin with the lighter. When Jeff nodded, I squeezed the peel and flicked the lighter.

To my joy, the lemon oil burst into flame. To my chagrin, the blast of fire surprised me. I lost my grasp on the peel, flinging it into the air.

It landed on the tower of paper.

"Where's the fire extinguisher?" Clancy slurred her words.

Smoke alarms shrieked so loudly I couldn't hear her. "The what?"

Drops of water ran down my nose. In my inebriated state, I wiped them off and stared in wonder at the wet spot on my hand. But not for long. The sprinkler system kicked into action. Water gushed from the metal heads overhead.

Six interns converged on the center of my store. "This isn't a drill. Get out. Go on," I yelled as I pointed them toward the front door.

"Go outside. I've got this under control. Kids? Outside. Everyone. Now." The ever resourceful Jeff had located my fire extinguisher, which had been mounted on the support beam six feet to my right. With the grace of a man who knew what he was doing, he swept the foam mixture up and down.

"Come on, Kiki," Clancy tugged on my right arm and Lee tugged on the left.

"It's melting, awwww..." I did my best Wicked Witch of the West imitation.

"Not funny." Clancy glared at me. "Not even remotely amusing. You're drunk, aren't you?"

"A little," I admitted while Lee held the door open for me.

"Out! Out!" Jeff shooed me toward the exit. "Lee? Get her out of here, please." With Clancy's help and Lee's encouragement, I staggered onto our sidewalk as two firetrucks and an ambulance showed up.

11

A s promised, Jennifer Moore tapped on the store's back door promptly at noon. She took one look at me, squinted, and looked harder. "What on earth happened to you? Two different shoes. A black smudge on your face. I think you've hit a new personal grooming low."

"Long story. Come on in and I'll tell you. Especially if you brought food."

She held up a brown paper bag with the St. Louis Bread Co. logo on the front.

"That just happens to be the magic password. Enter," and I executed a sweeping bow to usher my friend inside. As I moved, my feet made squishy noises. The sprinkler had filled my shoes with water. Wet shoes are never pleasant, and highly undesirable on a cold winter day.

"Now that Jennifer is here, I'm going to run errands. I'll be back." Clancy shrugged on her Burberry coat and wrapped her scarf around her neck.

I seriously doubted that she had errands to run. She was probably being polite and giving me some privacy. As Clancy shut the door behind her, I turned my full attention to Jennifer.

Snowflakes dotted the shoulders of her dark green coat, and her high-heeled Steve Madden boots left wet marks on the floor. "Brrr," she said, as she tugged off a pair of dark green leather gloves. "Cold and getting colder. I love this time of year. Is that smoke I smell?"

I fought the urge to say, "I hate it," although I do. I'll never appreciate cold weather, even when a fresh snowfall blankets the ground in such a poetic way as it had this morning. On the other hand, I love living in St. Louis, and that means I have to put up with our extreme weather. Face-slapping cold like now, and in the summer we get muggy heat. You don't stay here for the climate, I guess. However, once you realize how much the area has to offer in terms of culture, art, wildlife, beauty, history, and education, you're more than willing to overlook the short-comings of temperature and humidity.

"What is that black mark on your face? Are you planning to start teaching face painting?" she asked, moving closer so she could see it better. After examining me up close and personal, she set the paper bag on the break table.

My eyes stayed glued to the bag. I was starving. "It's probably just soot on my nose. Can we eat?"

"Not until you tell me what happened." She pulled off her cashmere scarf and pulled up a chair. Her perfectly made-up face must have been quite a contrast to my make-up free but sooty skin.

"I set a rack of paper on fire." My chin trembled.

"How on earth did you manage to do that?"

"I'd been drinking."

Her eyes opened so wide that her lashes looked like spiders against her skin. "Drinking? Really?"

"Uh-huh."

"By yourself?"

"No."

"Hmmm," she said with a nod. "Okay. I get the drinking part. You've had a bit of a shock with Brawny and all. And yes, before you ask, Anya told me everything. I don't understand where the fire comes in. Did you light up a joint to relax?"

I was shocked. "No!"

"Was there a candle-lighting ceremony that got out of hand?" Jennifer looked honestly perplexed, and I was having a difficult time forming coherent thoughts.

"There was no ceremony. Jeff Alderton was teaching me to make fancy cocktails."

"Really? I thought you were taking inventory. Instead, you were taking bartending lessons? What drinks were you making? Let me guess. Smoke Gets in Your Eyes? Hot Stuff? Blue Blazes?"

"You laugh, but Jeff was practicing to be a celebrity bartender."

"Why would you need a celebrity bartender here?"

This conversation was taking on "Who's on First" aspects. I made the universal time-out symbol with my hands and suggested that I begin at the beginning. Jennifer listened carefully. I concluded my recitation with, "I was curious about how Jeff set the lemon peel on fire, and so he showed me. But I'd had a lemon drop martini first, so maybe I wasn't as careful as I should have been.

"Right." Jennifer's mouth formed a capital "O." After a deep inhale and exhale, she added, "Well. Setting your store on fire is a very unoriginal way to get out of doing inventory. As your unofficial-official business advisor, I wouldn't ever recommend it. I think you've figured that out already. Before you eat, show me the damages."

She did a slow tour of the store, taking in all the damage and shaking her head. "Drinking fancy cocktails. Lighting lemon peels. Setting inventory on fire. Wow, and it isn't even noon. You have been a very, very busy girl." Jennifer started giggling and couldn't stop. "They don't teach this in business school. No way."

When she got control of herself, she did a quick circuit of the store. "Not too bad. I'd say fifty percent of your paper is ruined. But we'd been discussing cutting that inventory and freeing up your space."

Yes, we had. I still dearly love scrapbooking. Really I do. However, the hottest trend is altered journals, and tiny altered scenes. Fairy houses and fairy doors are big. So are fairy gardens. Jennifer and I had looked over my figures. Scrapbooking was barely recouping its expenses. "The beauty of your business is that you are small and nimble," she'd said. "Sit down with your crew and brainstorm ways you can keep up with the on-point trends. Too many business owners fall into the trap of thinking of their businesses written in stone. This isn't one of the Ten Commandments. You don't have to revere every item you've ever sold. Be a trendsetter."

Down in Florida, my friend Cara Mia Delgatto was doing all kinds of cool stuff. They'd started a weekly Coloring Club for adults. One of her employees made miniatures. Another taught DIY classes. As much as I hated to admit it to Jennifer, she was right: Scrapbooking had evolved. More and more people scrapbooked digitally. They kept their photos on their phones.

Yet at the same time, the love for all things handmade had never ever been stronger. It was as if we were surrounded by digital this and digital that, and we had this very primal craving for what we could touch, stroke, and hold.

"I don't even know how to file an insurance claim," I said, pulling off one shoe and dumping out the water.

"I can help you with the claim." Jennifer gave me a hug. "I've also got the phone number of a service that cleans up messes like this."

I covered my face with my hands and burst into tears.

"Hey, hey, hey," Jennifer gave me a side-hug. I got a good whiff of her Prada perfume. It smelled a lot better than the burnt paper. "It'll all be fine. This might have been the best thing that could have happened. It frees you to move on down the highway."

"I d-d-don't care about the p-p-paper. I'm worried about Anya," I said, between sobs.

"Yeah, I figured as much. Come on. Let's go sit down in the back. You can eat the lunch I brought you while we have a talk. Mind if I help myself to coffee?"

All my friends know that I buy beans from Kaldi's, a local purveyor of fabulous coffee. I've tried to cheap-out and buy whatever is on sale at the grocery store or Walmart, but that never works. Everyone notices and no one is happy when I do. The circuit breakers had turned off when the sprinklers went on, but I'd reset them and brewed fresh coffee because I knew Jennifer would be here.

"Of course I don't mind. You can drink all the coffee you want. I already owe you for the lunch. Seeing as how you're feeding and housing my daughter, help yourself. While you do, let me call Brawny and see how the boys are doing."

It was a quick conversation. The boys were resting, and Brawny had gotten Erik to drink chicken broth and ginger ale, while Ty drank a little Pedialyte from his bottle. Today was one of those moments, I was happy that I'd accustomed my infant son both to the bottle and to breastfeeding. I thanked the nanny and turned my attention to Jennifer.

"It's going to be all right. Your daughter is processing emotionally heavy information. An overload."

"Promise?"

"Promise. You remember how stressed out I was when I decided to tell my husband that our son is gay."

Yes, I remembered that well. It marked the start of our real friendship because I stood by Jennifer and supported her. However, the situations were different. Vastly so. I blurted out, "But Stevie is your son, and you already knew he was gay. So it wasn't exactly a shock. This is different. Brawny is the caregiver to our kids. This was a total curveball for all of us. We had no idea."

Jennifer looked at me curiously. "No idea that she once was a he, right? Anya was light on the details."

Jennifer looked over our stunning selection of mugs with sayings on them. This has become one of those inside jokes that makes Time in a Bottle a gathering spot for friends. People keep bringing us mugs with messages on them. The trend began when my friend and former cleaning lady, Mert Chambers, brought me a cup that said, "No more Mrs. Nice Guy!" Since then we've added everything from, "Sometimes I wake up GRUMPY and sometimes I let him sleep" to "As long as I get my own way, I'm totally flexible." Those crazy, silly mugs have become a way for us to signal our moods, our politics, and our intentions.

Jennifer held up the mug she'd chosen and admired the slogan: "When life hands you lemons, you still need sugar and water to make lemonade. Or maybe even a lemon-drop martini, eh?"

"Is that a message directed at me?"

"Yes, it is." Jennifer used a paper towel and wiped off a chair before sitting down. I thought I'd gotten them all dry, but I hadn't. She kept talking. "Like I said, Anya was light on the details about Brawny. I'm not asking you to reveal any personal secrets, but it might help me if I knew more."

I explained about Brawny's "birth defect." Jennifer's eyes narrowed, and she seemed increasingly uncomfortable. Finally, I put my turkey and Cheddar sandwich down and said, "You look upset. Upset with me."

"Well..." She hesitated. "I'm trying to be fair to you. I've learned so much about gender assignment issues because of Stevie's involvement with the LGBTQ community. I'm surprised you're not better informed. Then I remind myself, this has been my life since Stevie came out. I feel for Brawny, and of course, I feel for you. All your reactions are understandable, but this isn't the Kiki Lowenstein I know and love. I suspect your feelings about Brawny are tangled up in Anya's reaction and that lingering post-partum depression you've been struggling with."

Her implied criticism stung, and I reacted angrily. "You aren't the one who discovered a transvestite was living under your roof, and that you, as the responsible parent you think you are, didn't have a clue!"

"Transvestite?" Jennifer echoed. "She isn't a transvestite, Kiki. You need to get your facts right. Brawny isn't a person who's driven to dress in the clothes usually worn by the opposite gender. She was born with an unusual physical appearance. Then she was assigned a gender that did not match who she was, gender-wise. This situation was and is entirely out of her control. You don't seriously think that anyone would choose this for herself, do you? What if Anya had been born with the same problems as Brawny?"

Before I could answer, she continued in an increasingly passionate voice, "Can you imagine the misery that Brawny has endured? Being forced to act like someone she wasn't? Can you imagine what it would be like when such a fundamental part of you is at odds? Put yourself in Brawny's shoes. What if you'd grown up with parents who kept telling you that you were a boy? How would that mess with your head?"

I felt instantly and totally ashamed. "I hadn't looked at it that way. I tried, but I got all caught up in Anya being upset, and then in the boys getting sick. I just didn't have enough empathy to go around. I am trying, Jennifer. I really am. This is all so new to me."

"I guess." Jennifer pulled away from me. I could hear the disappointment in her voice.

Not only is her oldest child Stevie gay, but Jennifer's older brother was gay, too. Her father's lack of understanding drove Phil to join the service. He died three months later while in Vietnam.

"If you found out Brawny was gay, would you let her go?" Jennifer stirred her coffee gently, taking care not to slosh any of it over the side of the cup.

"No." My face got hot. "That's not fair, Jennifer, and you know it."

For an uncomfortable tick of the clock, we sat there. I wondered, "Will this be the end of our friendship?" The silence seemed louder than the sirens had been earlier.

With a tiny huff, Jennifer said, "Maybe you're right. Maybe I'm being too hard on you. I just get tired of trying to explain to people that gays don't make a conscious choice to be gay. Just because someone is gay, doesn't mean they abuse children. The same with transgender folk and transvestites. People lump everything into one category. They would rather be ignorant than educate themselves."

"Give me a little credit, Jennifer. I know more than most. But I'll admit, this is new to me." I sounded huffy. "I'm trying to come to grips with this. Trying to listen to my better angels. I can't tell what's behind Anya's reaction. Is it that she's stunned as we are? Is she feeling betrayed? Or did something happen that I need to address. I've never had my daughter run away from home. I'm scared and hurt. Please be fair to me."

A tight smile crossed Jennifer's face. "I guess this is where your problem bumps into my life and steps on its toe."

I laughed at that image. "I guess. I deserve some of these

slings and arrows. But not all of them. Please give me some credit, too. I've always been fine with Stevie. He's a terrific kid. A natural born leader."

"That's right; you have been good to him. I'm glad you like Stevie. Your Anya is a smart, thoughtful, kind young lady," Jennifer returned the compliment. "You have every reason to be proud of her. Sure, she's emotional. What thirteen-year-old girl isn't a hormonal disaster anyway? She's trying desperately to be grown-up about this."

"It's my job to protect her, and she's angry with me. With all of us. She thinks we messed up. Maybe she even thinks that we tricked her."

"No. She's embarrassed," Jennifer corrected me. "I worked in the school library this morning. Anya and I talked when she had free time before her lunch period. Anya told me she's paraded around half-naked in front of Brawny. She's also shared personal stuff like needing to go and buy tampons. Things that send a young teen into paroxysms of self-consciousness. Remember those days? I would buy twenty dollars-worth of junk food rather than plunk down a single box of Kotex when the grocery clerk was a cute guy. There were times when I'd change lines and stand there for hours rather than having to face a guy who was behind the register."

"I know!" I said. "I hated that. Our local grocery store baggers were all guys. I'd hide the Kotex under a magazine, which was totally dumb. The bagger still had to pick up the box. What made it worse is that the baggers were usually boys from my school. It was embarrassing times two." I'd sort of pushed all those memories to the side. After growing up with two sisters, I should have been more understanding.

"I remember one time when we were on vacation. Nicci sent Stevie into the drugstore to buy tampons for her while we waited outside in the car. She thought she'd figured out a way around her problem. Then, all of a sudden, the front door of the store flies open. Stevie sticks his head out and yells, *Regular or Super Absorbent?* I thought Nicci would die. She crouched down between the front and back seats and refused to climb into her seat until we were back to our condo. She wouldn't go outside for days."

Slowly, I saw Anya's distress in another light. Anya must have talked to Brawny as though she was speaking to a kindly aunt or a big sister. How exposed my daughter must feel! That would add another layer of discomfort to the sense of betrayal we all were trying to overcome.

"Jennifer, thanks for bringing me back to reality. I forget that Anya's been through a lot of changes. Detweiler moving in. Us moving to the big house. Erik joining our family. Brawny coming with him. And then the arrival of Baby Ty. Maybe this last bit with Brawny was the tipping point for her. Maybe I just need to back off and give her space." I rubbed a spot on my chest, realizing that Anya's defection had hit me hard, personally. Since the death of George Lowenstein, my first husband and Anya's father, my daughter and I had relied on each other. The idea that she would walk out, would go to another mother for comfort, and would refuse to come home to me stung like a slap across my face. The sting went bone marrow deep.

For a long while, Jennifer and I just sat there, deep in our own thoughts. Finally, she said, "Anya will always come home to you, Kiki. She loves you. You don't need to worry about that. She's trying to come to grips with this new reality. Think of it this way: She put herself in time-out. She's taking a break. That's all."

"Is it okay for her to hang out at your house?"

But before Jennifer could respond, our back door flew open. A blast of sub-zero air lifted my paper napkin up as neatly as the

Wright Brothers took flight, and slapped me breathless. The cold literally knocked the wind out of my lungs.

Which was fine, because Laurel Wilkins came barreling into the back room with big news. Screaming at the top of her lungs, she shouted, "Guess what, everybody? I am pregnant!"

12

S o as it happened, Laurel didn't have the stomach flu. She also couldn't stick around and talk. She'd only dropped by to share the good news and leave.

"Wait a minute. How's Joe taking this?"

Joe Riley is her fiancé and an Episcopal priest.

"He's thrilled. Hey, I've got to run."

Jennifer pulled on her coat. "I have to go, too. Look, try not to stress out too much about Anya. Give her time. I'll let you know if anything big comes up."

After my friends left, the rest of my day was blessedly anti-climatic. Because I had put a sign in the in front door that we were closed for inventory, there were no interruptions from the door minder. As I worked and worked and worked on that pile of inventories, I found myself praying for a reason to stop. None came. Even though Clancy returned from her fake errands, she was unusually quiet. She came in, said hello, asked if Anya was okay, and went about the business of checking over our yarn supplies to see what could be salvaged. Her body language made it clear she wasn't in the mood to talk.

Without our conversations, or a new project, or a customer

to break up the tedium, the day dragged along. I was never so happy to leave Time in a Bottle behind me. Detweiler and I had agreed to meet at a restaurant on The Hill, the Italian neighborhood in St. Louis. We figured we might as well eat out while we debated whether or not Brawny should keep her job as our nanny.

I phoned Brawny as soon as I was shown to our table. The nanny told me that the little boys were still running low temps. The vomiting had stopped, but both Erik and Ty were fretful. The virus was tiring them out. Erik had burst into tears twice. Ty was fussy. But Brawny was on the job and doing just fine, thank you. Then she asked about Anya. I tried to keep it light. "Considering that Anya doesn't want to get that tummy bug, it's probably best that she stay at the Moores' house for a day or two."

"Makes sense," Brawny said.

I couldn't help but think that Anya had picked a good day to run away from home. I was amusing myself by looking on my phone at other places I might want to live when Detweiler finally walked through the door.

"When you have a bad day, you have a really, really bad day," Detweiler said after he and I placed our orders, and I had given him a rundown of my no good, horrible day, including Anya's threat to never darken our door again. "I heard about the shooting up in Ferguson. At the very least, your friend's death is a good reminder not to sit around in your car with your window down and your engine running. Although that seems beside the point, considering no one took her car."

I didn't correct him and explain that Nancy and I weren't friends. It didn't really matter.

Our waiter brought me a tall glass of ice water and Detweiler an ice water and a glass of tomato juice.

My husband continued, "I don't envy Margit clearing out her mother's room. That's such a sad task. Let's make it a point to check on Horace later this week and see how he's doing. Maybe invite him and Rebekkah over for dinner. As for the store, I'm sorry about the fire, but paper can be replaced."

"Yes, it can."

"Taken as a whole, it wasn't such a bad day, was it? The fire could have been worse. We know that Anya is okay and Laurel had good news. I bet Joe is thrilled that he's going to be a father."

"Yup. She says he is. Although it could be a little uncomfortable for them. Him being an Episcopal priest and all. It's one thing to have premarital sex and another to parade the fruits of your labor around in front of a congregation."

"Good point. I'd completely pushed that out of my mind." Detweiler was raised Methodist. I was raised Episcopal, but I raised Anya as a Jew, in part because George asked me to.

"Do you think his congregation will be upset?" Detweiler asked.

A bus boy brought my water and a glass of tomato juice with no ice for Detweiler. Then our waiter arrived with a bread basket. I reached in, chose a warm roll, and buttered it. "I doubt that they'll be happy about Laurel's condition. Sex before marriage is frowned upon. A baby is living proof that Laurel and Joe weren't practicing abstinence. I have no idea how liberal Joe's congregation is."

"Could he lose his job?" Detweiler sipped his tomato juice.

"I would guess that's up to the vestry to decide. As I recall from my Sunday school days, a priest is called to a parish for life. I imagine they could fire him or they might consult the bishop first and then ask Joe to leave. I don't really have an answer, but I would guess the answer would be yes, Joe could be asked or forced to leave his job." Suddenly, I didn't feel so joyous about Laurel's announcement. Sure, I was happy that she and Joe were happy about the baby, but I could also see the tough times ahead.

"Whatever happens," Detweiler said, reaching for my hand, "they'll be fine. They have each other, and they have our friendship."

"Right."

It was half past five, early for most diners, but fine for us. My husband and I liked this particular restaurant. The food was good and surprisingly inexpensive. This should have been a wonderful date night for me and my new husband, except that I still smelled like smoke. I hadn't had time to change my clothes before driving to The Hill. Sadly, romance was not on the menu, not tonight. Instead, several intense discussions stood in the wings, just off-stage, waiting for us to bring them out to take a bow.

"You look like you're all right, Kiki. Are you? You didn't inhale a lot of smoke, did you?" Detweiler looked me over carefully. He signaled our waiter and asked him for a glass of their house Malbec.

"I'm fine. Jeff Alderton was the hero of the hour. He got all the students out. Lee helped immensely. She calmed everyone down and directed the firemen. Clancy is okay. Jennifer arrived shortly afterward and brought me lunch. We had a good talk, and she called one of those clean-up services that makes the mess go away. They're coming to the store tomorrow at ten. She even volunteered to help me with my insurance claim. I am blessed with terrific friends."

A waiter delivered two gorgeous salads complete with sliced hearts of palm, olives, fresh arugula, and shavings of Parmesan cheese. A light herbal vinaigrette dressing added a pop of flavor, as did various fresh green herbs. A sommelier brought my husband his Malbec.

Detweiler smiled, his eyes soft as they looked at me. "Have you ever stopped to think that you have terrific friends because you are a terrific friend?"

"I try hard." I used my fork and picked up a piece of heart of palm that I chewed thoughtfully. On the phone on the way here, we'd agreed not to discuss Brawny or the government agents' request until our dessert arrived. We needed a break before handling such thorny manners.

Detweiler sipped his Malbec. Looking past him, I could see two women who'd just been seated in a nearby booth. The newcomers were giving my husband the once-over. He is a nice-looking man, thanks to his long legs, his strong features, and his gorgeous green eyes.

"Speaking of terrific friends, you've heard me talk about Lee Alderton? How much I like her? Well, poor Lee got into a disagreement with Nancy right before she was killed." I shared what I'd learned from Jeff about Nancy and Lee's tiff. "Lee feels horrible that they parted on such bad terms."

"We heard about Lee's fight with Nancy Owens."

A tickle of fear came over me. "Wait a minute. Why were you involved in the discussion? Ferguson isn't in your jurisdiction."

What people typically call "St. Louis" is actually a metropolitan area comprised of 91 separate entities, each with its own police force. As a St. Louis County cop, Detweiler occasionally gets called in to help one of them, but taken as a whole, the districts do not communicate with each other as well as they should.

I felt a frisson of fear trickle down my back. If they (meaning the police) had already heard about the disagreement between Lee and Nancy, someone was talking, and it sounded as if that person had pointed a finger at Lee.

"Just so you know, it wasn't *Lee* who fought with Nancy. It was *Nancy* who got upset with Lee. There's a big difference. Lee's a really peaceful person."

"Okay. Do you know what the fight was about?"

I explained about the missing money market check. "But

Nancy talked with Fareed, the president, and everything was straightened out. Fareed told Lee he was satisfied with how their conversation concluded."

"That's what we heard, too. Kiki? You need to stay out of this. That irregularity could be a motive for Mrs. Owens' death."

"Then you're thinking it wasn't a random shooting?"

"We don't know what to think. Not yet." Detweiler studied the dark raspberry-colored liquid in his wine glass. I knew that trick. He wasn't looking at me because he didn't want me to read his expression.

"But Lee didn't drive past Nancy's car and shoot her. You aren't suggesting that! She had no reason to shoot Nancy. The problem had been solved. Fareed said the missing check was a non-starter. So Nancy got a little testy in the bathroom. Big deal."

"That's what you've been told. Maybe that quarrel with Nancy Owens wasn't just a little disagreement. Maybe it escalated, Lee followed Nancy, and shot her. That would have been easy enough."

I pushed my chair back from the table. "Whoa. You have to be kidding! You don't actually believe that, do you? Where's all this coming from?"

"I don't know Lee like you do, and you of all people know how an investigation works. Our job is to follow up on every possibility. Track down every lead. Discuss every angle. Right now other detectives are requesting phone records and doing interviews. Until then, I suggest you stay clear of Lee Alderton."

I nearly threw down my napkin in disgust, but the waiter appeared with my pasta Pomodoro, and I was too hungry to storm off. Instead, I picked up my fork and did my best to twirl the strands of pasta around the tines. "You have to tell everybody that they're wasting their time looking into Lee. She's my friend. You'll do that, won't you?"

"No, I won't. I won't tell other cops how to run their investigation. Honey, you don't seriously expect me to step in, do you?"

Now that he put it out there so frankly, I agreed that I couldn't ask that of him. "I guess not. But you know how these volunteer groups work. People get roped into doing jobs that they are not necessarily qualified for. Mistakes get made. Lee wasn't accusing Nancy. She was trying to be responsible. That's why she brought it up to the president. It was Nancy who overreacted and yelled at Lee. Sane people don't go around shooting everyone they argue with! That's a gross overreaction."

"You don't know if that was the only provocation." He cut a piece of his chicken Parmesan. I could smell the pungent cheese from where I was sitting.

"Okay, I don't, but we've come full circle. I know Lee. I know she didn't do it. End of discussion."

For a while, we simply enjoyed our food. It had been a long time since I'd eaten anywhere other than my kitchen or my store.

"I'm sure the investigators will come to the same conclusion that you have, Kiki. Are you ready to order dessert?"

Over a huge chunk of tiramisu that we'd agreed to share, I eased into the big item looming over us. "I spoke with Jennifer about Anya today."

"How are you feeling about Anya running to Jennifer's house?" Detweiler asked.

"I get that she's upset. I understand she needs time to process this. But I bitterly hate being told she'll never come home again. That hurts."

To my surprise, Detweiler chuckled. "I think everybody should run away from home at least once. I remember running away. I don't remember why, but I remember I was mad. I made it as far as the haymow."

"What's a haymow?"

"The place you store hay in the barn."

"And then what?"

"Mom baked an apple pie."

Why was I not surprised? Thelma Detweiler could give Martha Stewart a run for her money. Thelma's pies were legendary. "And she used the pie to bribe you?"

"Sort of. She set it in the kitchen window to cool. We had screen windows back then, so the smell drifted out to me. I was hungry because I'd forgotten to pack food. The scent of cinnamon drove me nearly insane. Finally I decided it wasn't worth starving to make my point." He snickered. "To this day, I suspect that Mom knew exactly what she was doing and how well it would work."

I laughed. I had always liked Thelma Detweiler until recently. She'd gotten herself all worked up about the fact that I'd continued at the store until the last possible moment of my pregnancy. Later I'd learned that Thelma had carried her first child, a dead baby, to term, and that she blamed herself for losing that baby. She decided she'd been on her feet too much and she'd killed her child. Although learning about Thelma's ordeal had softened my feelings toward her, I still felt guarded in her presence. Even flesh wounds can take a long time to heal.

"Anya is smarter than I was. She figured out a place she could go and still get fed good food." Detweiler's words were cheerful but his smile was sad. "On the other hand, Anya must not have given it a whole lot of thought. Running away from a he-she nanny and going to the home of a friend with a brother who's openly gay? Anya's not going to get a lot of sympathy from the Moores."

"I think that's part of why she was so ticked off. Anya has always known Stevie was gay, and by contrast she feels tricked by Brawny. Although she's never said as much to me, I think she and Nicci have discussed how hard it's been for Stevie. But she hasn't given Brawny the chance to explain herself."

Detweiler signaled the waiter for our check, before turning his attention back to me. "I suspect, and I bet you do too, that this isn't about Brawny's gender."

"You're right. Jennifer thinks that Anya is more embarrassed than anything else. Clancy thinks it's all the stresses in Anya's life coming to an ugly head. My pregnancy, Erik's arrival, our marriage, Sheila marrying and going into rehab, and even our move into the big house."

"Plus the fact that she's become a young woman. I remember how hormones would make my sisters act weird."

Gosh, but I loved this man. "Where does that leave us? What do you think we need to do, if anything?"

"I've been thinking about this all day, and I think we need to give Anya time. On the other hand, I do need to know if anything inappropriate happened. I can't imagine that, can you?"

Detweiler's smile turned rueful. "No. Given Brawny's training at the Norland College for Nannies, three years of classes on child development, including food and nutrition, care and well-being, play and learning, as well as driving under hazardous conditions, plus the fact she finished her dissertation on 'Stress and the Young Child: Mitigating Factors, Intervention, and Character Building,' I think she's passed every possible test with flying colors. Beyond all that, we've watched how stable and responsible she is with our children. We've seen proof of her commitment with our own eyes."

"I still want Jennifer to find out if anything happened."

Looking up from the last bite of the tiramisu, Detweiler studied me. "Nothing happened."

"You can't say that for sure."

"As sure as you are about Lee Alderton, I'm equally sure that

Brawny did not do anything inappropriate with Anya. Or the boys."

He drummed his fingers on the table. "I appreciate that you still have concerns. I should have done a little research on Brawny. What we want in a childcare provider is not the same as what the FBI is looking for."

I put my hand over his. "This wasn't an ordinary situation."

"Right. But the rules don't just apply in ordinary situations. In fact, when there's an unusual situation, that's exactly the time the rules really must be applied, and I blew it. Hearing that you're worried reminds me that I didn't do my job."

"Off with your head," I said in my most regal voice. "Would that make you feel better?"

He chuckled. "No."

"Jennifer is perfectly happy to keep Anya for a while. I have a hunch my daughter will miss Seymour and his loud purring. She'll be lost without Gracie and want to come home." I didn't mention Martin, because he's my cat. I rescued him, raised him from a kitten, and he's decided I'm the only person in the world truly worthy of his attention and love. Most of the time.

"Good. In the meantime, we need to move this discussion along. What exactly do we want to do about Brawny?"

I'd thought about this off and on all day. "I don't see how we can do without her."

"Remember, sweetheart, that she's not the only nanny in the world. We can find somebody else. If you feel the tiniest bit of concern, keeping her won't work. It just won't."

"We won't find anyone as qualified. Not who fits into our household like she does. Not with a history with Erik."

"But we can certainly find someone else who's good with our kids."

I stared at him. "Do you really think she's that easily replaced?"

His hesitation told me all I needed to know, but I waited to hear what he said. "No. I know she isn't easily replaced, and when you hear why the government agents visited, you'll be even more confident that she's irreplaceable. Her hand-to-hand combat training is phenomenal. She's not only a fantastic child-care expert; she's also a kick-butt bodyguard."

I rolled my eyes. "You have to be kidding me, pal. I was there when she brought down a bad guy. I know she foiled a hired assassin. Babysitters like that don't grow on trees. Take today for example. She knew exactly how sick the boys were. She diagnosed them on the spot. She only took them to the pediatrician for a second opinion. If I'd been by myself, I would have been frantic. It's been ten years since Anya was that age. I'd forgotten how scary it is when they get a bug. With little kids, they get sick fast and go downhill even faster. But Brawny was on top of it. Not every sitter could handle a situation like that."

I hesitated. Then I realized what I really wanted to say, "Actually I wouldn't be comfortable with most babysitters. But I am with Brawny, despite what I said about wanting to make sure nothing happened, I trust her. So, no, she's not replaceable. In theory, yes. In practice, no. On top of that, I don't think that you, mister, have any idea how hard it can be to find good help with kids. Or the time it would take. In other countries, they train nannies. Not here. We say our kids are important, but we don't act like it. We don't support working mothers, and we don't have institutions that train and license nannies. I suppose if you are very, very rich, you can import somebody—"

"That's exactly what Van Lauber did, when you think about it." Detweiler played with his empty coffee cup.

"Yeah, you're right. We're benefiting from the fact he did his due diligence."

"Except we're not, because we're questioning his decision."

The waiter brought us our bill inside a leather folio.

Detweiler counted out enough cash for the food and a tip. He tucked the bills neatly into the folio.

A noisy group of diners had taken over the table next to ours. Detweiler's expression changed from relaxed to wary. I knew my husband. I knew that he valued his privacy. He'd learned the hard way that remarks said innocently in public could endanger people. Detweiler leaned close and gave me a kiss. "How about we finish this in the car?"

"Sounds like a plan."

13

St. Louis is a city of parks. Instead of sitting in the car and taking up a space in the parking lot of the restaurant on The Hill, we drove to Turtle Park, a favorite spot filled with huge concrete turtles that had been created by Bob Cassilly, the famous sculptor.

I climbed onto the head of the biggest turtle, sitting astride as though I was mounted on a horse. Detweiler leaned against the turtle's shoulders so that he was next to me. The night was cold and crisp. Beneath us, traffic on 40 hummed like an old sewing machine. Near the horizon, the stars were hidden by the ambient light, but as my eyes grew adjusted, I could see the belt of Orion, the Mighty Hunter. That particular constellation seemed fitting as my husband explained why the two federal agents had come knocking at our door.

"Those federal agents were an advance team. It's standard procedure when dignitaries come to town. They surveil the location and take note of local assets."

"So this is about Prince William and Kate Middleton's visit?"

"Yes, but there's more to it than what's common knowledge.

When William and Kate come to town, they'll be bringing their children, George and Charlotte."

"Wow! Boy, oh, boy. Anya would sure love to meet them. Heck, she'd be over-the-moon to even see them with her own two eyes."

"I know she would, but I don't see how that can happen. The young royals will be coming a week from this Sunday. They'll be the guests at a $1,000-a-plate dinner. It's all sold out. Every philanthropist in town will be in attendance. Publicly, the feds want to play their cards close to the vest. All that's been announced is that William and his wife will fly in, he'll speaking at the dinner, and then they'll fly out."

"Where does Brawny fit into all this? What did the FBI agents want with her?"

"Now that they know the children are coming, too, the federal agents want Brawny to help protect the royal heirs. I got roped into the conversation because I'm a local law enforcement officer and technically, I'm Brawny's employer. I guess they missed the news flash that we're married, and that you, too are Brawny's boss."

"That's so wonderful! What a super opportunity for Brawny. It's just terrific that the royals will bring their children. The whole town is being honored." I quickly imagined various scrapbook pages in my head. The colors of the monarchy united with blue for George and pink for Charlotte would make stunning layouts. My fantasy came to an abrupt halt as my more practical side kicked in. "Do you know their itinerary yet?"

"That's one of the things the advance agents were working on. In addition to William making a speech at the Coronado Ballroom to raise money for endangered rhinos, the entire family—William, Kate, George, and Charlotte—will make time to swing by our zoo."

Of course! Given the prince's love for endangered animals,

this expanded visit made a lot of sense. Founded in 1912, the Saint Louis Zoological Park has been rated America's #1 zoo by Zagat. Before he was tapped to become the famous host of Mutual of Omaha's Wild Kingdom, Marlin Perkins was hired as a groundskeeper. Perkins later became the director of the zoo. It was a perfect fit for a man whose mission was to protect and save endangered species.

"Our zoo has had eight black rhino babies born in captivity," Detweiler said. "We're one of 26 institutions globally that breeds black rhinos. The St. Louis Zoo is doing everything possible to keep black rhinos from extinction. Of course, Prince William would like to tour our zoo. I've been told he's specifically coming to raise money that will fund a new park in South Africa, a facility to help educate people about the rhinos."

I gave a hoot of laughter. "Educate people about rhinos? You mean knock sense into the heads of old men who believe powdered rhino horn works as an aphrodisiac!"

"Exactly."

I shivered, and Detweiler pulled up the collar on his jacket. We wouldn't be able to stay outside long because it was so cold. But I was still glad we'd come here. Having the place all to ourselves was a rare treat.

"For obvious reasons, we'll need to protect the royals when they visit. The trick is to do it in a way that doesn't scare their children. That's where Brawny comes in. If she can be at the event, that's one more layer of protection. To an outsider, she's nothing but a childcare giver. Her other training would be a real surprise to anyone who wants to create mischief."

"Is all this normal pre-VIP activity? I remember when the Pope visited. The city went all out. They even welded shut manhole covers to keep an assassin from popping up while the Pope drove by. So I totally get the fact we don't want to go down in history like Dallas did. We don't want to be remembered as the town where a high-profile assassination took place. But is that it? An abundance of caution? Or is there a bigger threat in the wind?"

He took a long slow inhale and blew it out before responding. "There's been terrorist chatter. No one knows how credible it is, who's doing it, and whether this is real or fake. The ability to verify the real aims of any online conversation is hit or miss. That's why multiple layers of protection are the most effective way to keep the royal family safe. The DSS—Diplomatic Security Service—is the arm of the Department of State that's charged with protecting foreign diplomats. Often they pull in the FBI and ATF, but DSS will ultimately be in charge.

"Whenever there's an event like this, all the agencies work together to control the variables. They shut off routes. They secure buildings. And so on. When it comes to human assets, it's imperative to work with people who are proven to be reliable, trustworthy, and if possible, well-trained. Locals have a special role to play because invariably things have to be fluid. You simply cannot plan for every contingency. Staying fluid and safe demands on-the-spot knowledge of the environment and options. Does that make sense?"

It did. "What's the plan?"

"Prince George and Princess Charlotte love animals so their parents want to bring them to the zoo for a visit next Sunday. While there, they'll mingle with other children and parents. As you know, this generation of royals believes in giving their children as normal of an upbringing as is possible. Because I'm local, I'm a dad, and I'm Brawny's employer, they've asked me to be one of the undercover officers who'll be onsite. Because Brawny lives with us, they decided to make one visit do the work of two. Because Brawny's trained to protect children, she'd be an essential part of the operation to keep the young royals safe.

Since she's had training in the military and as a nanny, she's a natural choice."

He didn't need to go on. I got the drift. "Is Brawny willing to help them?"

"Yes, as long as we allow it. Provided of course we don't fire her before that.

He went on to explain that for years, the Norland College for Nannies had worked with the Royalist and Special Protection group, which is part of Scotland Yard. On a regular basis, Norland provided Scotland Yard with a list of their graduates all over the world who might be called upon if the royal family needed assistance.

"Of course the young royals have their own nanny who's a graduate from Norland, but the Royalist and Special Protection group wanted to map out their resources. Not surprisingly, Brawny came highly recommended. Scotland Yard had actually gotten in touch with her when she worked for Van Lauber. They'd sent representatives who asked her if she would honor her commitment as a member of SAS who had sworn to protect and defend Crown and Country. At that time, they were clearing the way for a visit to California that never materialized. When doing their research for this visit, Brawny's name came up first thing."

"In the end, whether or not she participates is up to her. They can't force her, can they?"

"No."

I slid down off the turtle's nose. My backside was getting cold. Detweiler pulled me close to warm me up.

"But this does complicate matters, doesn't it? If we fire Brawny right now," I said, "it would look very suspicious for her to stick around St. Louis and show up at an event where the young royals are front and center."

"You're right. Especially since the goal of Scotland Yard is to make Brawny's appearance seem as natural as possible so she doesn't raise suspicions." Tucking my hand under his arm, Detweiler strolled us back to the car. He opened the door for me. He sighed and said, "I've been over and over this in my head. I can definitely see why they want her. Brawny will be a real asset when it comes to protecting our royal guests. She can fly under the radar because she actually is a nanny. Her training in close quarters hand-to-hand is beyond anything I've ever seen or experienced. For our local agencies to replace her as part of the protective detail would be difficult if not impossible."

He closed my door, got in, buckled up, and turned over the engine. The drive to our house was pleasantly quiet. We don't need to fill up the space when we're together. Instead, we simply enjoy each other's presence. I've learned to enjoy these special moments with my husband. Tonight my mind raced, running here and there, weighing options.

"I don't want to let Brawny go," I said as we made the turn onto our street in Webster Groves. "If we did let her go, that would be contrary to who we are as people. We both believe that everyone should have equal rights under the law. And equal protection and respect. Even if Brawny had chosen to change her sex, and there weren't so many extenuating circumstances, I want us to have compassion for others. Maybe acceptance is a better word. Whatever. I think it would send a really bad message to Anya if we fired Brawny while our daughter is having a hissy about this. It would be like saying, 'Okay, you got angry, jumped to several conclusions, and now here we are, doing exactly what you want.' She's not the parent. She's a kid. It's not up to her to make these decisions. These decisions are our call."

"You're betting she'll come around?"

"I sure hope so." I paused. "Anya's got a good heart. Jennifer asked for a few days to find out if anything untoward happened. That timing of that should be perfect, because Anya needs the space. She'll have to feel comfortable with Brawny or this will never work. I can't force it. If we can just hold on, I bet Anya'll do just fine."

"And the royals' visit? Since we want to keep Brawny, do we want to essentially loan her out?" He pulled into our driveway, hit the button for the garage door, and waited for the metallic squeak as it rolled up and out of our way.

"That's entirely up to Brawny. I'm sure she took an oath when she enlisted. I can appreciate her need to keep her word. I do get the impression from everything you've said that she really is uniquely qualified to help keep the royals safe."

Detweiler parked the car and we sat there, staring into the dark garage. "I never even knew there were people with mixed up sex organs, although Clancy says it isn't all that uncommon. She uses the term 'intersex.' I mean, it makes sense, but I just never thought about it. It seems strange that someone I know was once a boy and is now a girl, even if that's not exactly what happened. But when I push that aside, when I compartmentalize, I still trust Brawny down to my toes. Like tonight. We're out here, taking our time, deciding her fate, but we haven't once worried about the boys even though they have a tummy bug. I wouldn't have that level of confidence with a teenager or most babysitters."

"That's a good point. Look, if we decide to keep her that doesn't mean we can't ever let her go. It's not like we're making a lifetime commitment."

"Right." I tried to lean my head on his shoulder, but it was tough because the console came between us. "If we keep her, do we need to tell everybody about her gender dysphoria? What will your parents say?"

I thought about Anya's paternal grandmother, Sheila Lowenstein, who had recently married Robbie Holmes, our chief of police. "Sheila's still in rehab out west. Robbie's with her. What, if anything, do we tell them?"

"Is it their business?"

"No. Actually, it's not."

"Okay, just to be clear, we've decided to let Brawny stay, barring any information that she was inappropriate with Anya. We both assume that Anya will come around. If not, we'll deal with that later."

Although it was dark in the garage, the security lamp outside the window cast a cone of warm yellow light. I loved looking at the profile of my new husband. Point of fact, I loved everything about Detweiler. I particularly felt a thrill of pride in his belief that all of us can be of service in our lives. Not just cops or nurses. All of us.

"I admire how the young royals try to socialize their children and bring them out into the real world," he said. "Just like Princess Diana did. I also support what Prince William is trying to do to stop poaching."

"You know what a total animal lover, I am," I said. "Brawny really is the perfect person to protect the youngest royals."

"Yes, but this has to be her decision."

"I agree."

"Let's shake on it." Detweiler put his hand in mine. First we shook and then we kissed.

I laughed. This was our newest ritual, a way of signing off on any disagreement. With that handshake, our course of action became clear.

14

Not surprisingly, we discovered that Brawny had been waiting up for us in the family room. She'd taken a wingback chair, facing the fireplace. On her lap was a pair of navy blue socks she was knitting on four needles. I thought they were for me, but I didn't ask. Her face was drawn; her eyes ringed with plum-colored circles. There was an air around her, a suggestion of defeat. Even so, her posture was ramrod straight, almost as if she were facing a firing squad. She stood to welcome us and then sat back down in front of the modest fire she'd started in our fireplace. The crackling logs and cheerful glow helped to drive the chill from my bones.

"How are the boys?" I asked.

"Better. Their temperatures are down. Erik drank a bowl of chicken soup broth and kept it down. He had an ice pop before he went to bed. Ty has been fussy, but he drank Pedialyte, and kept it down. As the doctor said, it was naught but a tummy bug. Both will be right as rain. 'Tis probably just as well that Anya," and here her voice broke with emotion. She gathered herself and continued, "that Anya isn't here. I imagine this is something she's already developed an immunity toward, but you never know."

"Kiki? I'm going to get a cup of decaf. Do you want anything? To warm you up?" Detweiler asked as I sank down onto the sofa. Gracie had greeted us at the door. Now she jumped up and sat beside me with her head resting on the back of the sofa.

"Decaf tea, please. Brawny? Yes? One for her, too, please."

"What else have you been doing this evening?" I asked, trying to make conversation until Detweiler joined us. "Working on socks?"

"Aye. Knitting is soothing. So is crochet. I hope to get these done for ye this week."

"Thank you. You might want to make a baby afghan next."

"Are you?" Her face lit up, a study in pure joy. Brawny loved children. You could tell by the way she spoke to them, the care she took, and how she perked up at the mention of a child. Now I sort of felt bad because she was so excited about me having another baby. As far as I knew, that wasn't happening.

"Not me. Laurel. She and Joe had planned to start a family as soon as they got married, but I guess the stork moved faster than their wedding planner. They'd been discussing what to do, what sort of ceremony to have, but every option seems problematic. There are a lot of factions to keep happy." I took a cup of hot tea from Detweiler. He delivered a second mug to Brawny, and then went back into the kitchen for his coffee. When he'd joined me on the sofa, Brawny turned sad eyes on us.

"We want you to stay," I said in a rush. There was no good reason to prolong her misery. "Yes, we've had a shock. Yes, Anya's having trouble getting over being embarrassed, but we think the world of you. We know how dedicated you are to our children. You've proven you'd give your life to protect any of us. We can't imagine finding anyone more capable, reliable, or kind."

To my horror, she burst into sobs. Seeing the strong, warrior-like nanny go to pieces sent my head spinning. I went to her side and hugged her. "It was just a shock," I repeated. "That's all. It took us a while to process this. I'd never heard of intersex. Now I have, and I'm sorry that you were put through that. It must have been horrible."

Brawny pulled a white cotton handkerchief from a pocket of her gray sweatpants, her after-work uniform. Wiping her eyes, she said, "I regret that I didn't tell you earlier. Truly I do. Aye, it's been hard. I can best describe it as wearing somebody else's clothes or shoes. Being a man never fit me properly. No matter how hard I tried. No matter how many mornings I woke up and rededicated myself to being masculine. I couldn't be someone I wasn't."

After giving her a pat on the shoulder, I went back to my spot on the sofa. In my absence, Gracie had gotten up, turned around, and rested her head in Detweiler's lap. Fortunately, she'd left space for me, but only because she was nearly on top of my husband.

"I can't imagine what that must have been like for you," Detweiler said, "Or for your parents. They must have been just as confused and frightened as you were."

Brawny's hands shook as she lifted the cup of tea to her mouth. "I was lucky, actually. I've since learned that a lot of doctors took it upon themselves to do surgery immediately. They called it 'corrective,' but effectively it took away a person's right to make a choice when they were older. It's still a battle for many. There are doctors who label intersex as belligerent when they refuse surgery or when they disagree with the gender they're assigned."

"How hard it must be for parents facing a decision like that for their baby. The option of a boy or a girl is something most of us are content to leave in God's hands." I sipped my tea and thought about my two little boys upstairs.

"Most parents are told it is a sort of birth defect. They want to hurry the process along rather than deal with the indecision," Brawny said. "I was lucky that my parents didn't allow the doctor to carve me up. If I were born today, I would probably be allowed to choose my gender when I was old enough, and then I'd be given hormones to help bring my body into compliance. As it is, I muddle through."

Detweiler faintly colored, so I changed the subject. "I spoke to Jennifer Moore today. She's confident that Anya will come around. Evidently, she's embarrassed about the personal matters she shared with you."

"Aye, I hope Anya will give me another chance. I felt torn over that. I considered trying to stop her from sharing, but I lacked the courage. I am trained to care for children of all ages, but I used my education as an excuse. To my mind, 'twas nothing more than she would tell a doctor or a nurse, but now I see that might have been the wrong decision. I don't blame her for being angry. I am sorry she feels that I misled her."

"She'll get over it," I said with a confidence I didn't feel. "She'll need time. That's all. If anyone can judge how Anya is taking this, Jennifer's the one."

"I'm hoping young Stevie can help her come to grips with it. They text each other all the time."

"Moving on to the visit from the royals," Detweiler said in true left-brain fashion. "I explained what little I know to Kiki. The big question in our minds is, 'Do you want to be involved?' I know they brought up your time in service to the Crown as leverage, but as long as we remain your employers, it's well within our rights to refuse giving our permission. Not that we would do that. I'm just saying there's a reasonable excuse if you don't want to help out. Don't let the authorities back you into a corner."

Brawny stared long and hard into the fire. The sweet

fragrance of cedar drifted up. Unlike the fire at my store, this one made me happy. I loved staring into the flames. "I do feel it's my obligation to do what I can to help the young royals. You see, I met Prince William years ago. We were both stationed in Belize as part of the British Army. He's a good lad, the kind of fellow anyone would be proud to call a mate. Of course, I don't know what sort of plans have been made by your country's diplomatic protection service. I imagine they'll do everything in their power to keep the royals safe."

"Of course they will." Detweiler sounded confident, and that gave my spirits a lift.

It had been such a long and draining day, that we all said goodnight.

15

Not surprisingly, I found it difficult to get to sleep. The emotional stresses of the day had kicked my body into high gear. If it hadn't been so cold outside, I would have grabbed Gracie and gone for a long walk. Instead, I snuggled next to my husband and did my best to get a little rest.

The next morning, after Detweiler got up to run, I dressed and went down into the kitchen for a cup of tea. Brawny was already up. She announced that the boys' fevers had broken. She'd used one of those flexible thin-strip thermometers so she didn't have to wake them. As usual, I ate a slice of Ezekiel cinnamon-raisin toast with peanut butter and apple slices. Then I woke Ty up. He nursed for just a little bit and then promptly fell back to sleep. Erik was zonked when I tried to wake him.

"Brawny, is it okay with you if I let the little boys stay home and rest up? I know you usually run errands on Tuesdays. Will that mess with your schedule?"

"'Tis nothing that won't keep." She poured a glass of orange juice. "Have ye heard anything this morning from Anya?"

"No." I put a second slice of Ezekiel bread in the toaster. "But you have to remember, she's Sheila Lowenstein's granddaughter.

If anyone can hold a grudge, it'll be Anya. Her pouts are legendary."

"I miss her. I want to apologize to her and ask her forgiveness." The emotion in Brawny's voice surprised me. I knew she was upset, but obviously this estrangement with Anya bothered our nanny more than I would have guessed."

"Sooner or later, she's going to miss her cat and Gracie. I bet she'll also miss Erik. Maybe even Ty. Try not to take her behavior too hard. Remember, she's been through a lot of changes recently."

Brawny gave me a sad nod of agreement.

A glance up at the kitchen clock sent me hurrying around like a crazy woman. "Gee, without the kids underfoot you'd think I'd be ready for work in nothing flat."

"Will ye be working all by yourself? How's the mess from the fire?"

"Laurel is coming in." I stood with one hand on Gracie's leash and the other on the doorknob.

"Why not leave Gracie here? The little boys will enjoy her company."

"All right," I said, handing her the leash.

"Can the two of ye clean up the mess from the fire?"

"We won't need to. Jennifer texted me with the number of a man whose company specializes in disaster clean-up. He's even got a general contractor's license, so if there's structural damage he can fix it. Jennifer has used him and likes him a lot. I'm supposed to meet him at the store. If Laurel makes it in, she can wait on customers while Clancy and I finish taking inventory."

"I hope she's back to feeling bright as a copper penny." Brawny paused. "It must be wonderful to be in a family way. I can't imagine…"

The wistful tone in her voice reminded me that she probably couldn't have children of her own. It's one thing to make a decision not to have children, and another whole thing to have the decision made for you. Considering how much Brawny loved kids, the inability to conceive must have broken her heart.

How easily I'd taken my fertility for granted!

ON MY WAY to the store, my phone rang.

"Anya is fine," Jennifer reported without the preamble of a salutation.

"Thank goodness. We're planning to keep Brawny. We decided last night that she's a terrific person, a fabulous care-giver, and her gender history is nobody's business."

"I thought you'd come around. You just needed time to get over your shock."

"Okay, I'm over it. How's my daughter doing?"

I could almost hear a grin in Jennifer's voice. "She Skyped Stevie, and he told her in no uncertain terms that she was being a brat. He sent her all kinds of information on gender and iden-tity. I have to tell you, that kid of yours takes after her grand-mother. She was resistant to the bitter end, but finally Stevie hit her with, 'Where's your sense of compassion?' Anya told him that she deserved compassion, too. She said she was embar-rassed by what she'd shared with Brawny."

"Wow. I'm glad she opened up to your son."

"Stevie took advantage of her confession. He asked her point-blank, 'Your embarrassment is more important than a person's livelihood? Than her character? Than the struggle she's had?'"

"Double-wow."

"I have to tell you, more and more I'm seeing that my son has a future as a talented activist. When Stevie was little, he was so quiet and shy. Now, he's a man on a mission. He is knowledgeable about the LGBTQ community and their issues. He is totally driven to help people understand that gender is not a binary construct. People of our generation were raised to think in terms of boy or girl, either or, and that was the end of the conversation. Life is much more nuanced than that."

"It certainly is. I can't thank you and Stevie enough for helping Anya through this tough time."

"I still haven't asked Anya if there was anything else that happened. Anything inappropriate. I'm pretty confident the answer is no, but you asked me to find out for sure, and I promise you that I will. I think I'll get the chance this afternoon when I pick her and Nicci up from school. Hey, I've got somebody on the other line. Got to go!"

With a sigh of relief, I arrived at Time in a Bottle. I parked and rested my forehead against the steering wheel of my old red BMW convertible.

"Dear God, thank you for my friends who love my children. Please help me to be compassionate toward those who are different from me. I ask you to help me be generous of spirit so that they might have an easier path to travel. Amen."

I looked up to see a van with the Speedy Service Cleaners logo on its side, pulling into the lot at Time in a Bottle. This would not be a fun experience, going through the mess the sprinklers and the fire had made, but it had to be done. Getting out of the car, I picked my way across the icy patches. As the sun rose in the sky, ice and snow in the shade would melt, only to re-freeze later as the sun went down. Because our parking lot is asphalt, you can't always tell you're walking on ice until too late. I've slipped and fallen more than my fair share of times. That's caused me to be extra, extra cautious. Anya says I move like an old lady. And she's right. I do.

The man who got out of the van met me at the back door. He wore a white shirt with Speedy Service Cleaners embroidered in blue over the pocket. His navy pants sagged a little at the knees, but all in all, he projected the sort of capable personality that would run a cleaning service. "You Mrs. Lowenstein-Detweiler?" is what he tried to say. Instead, he totally mangled both names, calling me, "Low-stine-de-why-lair."

Holding out my gloved hand for a shake, I decided to make his life easy. "Call me Kiki."

"I'm Curtis Priva," he responded, looking me straight in the eyes. His were a watery blue and he had a tiny scar above his left eyebrow. The color of his hair was hard to define, somewhere between black and dark brown. Most striking about the man was the chiseled structure of his face. Curtis looked as though he'd lived a hard life, and it had taken a lot out of him.

"Heard you had a fire and then the sprinklers turned on. Plus," and he consulted a clipboard, "a fire extinguisher was used. That right?"

"Yes." I unlocked the back door and let him in. There I shrugged off my coat and pulled off my gloves to hang them up. I felt strangely vulnerable without my big dog at my side.

But I didn't have to feel that way long because a heavy knock on the back door demanded my attention. Another man greeted me. This one wore a black cashmere topcoat and fancy dress shoes. "Mrs. Detweiler? I'm Frank Folger, your insurance agent."

Not surprisingly, both men wanted coffee. Frank carefully hung up his nice coat next to mine on the small rack we used as a closet. Curtis seemed impervious to the temps outside.

"I'll take a quick look around to see what needs doing, but I won't get down to the nitty-gritty until your agent has had the chance to take photos," Curtis explained.

Both men wandered around while I put on the coffee pot. It felt totally weird to have two guys I'd never met before wandering around my store. Most of our customers are women. We have a few gay men who shop with us. Once in a while, a guy will come in and shop for his wife, but typically, this is Girl Land.

Frank did his circuit and returned to the back room. He reached eagerly for his cup of coffee. After draining the cup, he ran through what we needed to give him for a claim. "Here's a brochure to help you. I've taken pictures of the mess. The clean-up can start. However, you will have to document the value of what you've lost. Invoices are the best proof, but obviously you'll need to inventory the losses first."

Luckily, Clancy had done a count of the paper rack before I'd set it on fire. I'd planned to put a lot of the paper on sale after the inventory. However, my invoices would reflect the full cost, the retail cost, of what I'd lost. If I was really lucky, that extra money would cover my deductible.

After Frank finished his coffee, he handed me three copies of his business card and left. "Call my office and talk to my girl, Paula, if you have any questions."

I said I would, although I nearly choked on that word, "girl." For a grown man to call his secretary "his girl" in this day and age was ridiculous. I was still steaming as I carried a cup of coffee out to Curtis.

"Thank you very much. This looks worse than it is," he said with a sweeping gesture of the hand not holding the mug of coffee. "Sure you lost a couple racks of paper, but the sprinklers turned off quickly. I can toss all the paper in plastic bags so you can take an inventory, if you'd like. There isn't a lot of standing water. Let me turn on a couple of industrial size fans and small heaters to dry up the moisture. You'll probably have trouble waiting on customers with the noise and the wind."

I made a small sign to tape to our front door: *In case of a crafting emergency, come around to the back door and knock hard!*

"Does that really happen?" he asked, rubbing his jaw.

"Does *what* really happen?"

"A crafting emergency?"

"You'd be amazed," I said. "When it does happen, I want my customers to know I'm here for them."

"Good thinking." Curtis gave me a wink. "I'll try to make this as painless as possible for you. Once the areas are dry, you'll be able to see what's what."

I'd made a cup of decaf for myself when Laurel flew in through the back door. Her cheeks were pink from the cold, but her skin was more pale than I can ever remember. I hugged her and noticed how her shoulder blades stuck out, even when muffled by her heavy winter jacket. Laurel has always been thin, at least since I've known her, but now she felt like skin and bones under my touch.

"How about a cup of mint tea? That should help you with morning sickness."

She took a seat at the table we use for breaks. I started the electric water kettle and got her up-to-speed on the situation at my house. Because Laurel and Father Joe have agreed to be my children's legal guardians, they had more than a passing interest in how my kids were doing.

"Anya'll come around. I remember getting embarrassed easily when I was younger. Don't you?"

"I hope so." I put a tea bag into the mug of hot water and then I covered the mug with a plate so the mint would steep.

"How are you feeling?"

"Not good. I've been sick a lot. I don't know why they call it 'morning sickness,' because I've been puking all day and all night long."

Curtis walked into the back room to pour himself a second cup. The aroma of the coffee must have turned Laurel's stomach because she raced past him, slammed the bathroom door, and puked so violently we could hear it twenty feet away.

"She hasn't been feeling well," I said, by way of explanation.

Curtis stared at the door. "Geez. Poor kid."

Laurel wobbled her way out of the bathroom. I introduced her to Curtis. She nearly fell into her chair when she went to sit down. "I hope this gets better."

"When was the last time you kept down any food or water?"

She shrugged. "Three days ago."

"Have you talked to your doctor?" I didn't want to be a nag, but I was worried.

"Yes." She unwrapped a ginger-infused hard candy and popped it into her mouth. "He's really nice."

"Laurel, nice doesn't cut it. He needs to be responsive. Did you explain to him that you have not been able to keep anything down for three days? If you stay sick like this, you'll wind up seriously dehydrated. "

With a little shrug, she ignored me.

I sat down across from her. "Hey. You need to force your doctor to pay attention."

"Okay, all right. I'm seeing him tomorrow morning. I'll tell him that I've been sick."

"Not good enough. You need to be specific. Tell him that you haven't kept any food or drink down for three days. That's a long time! Promise!"

She looked irritated, but finally she nodded. "Now, what work can I do?" There was an edge to her voice that urged me to back off. Laurel might look like a fluffy bunny, but she had a backbone of pure steel, a spine she'd grown through early adversity.

I filled her in on the steps necessary for us to make an insurance claim.

"Most of this I can do from home," Laurel said. "I'll pull the inventory sheets for the areas that were ruined. We've got a copier at the apartment that I can use to make duplicates. Is it okay if I bring these back tomorrow after my doctor's appointment?"

"Yes, as long as you agreed to tell your doctor how sick you've been. I also expect you to promise to drink a lot of liquids and put your feet up."

"Promise."

Laurel had already left when Clancy arrived at ten. Her eyes and nose were both red. Her hands trembled as she poured herself a cup of coffee.

"What's wrong?" I asked, as she pulled up a chair across from my stack of paperwork.

"Nothing," she mumbled.

"Clancy? Don't give me that. Come on. You know everything that happens in my life."

"Since you insist."

"I insist."

"As you know, James, my ex, took the kids on a two-week for the holidays." Using both hands, she raised the mug to her lips.

I nodded. After hearing about her ex-husband's plans, Detweiler and I had invited Clancy to join us Christmas Day. I wasn't sure if she would accept, but she did. Several times, she thanked me. If I hadn't intervened, she would have been home alone.

"James told me that he wanted to introduce our kids to his new girlfriend, who's the same age as our daughter, Elizabeth, and a year older than our son, Charles." Clancy paused and shook her head. "I hated the whole idea, but I finally reconciled myself to it. When he left me, they quit talking to him. They are his children, too. I can't blame him for wanting to salvage his relationship, but I was upset that he planned to take them during the holidays so I couldn't see them at all."

"That seems pretty cruel to me."

"I thought so, too. Anyway, I haven't heard a word from the

kids since they left. Not a peep. They didn't even try to Skype me on Christmas Day. I've seen a few photos on Instagram, but that's it, and it's really getting to me. Finally, I gave in and phoned James. He says they had internet connection problems on the cruise ship. I get that. I've been on cruises before. They always tell you that there's WiFi, but then they make you pay for it with solid gold bars. Sometimes you have to line up to use the ship's computers to connect. You stand there waiting while kids play video games."

"So there's a technical reason they can't contact you."

She gave me a look so filled with anger I nearly dropped my coffee cup. "Baloney. There's no reason at all. None. They've been back to school for nearly a month now. My kids still haven't contacted me. I'm sure they are okay, but it hurts that they can't find the time to call me. It's like a knife wound to the heart."

I went around the table to hug her. She accepted it with the sort of stiff posture that she always grants my affection. Even so, I could tell she appreciated the gesture. I couldn't imagine how badly she must be feeling. I knew where Anya was and how she was doing, but I still felt miserable, and it had only been a short while that she'd been gone!

"Clancy, I am so, so sorry." I still had my arms around her.

She talked into my hair. "So am I. I really thought I'd raised them better than that. I thought they loved me, no matter what. Now it feels like they've kicked me to the curb because their dad can offer them more goodies than I can."

I squatted next to her chair, putting myself a tad lower than she was. "You don't know that. You can't be sure what's happened."

"You're right." Her sigh was deep, and silver crescents of tears sparkled in her eyes. "I don't know what's happening. Or more correctly, what has happened."

"How about texting your kids?" I asked.

"I tried. Not a peep. They aren't answering my calls now. My ex seems to be dodging my calls, too." She ran a shaking hand through her auburn bob.

"What's your best guess?"

"He's trying to turn them against me. It's the old Disneyland Dad syndrome."

"The what?"

Sighing, she wiggled free of my hug. I let her go and walked back to my chair. After another gulp of coffee, she explained, "A Disneyland Dad is a man who tries to buy the love of his kids by pulling out all the stops when they're together. I can't tell you where the phrase originated, but I can say that as a teacher, I saw it all the time. A father's guilt can translate into a spoiled rotten kid. Besides bribing the child with vacations, toys, clothes, and even cars, some dads purposely suspend all the mothers' rules when the kids visit. It's a nasty, destructive way of endearing the kids to their father and making Mom out to be the bad guy."

"Is that what you think is happening?"

"Yes, I do. I suspect that James really laid it on thick. He truly does love our children. When he ran off with his girlfriend, our kids were furious with him. He had a lot of groveling to do before they would *even* talk with him. Initially, I encouraged them to go on the cruise. I didn't want them to be estranged. I wanted them to move on and forgive their dad for starting a new life with Bambi."

I hooted with laughter. "Bambi? I don't think you've ever used her given name before. You've called her the Hussy and the Homewrecker, but I didn't know her name was Bambi. Is that a joke?"

"I wish it was. No, the name on her birth certificate is Bambi. I'm surprised her mother didn't name her Jane Doe. Can you imagine? How dumb is that?"

"Bambi." I marveled at the name. Actually, it really was a pretty name. It brought to mind big brown eyes, and an innate sweetness. But it sent the wrong vibes entirely.

"Get this: she looks exactly like you'd expect her to. She could be a Playboy centerfold. It's not surprising that James fell for her. He always was a complete fool when it came to women. Not that he'd ever strayed before, but he always was the type of guy who got whiplash when a pretty face or a nice body walked past."

"Excuse me. This will be loud," Curtis said. He had walked past us, carrying the tank from his wet vac. With practiced ease, he drained the contents into the sink. Because the sink was only four feet from where Clancy and I were sitting, the noise drowned out any further conversation.

When the gurgle stopped, Curtis righted the tank. He turned to face Clancy. "I shouldn't be eavesdropping, but lady, any man who'd run after another woman when he was married to you has to be dumber than a goldfish. You're well rid of that sorry excuse for a husband. You deserve a guy who treats you like a queen. Not a numbskull who chases kids in skirts."

Clancy and I were wide-eyed with surprise. I struggled not to giggle, while my friend colored from her neck to her hairline.

His momentary lapse of good manners must have surprised Curtis too, because he turned the shade of a ripe tomato. "Sorry," he added before hustling out of the back room.

"Smart man. My sentiments exactly," I said. "As for kids, this seems to be the season for selfish offspring, doesn't it? I can't imagine how badly you feel about this. Let's hope our kids regain their senses, and they do it quickly."

Dabbing her eyes with a paper napkin, Clancy nodded. "Thank goodness for this job. I would go out of my mind if I didn't have this as a distraction. Well, this and the ongoing drama at the Detweiler house."

"Glad I could provide entertainment value."

"You always do. You're a walking-talking highlight reel. Enough feeling sorry for ourselves. Let's go over what we need to do to get ready for our regular Friday night crop."

For the rest of the morning, the three of us did our jobs companionably, not bothering each other. Curtis worked out on the sales floor, I sat at the break table, Clancy moved around the store. With a little help from the insurance agent's brochure, my friend created a form that would help us organize our list of damages. Meanwhile Curtis worked his magic, sucking up standing water and circulating fresh air. Around noon, I waved him down.

"You're welcome to join us in the back for lunch," I said.

"I appreciate that. May I use your microwave?"

"Help yourself."

After making a trip to his van, he brought in a small cooler. From it he removed a glass container full of reddish sauce and what looked like a chicken with vegetables dish. His food smelled terrific as it heated. Meanwhile I had a tuna fish sandwich and a dish of sliced cucumbers. Clancy had her usual salad, but that didn't inoculate her from the charms of Curtis's food.

"That looks terrific," Clancy said. "What is it?"

"Hungarian goulash. Just like my mother used to make."

That led to a discussion about my favorite subject: food. From food, we naturally discussed travel, since the goulash was a beloved native dish. Before her divorce, Clancy had done a lot of traveling. She and Curtis discussed the Rhine River valley while I listened with envy. The conversation made for a pleasant lunch, and it definitely took Clancy's mind off her adult children.

"Back to the salt mills," I said.

"That's salt mines," Clancy corrected me.

Rebekkah dropped by at two. She looked like a hot mess with her curls flying around her head in a dark halo. From the back, her body was so similar to her mother's that I felt a fresh ache of sadness. I never walked into the store without thinking about Dodie and her devotion to saving and making memories. Rebekkah seemed distracted as she hung her navy pea jacket haphazardly on a hanger from the coat rack. As she stepped away, it fell to the floor. Clancy, however, retrieved and re-hung it properly. She also straightened all our coats and arranged the hangers an equal distance apart. This unnecessary organizing was a symptom that her OCD was raising its ugly head.

With a sigh, I asked Rebekkah how her father was.

"*Abba* has walking pneumonia. They're keeping him in the hospital for a few days because he's pretty weak." Sighing, she ran a hand through the unruly curls that spilled onto the infinity scarf wound around her throat. She'd made the piece herself, using a variety of blue yarns in different textures. Brawny had patiently taught the girl to crochet, a real feat because Rebekkah, bless her heart, was all thumbs. But she had been motivated to learn, and she kept at it. "This will help me keep calm. I love blue, and I figured the soothing colors would help, too. With *Bubbe* gone, I need to help *Abba*, and I can't do that if I'm overly emotional."

Her rationale brought tears to my eyes. She was so sweet and so lost.

Clancy and I offered our support, but it had been Brawny who'd taught Rebekkah the art of crochet. At first, like many beginners, Rebekkah kept her knots too tight. She worried they'd slip off the hook. Trusting the process comes with practice. So did learning to "read" the knots, so she could see her stitches.

"How did inventory go?" she asked. "Wait a minute. Do I smell smoke?"

We explained what had happened. Then Clancy dragged out a plastic tub full of items that needed to be assessed for damage. I copied a couple of the insurance claim forms that Clancy had created and gave them to Rebekkah. Already I could tell that using them kept us all on track. The form made it easy to see at a glance what had been counted and what still needed our attention.

Armed with the proper supplies, we all got back to work.

I had trouble focusing. I kept glancing at the clock and thinking about Anya. Jennifer had promised to talk with her, to make sure nothing inappropriate had happened with Brawny. How would that conversation go? Had Stevie's blitz of information been enough to help Brawny's cause? Would my baby ever come home?

That led me to ponder Clancy's problem. How could she compete with a husband who was determined to "buy" his adult kids? Why weren't Elizabeth and Charles smart enough to realize what their dad was doing? Would they ever "come home?" Why weren't they polite or kind enough to stay in touch with their mother? Was there more to this than inconvenience? Was Clancy being totally honest with me?

I knew Clancy could be difficult. She lacked flexibility. She was judgmental. She had borderline OCD, and she walked around picking up after people, which often created problems because she didn't put stuff where you wanted it. More than once, she had dismantled a project that I was working on, scrambled all the parts, and made a hash of them, simply because she couldn't take looking at the mess. Had she driven her children away?

Was I doing something similar with Anya? Was I somehow overlooking her needs for autonomy? Was I overbearing? Had I paid my oldest child enough attention? She'd been through so much in the past few months.

If only Sheila was out of rehab! She had been a stabilizing factor in Anya's life. Although the late George Lowenstein's mother could be a real harpy to me, she was a never-ending source of love for Anya. Right this minute, Anya really, really needed her grandmother. It would be easy to be ticked off at Sheila, but in truth, she was stuck in rehab fighting for her life. Briefly, I considered calling Robbie and asking him if there was some way that Sheila and Anya could get together. Just as quickly, I ditched that idea. Sheila had already had one big setback, drinking Aqua Net hairspray of all things. Better to wait until Robbie gave us the okay. He knew how close she was to Anya. We'd talked about it many times—and concluded that Anya was Sheila's number one reason for agreeing to dry out. If for any reason a meeting between them backfired, such a risky move might cost Sheila her life.

I mulled all this over while counting wet sheets of paper in the back room. Rebekkah labored over the plastic tub of assorted damaged items. A couple of hours passed by slowly. I was finishing one more inventory sheet when Rebekkah set her clipboard down on the break table. "I'm sorry, Kiki, but *Abba* is expecting me. I promised him I'd come visit this afternoon. I have to get going."

"Of course. Please give him our best."

After she left, Clancy continued taking inventory, spending most of her time out on the sales floor. She and Curtis developed an easy camaraderie, allowing her to direct his efforts while she did what we needed to make our insurance claim.

AT FOUR, we heard an insistent pounding on the back door. I opened it and Lee Alderton stumbled in. If I hadn't grabbed her by the arm, she would have done a face-plant.

"Lee? You okay?" I slipped an arm around her waist and led her to a chair. Lee sat down with a plunk that suggested she was about to keel over.

Her knit scarf had been pulled up around her face like a cowl. You could barely see her features. With mittened hands, she pulled it down. A pair of red-rimmed eyes and a nose suitable for Rudolph the Red-Nosed Reindeer appeared. Red blotches marred her skin.

"Lee? Are you all right?" I crouched beside her chair. Seeing the normally competent woman this discombobulated had me worried.

She looked at me as if seeing me for the first time. After blinking a couple of times, she seemed to get a hold of herself. "You have to swear not to tell anyone. Promise?"

Rebekkah, Clancy, and I raised our right hands and promised to keep our mouths shut.

"I just met with Fareed. We have a problem. A big problem. The cashier's check that he and Nancy co-signed for a million dollars is missing."

"A cashier's check for a million dollars?" Clancy's voice was a notch higher than usual. "And you lost it?"

Lee explained how Zoo Keepers had been doing fundraising all year, tapping big donors, hosting events, and asking for pledges. "It was Nancy's dream to give a substantial amount to the Tusk Trust, the prince's own conservation organization. She wanted to personally hand that check to Prince William."

"It's missing? Who had it last?" I asked.

"Fareed and Nancy showed it off at our board meeting. They'd gone together to the bank, signed for it, and brought it back so the board could see it. It's the culmination of three years' work. We all signed a card for the prince. Nancy tucked the check inside the card and put it in her purse. Since she's the longest serving board member, she would see her dream come true. She and Fareed were going to personally hand it to Prince William after his speech in the Coronado Ballroom."

"So you actually saw it at your board meeting. Did you watch Nancy put it in her purse?"

"Yes. We all did. She was going to take it home and lock it in a wall safe."

"The news reports said that nothing was missing from Nancy's car, but they could have been misinformed. Sometimes the police hold back information. Lee, do you know whether Nancy had the check on her person when she was shot?"

"I don't know, but I would assume so. She must have gone directly from our board meeting to Ferguson." Lee dabbed her eyes with a paper napkin.

I really needed to keep a box of tissues back here. Either that, or we all needed to quit crying.

Lee continued, "The last we saw of the check was when Nancy tucked it inside the card and put the card in her purse. Fareed is going to the police as we speak, but he suspects that the person who shot Nancy took the cashier's check."

"Okay, then," Clancy said. I could see she was shifting into her practical mode. "Just call the bank and stop the payment."

"We can't."

"If they won't do it over the phone, get there tomorrow when the bank opens and—"

Lee waved the suggestion away. "It doesn't work like that. The whole point of a cashier's check is that it's just like having cash in your hand. The money to back it up is held in escrow. If a bank does not honor the cashier's check, they get fined."

"Back up a minute," I said. "Are you one hundred percent positive that's correct? About the cashier's check being like cash?"

"Absolutely." Lee sniffed and dabbed her eyes again. "Fareed even put the bank president on speaker phone so we could both ask him questions."

"Then you're telling us that somebody killed and robbed Nancy for a piece of paper worth a million bucks?"

"No," and Lee sobbed. "It's not really about the money. You have to have a payee or the bank won't write a cashier's check. We had the payee. It's the Tusk Trust."

"So no one can deposit that check but the Tusk Trust. And that's who was supposed to get it, right?"

"Right, but that's not the problem."

Now I was totally confused. "Okay, I'm officially lost."

Clancy went over to the refrigerator, grabbed a Diet Dr Pepper, popped the top, and handed it to Lee. "Drink this. Collect yourself. Start over."

"I'll have one, too," I said, but I didn't get up.

"Aren't you over your limit?" Clancy gave me a querying look.

I hopped to my feet and marched past her to the refrigerator. Once there, I grabbed can of my favorite cola. "Ty will just have to deal with it."

Several fortifying sips later, Lee had calmed down. "Okay. Take two. Here goes. Fareed and Nancy are—were—authorized signatories for the Zoo Keepers. They went to our bank and had a cashier's check made out to the Tusk Trust. That's the conservation trust that the prince started. They got the check because we wanted to give it to Prince William. He knows it's coming. That's a big reason he is flying to St. Louis. So he can officially receive the check. Are you with me so far?"

We nodded.

"The funds backing up a cashier's check are held in escrow. When a cashier's check is presented, the bank receiving it must honor it just as though cash was being exchanged. So you can't stop payment on a cashier's check, because you can't stop payment on a dollar bill, right?"

"Right," I agreed.

"Nancy and Fareed brought the cashier's check to our meeting so everyone could see it. After all, it's not every day you write a check for a million dollars to a worthy cause. While we watched, Nancy put it inside a card. She put the card in her purse. She drove to Ferguson and was killed. Now the check and the card are missing."

"And that's why you're upset. Because the check is missing, right?"

Lee gave an exasperated sigh. "Not exactly. No one can do anything with that check except to deposit it in the Tusk Trust. That check is worthless to anybody but the Tusk Trust."

"So what's the big deal?" I asked, rolling over my palms.

Clancy shuddered. "I'll tell you what the big deal is. Prince William and his wife are flying here to accept a check that's gone missing. He's making this trip, which is a huge big deal, and Zoo Keepers won't be able to deliver on their promise."

"Yes!" Lee nearly jumped out of her chair. "You've got it. And that's not the worst part. The very, very worst part is that the event is sold out. Every place at every table will be filled with someone who paid $1000-a-plate to see that check delivered. Many of the biggest donors were promised a photo op with the royals."

Suddenly the problem was really clear to me. "And there's going to be a lot of egg on everyone's face."

That brought Lee to her feet, and she gestured wildly with both hands. "We will lose all kinds of face with those patrons. They will never, ever want to make a contribution to Zoo Keepers again. Why would they? We'll look like we were careless with their money! And here's another kick in the shins: What does Fareed do? Get up there and hand the prince an empty envelope with an IOU inside? Does he say, 'Yes, we dragged you out here to the Heartland, Your Highness, but no, we can't come up with the money we promised you. How about a train ride around our zoo. Isn't that a fair trade?'"

I was still stuck on the do-re-mi. "But eventually you can get the money. Am I right?"

"Yes. The key word is eventually. We can take out an indemnity bond for the amount. However, most banks won't reissue the cashier's check for 30 to 90 days. I doubt that Prince William will hang around St. Louis that long."

"How many people are scheduled to attend the dinner event?"

"Two hundred." Lee buried her face in her hands. Through her fingers, she said, "The cream of St. Louis society. All the major philanthropists. Every big donor we've ever tapped. And we're going to look like such a bunch of idiots."

"Could be worse." Clancy ran a fingertip around the rim of her coffee cup. "You might look like idiots, but at least you're still alive. Nancy Owens was killed for a check that can't even be cashed. I wonder if her killer knew that?"

I couldn't even go there. Was it possible that Nancy had been the ultimate victim of a senseless crime?

"In the meantime, you have to do as the Brits did in the war," Clancy said. "Keep calm and carry on."

"You're right." Lee nodded. "That's a great motto. Fingers crossed that someone tries to cash that check. All the banks have been alerted. Maybe we'll get it back somehow. Maybe."

"Look, Lee, I can't replace the money you've lost, but I can do my part. I'll dedicate all the proceeds from the crop on Friday night to Zoo Keepers."

"That's very kind of you." For the first time since she'd arrived, Lee managed a smile. "Let me check with Fareed, just to make sure it's okay. I bet we can send out a notice to all our members and donors. Maybe some of them will come."

Trust Clancy to rein me in and be sensible. "We can't accommodate more than 30 people at a time."

"Okay, but I can make page kits, and those are only limited by the amount of stock we have. What about if I create a page kit that Zoo Keepers can promote to their mailing list? I'll focus on Prince William's visit, which will give people a really great reason to get this particular kit. We'll donate everything we make off it except for the cost of the supplies."

Lee's smile grew bigger. "That's wonderful. We have brochures that explain our mission. Can I bring them for you to pass out?"

"Of course you can."

"Do you have any donation forms?" Clancy asked. "Those would really get you the most bang for your efforts. Maybe paperwork explaining how bequests and gifts work? There might even be a big donor out there who'll be persuaded to change his or her will. I remember when I worked with the board of a non-profit. We kept hitting up the same people over and over for money. Linking your requests to people who want to save their memories of William and Kate's visit might expand your audience."

Before she left Lee dispensed hugs all around. "Keep calm and carry on," she kept repeating. It was as if that slogan had become her new mantra.

BY FIVE O'CLOCK, I was drained, literally and figuratively. Clancy shook a finger in my face. "You are going to wear yourself out and then get sick."

"I know, I know."

My car was freezing when I climbed in. The tires didn't want to move. They were frozen to the parking lot. Slowly I moved forward, hearing the crunch of snow beneath my tread.

I waved to Clancy and Curtis and hit the road feeling bluer than the ocean on a perfect summer day. I missed Anya so much! Sheila once told me that she thanked her lucky stars that she'd had a boy and not a girl. "Girls are harder to raise than boys. Women can be much more vicious because we're more attuned to pleasing people. We know what will really, really hurt."

That got me thinking back to that night at the Webster Groves Library when Nancy Owens asked me if I had time for a coffee. In retrospect, I was really glad that I had made the time for her.

We drove separately to the closest coffee shop, a little place call Java Java Ging Ging Ging. I'd never been there before, but Nancy said it was nice.

My first impression was that I'd walked into a dollhouse, the shop was that cute. White squares trimmed with lace sat on top of red-and-white gingham table skirts. The white table settings were framed by black mats. White damask napkins were cinched by black, red, and white braided ribbons. One of those comical black cat clocks, the kind with a tail that swings back and forth, watched us from one wall. Other walls were decorated with black silhouettes on white paper, framed in black. An efficient young woman with a cute bobbed hairstyle swished out of the kitchen. A frilly white underskirt peeped out from under her red-and-white gingham skirt, but her simple black tee shirt added an edgy vibe.

"Hiya," she said as she slid menus our way.

I hadn't intended on eating, but the Peanut Butter Rice Crispy Treats sounded fabulous, so I ordered one along with a cup of decaf. Nancy ordered Fudgy Healthy Brownies, made with black beans! She ordered regular coffee.

"Won't you have trouble sleeping?" I asked Nancy as the waitress walked away.

"I never sleep. I can't. She won't let me."

"She?"

"Rochelle. My stepdaughter. She makes certain I never get any sleep. My husband can sleep through anything. A freight train could plow right through our bedroom, and Bert wouldn't wake up. But I'm a light sleeper. Rochelle figured that out right away. She's certainly using that knowledge to her advantage."

"What do you mean?"

"Rochelle has decided to torture me by keeping me up. She sets our alarm clocks to go off in the middle of the night. She rattles the doorknob at odd hours. She turns the heat up or down. She calls my husband on his cell phone at three a.m. When he doesn't answer, she calls mine. I don't think I've had more than four consecutive hours of sleep since Bert and I got married."

"She's doing this on purpose?"

"Absolutely. She's admitted as much to me."

"Your husband lets her get away with this?"

"He doesn't believe it's happening. He says I'm overreacting,"

I knew what sleep deprivation could do to you. There's a reason it's a technique used to torture people. Lack of sleep can seriously mess with your head and wear you down physically. New research suggests that your brain actually begins to eat itself when you go too long without sleep. "Isn't there anything you can do?"

Nancy gave me a weak smile. "I could go away. Divorce her dad. Drop dead."

"Here you go." Our waitress slid our desserts onto the table. "Be right back to warm up your coffee."

"You're a widow, aren't you, Kiki? But you're obviously in a relationship."

"Yes, the belly bump is a dead giveaway, isn't it? My first husband was murdered."

"I remember that! Was your partner married before, too?"

"Twice. And we got married on December 27th. I'm not wearing my ring because my hands are swollen."

"Does your husband have any children?"

"That's complicated." I explained how Detweiler's first wife had cheated on him, but run off when she discovered she was pregnant. "Erik is legally Detweiler's child, but not biologically."

"How old is Erik?"

"Five. I have to say that he's integrated well into his new life. He adores his older sister, Anya, and now the kids are both excited about the arrival of our new baby. Detweiler always wanted a lot of children. Seems like we're on our way to raising quite a brood."

Nancy's next comment surprised me. "Be careful what you wish for," she said. "My grandmother always told me that, and I didn't listen. But she was right. Truer words have never been spoken."

"Huh?" I wasn't sure that I understood. I could feel the intensity of her gaze as her mouth turned down in an angry grimace. Confusion set in, and I wondered if somehow I'd offended her. "Did I say something wrong?"

"No," she said as she brushed away my question. "Not at all. It's just that I felt exactly like you. I thought my handsome prince would come along, and our love would conquer all obstacles."

"But it didn't?"

"Ha! It not only failed at conquering obstacles, it dragged along its own ugly bag of garbage. Let me give you a bit of unsolicited advice. Are you ready? Listen carefully. Never, ever marry a man who has a teenage daughter from a previous marriage. Ever. Especially if that man feels guilty about his divorce. And if his daughter despises you, don't even try to make things work. Trust me. He will always choose her over you. You and your marriage are doomed from the start."

"Wow." I couldn't think of anything else to say, so I repeated myself with, "Wow."

I turned the subject to other topics. To an outsider, I probably sounded like I was giving a commercial for my store. That's because I didn't know what to say to Nancy. I didn't want to share more about my marriage. I wasn't interested in hearing how Detweiler and I couldn't possibly hope for a happy future together. Now I keenly regretted that I had agreed to spend more time with Nancy. Here I'd thought of her as a sweet woman who just needed a shoulder to cry on, and instead, I'd gone for coffee with an unhappy person, who had cheerfully predicted that my marriage was doomed.

When the waitress set down our bill, I snatched it up. I didn't want to linger here any longer. I paid for it with a twenty-dollar bill. "Keep the change," I told our waitress, hoping that this would speed our exit. But Nancy obviously wanted to linger. She took her time putting on her coat. To head off any more unpleasant glimpses into my future, I turned the conversation back to her.

"So you married Bert Owens, thinking his daughter would get over it? But she hasn't?"

"I fell in love with Bert for many reasons, not the least of which was how much he adored his daughter. That was my mistake. I thought that if he could love me half as much, I'd be happy. But Rochelle wasn't willing to share her father. She liked being Daddy's Little Princess, and she resents every second he spent with me."

"Have you tried counseling?" I stood to indicate I was ready to leave. Because Nancy didn't, I added, "I need to be getting back."

"Bert isn't interested in counseling. He says it's natural for him to love his daughter, and that she's just having trouble adjusting. Bert still feels guilty for divorcing Rochelle's mother. Of course, Rochelle plays on that."

What an ugly future was in store for the Owens family.

Nancy fiddled around in the area of her seat cushion and brought up her scarf. Winding it slowly around her neck, she said, "Rochelle has told me in no uncertain terms that she'll never, ever get over her dad marrying me. She's gone as far as telling me that I'll regret this as long as I live."

By mutual agreement, Nancy and I gathered our belongings and walked to the door. In the soft glow of the sodium-vapor lamps, snowflakes spun their way to earth. The day had been cold and heavy; the night was colder still and oppressive. The moist and damp atmosphere seemed to pin us down. Instead of enjoying the expansiveness associated with the out-of-doors, I felt claustrophobia. I couldn't get over the sad story that Nancy had shared, and I wished—oh, how I wished!—that she hadn't burdened me with her misery. The thought of living under the same roof with someone who actively wanted you dead made me weak in the knees. Hadn't I grown up in a similar environment? With a father who was dangerous?

How bizarre it would be to hear such threats from the mouth of a teen. How frightening it would be to know your husband didn't believe his daughter plotted against you. The whole story sounded like something straight out of *Rebecca!*

Coming back to the here and now, I shook my head. Just the memory of Nancy Owens' misery cast a pall over me. I told myself, "She's dead and I'm not. I have to cheer up."

My gloomy thoughts traveled with me as I drove home. I took the back way, avoiding heavy traffic. I needed to calm down and clear my head. But my plan didn't work. Instead, I grew more and more anxious as my old BMW moved along from one darkened street to the next. I pulled into the garage with a sigh of relief. Our house seemed strangely quiet as I walked from the garage past the laundry room and into our kitchen. Usually Anya and Erik are buzzing around, hopping up and down while doing their homework at the dining room table.

Not tonight.

I missed my daughter. This gave me a sudden empathy for Bert Owens. No wonder he had bent over backwards to keep his child happy. What parent wouldn't? Especially if that parent felt responsible for creating chaos in a child's life?

Entering the kitchen, I realized I'd brought along my very own little cloud of freezing air. Gracie galloped down the stairs and greeted me by standing on two feet and putting a front paw on each of my shoulders. Her tail thumped the wall repeatedly, indicating how happy she was to see me. The warmth of my home blanketed me as I sniffed the air appreciatively. The savory fragrances of garlic, onion, celery, and chicken set my mouth to watering. Brawny must have put on a pot of chicken noodle soup. How wonderful it was to come home to a hot meal! From the oven came the fragrance of popovers.

"What have ye heard from Anya?" Brawny had followed Gracie down the stairs. Standing before me, she was wringing her hands, a motion you read about but rarely see.

"Nothing. Not a peep. How are the boys?"

"Better, but they both have had a bit of a temperature off and on. They're asleep right now." Her head tilted as she regarded me seriously. "Anya hasn't had any communication with you at all?"

"No. Has she texted you?"

After watching Brawny shake her head in the negative, I said,

"Me neither. I've texted her. Usually she texts a message or two between classes. Not today."

I turned my back on Brawny because I was struggling with tears, but Gracie saw me. The big black-and-white giant stood on two legs, putting her blocky muzzle at eye-level with me. Those brown eyes searched my soul. Sensing how hurt I was, Gracie did something I've rarely seen her do—she yodeled.

"My, my." Brawny stared at the dog in wonder.

"It's okay, girl." I rubbed the big dog's ears and eased her back to a four-paw structure.

"She's not happy that you're upset."

"Nope."

"Have you spoken to Mrs. Moore?"

"Yes. Earlier today. She assures me that Anya is coming around."

"I hope so."

"I do, too."

For the next two hours, I kept myself busy, washing and folding clothes, hoping the distraction would help. It didn't. Not much. In fact, I was getting more and more depressed when Jennifer called.

"Sorry, but I wanted to speak to you without the kids over-hearing," she explained.

"No problem," I lied.

"Anya is fine, but I can tell she's sad. On the way home from school, Nicci asked Anya to help her re-organize her closet. You can imagine how excited Anya is about that!"

Despite myself, I laughed. Sheila has always made sure that Anya has adorable clothes to wear. My child is appreciative of her grandmother's generosity, but Anya has never shown the same level of interest in her wardrobe that most of her female classmates have. In fact, my daughter has told me that she finds Nicci's passion for fashion to be tedious.

"We both know that Anya would rather have a tooth filled than help Nicci organize her closet. She's only being agreeable so she can play the part of a good guest. You've taught her well, Kiki."

"Thanks, I think. What should I do, Jennifer?" I couldn't help myself. I hated the fact that Anya and I were estranged.

"You have the hardest job possible. You have to do nothing. Nothing at all. You have to wait Anya out. This is going to get old for Anya really fast. Hang in there."

WITH THREE KIDS and three adults, laundry is an ongoing process, not a task that ever ceases. Erik woke up grumpy, but now he was happily watching *Sponge Bob Square Pants* in the family room. I dumped a warm basket of clothes on the sofa next to him and folded as he watched.

Erik asked me if he could help. I gave him the washcloths to fold.

I could tell that he was both lonely and happy that Anya was gone. After all, he'd gone from being an only child to one of three in the space of six months. His idea of heaven was not having to share any attention, having both me and Brawny to himself. Especially since he was getting over being sick, he acted clingy. I couldn't blame him. Poor dude. After dinner, we went back into the family room. He crawled up into my lap and snuggled in. At his behest, I read him one book after another. When I needed him to hop down so I could nurse Ty, he left me reluctantly and crawled into Brawny's lap. It was her turn to read to him, and she did until his bedtime. Ty was already asleep in my arms.

"Let me check Erik's temperature and then I'll take the baby upstairs to bed." From a pocket of her sweatpants, she withdrew the flat thermometer and pressed it against Erik's forehead. "Still one hundred degrees. No school for you tomorrow, young sir."

The nanny waved the flat thermometer at me. "Let me check Ty."

The baby's temperature was slightly higher than normal, too. Now she gave me a once-over. "How are you feeling?"

"Tired." Realizing she needed the truth, I added, "A little sore."

"Not surprising. You shouldn't be lifting anything or working so hard. Not to mention climbing stairs with the baby in your arms. Hand Ty to me and I'll put him in his crib."

The transfer was made without waking the baby. Brawny stared down at me. "You should try to get some sleep. You have a crop on Friday, right?"

"Right. Also one on Saturday. Just call me a glutton for punishment. Erik?" I beckoned to the little boy as the nanny left the room. "Would you walk upstairs with me?"

Even though his eyes were droopy, he wasn't ready to give in. "I don't want to go to my room. I'm not sleepy."

"Well, I sure am." I held out my hand. He obligingly hopped off the sofa and came to me. "Would you mind if I lie down on your bed? Just for a minute or two? I am so tired. Maybe we could read together."

Of course, he couldn't read. Not yet. But he liked to pretend he could. He especially enjoyed the Where's Waldo series that had once enthralled Anya.

Anya.

Was I just tired? Had I overexerted myself? Or was the ache I felt a symptom of missing my daughter?

Keeping a strong grip on my fingers, Erik led me up the stairs. Once we made it to his room, I put the overhead light on low by using the dimmer switch. "Erik, honey, can you go and get me my Kindle? It's beside the bed."

The self-important way he walked suggested that he was thrilled to be my big helper. He came back with the e-reader in hand and solemnly presented it to me. I thanked him, and we snuggled together on his big boy bed, a twin-sized mattress we'd put on the floor just in case he rolled off it.

As the warm skin of his neck rested against my arm, I reminded myself to cherish these moments. Since coming to live with us last summer, he's slowly come to accept me. I wasn't his birth mother, and I hoped that he would never forget Gina, but he called me Mama Kiki, and on occasion, just plain Mama. Those first few months, he would only go to Brawny if he needed comfort. Now it was Brawny first, then Detweiler, and I was running a close third.

He was clingy now because he was sick. When kids don't feel well, a parent is a source of great comfort. I realized that many businesses don't understand why working women need to stay home with their sick children, but the reality is that no one knows your child like you do. No one can comfort a sick kid like a mother or primary caregiver. If you are forced to go to work and leave that child with a caregiver, you won't be able to concentrate anyway.

I think it's funny that companies want to hire "good" people but then they want those same people to ignore other priorities in their lives. How could a responsible person ignore his/her aging parent or sick child? They couldn't. A person who would ignore the needs of family is hardly likely to be loyal to co-workers. Yet, many businesses penalize people for showing responsibility when a family member needs help. That flat out doesn't make any sense.

Considering both boys were still feverish, Anya's absence was well-timed. Because she was out of the house, she probably wouldn't get the tummy bug her brothers had contracted. I could spend quality time with Erik. I didn't need to worry about

Anya's needs, so my attention wasn't divided between them. At this stage of his life, Ty was an eating and pooping machine. Sure, he was learning all sorts of things like what his fist tasted like and that crying helped you get what you want, but his need for my attention was limited. Since babies sleep so much, I could concentrate on Erik.

I told myself this was a good thing. A very good thing.

So why did I feel empty inside?

16

D etweiler came home and slept on the sofa rather than wake me up. He planted a kiss on my cheek before he left for work, since I had to get up then anyway. I had dreamed about Anya, and consequently, I woke up with a dream hangover, a fog that sticks around even after you're up and back to the world of the living. Regardless, I got ready for work and slapped on a cheery face when talking to Erik over breakfast. His temp was down a degree. Not yet normal, but definitely on the mend. Ty nursed and fussed. His temp was unchanged. Brawny gave them both doses of liquid Tylenol. We'd decided that only one of us should do the dispensing so there couldn't possibly be a mistake. Once again, I found myself grateful that she was a part of our lives.

As I walked past Anya's empty room, I suddenly remembered that poor Clancy hadn't heard from her adult children in weeks. Who was I to be whining about my daughter? After my toast with almond butter, a bowl of fresh fruit, and my coffee, I hustled Gracie into my car. On my way to work, I practiced smiling. I even sang silly songs to get my spirits up. We have a simple rule at the store: Only one person can be down in the dumps at a time.

I had to pull up my big girl panties and get a grip on my life.

Clancy must have come to the same conclusion. She seemed totally energized. When I asked her what she'd put in her coffee, she answered, "Matcha. My spirits were dragging and I was having trouble waking up, so I stopped by a grocery store and bought a bottle of matcha. It's a superfood made from dried and ground up green tea leaves. The antioxidants in it are off the chart. So's the caffeine, but it doesn't give me the jitters. Matcha helps me focus and stay in a good mood."

I was impressed. After that little commercial, I busied myself planning the Friday and Saturday night fundraising crops for Zoo Keepers. First I went to my computer and pulled up everything that was public knowledge about the event and the people who were involved. I learned there would be an appearance by one of the local high schools' marching bands. Further research pulled up more interesting facts. Not only was the Budapest zoo one of the oldest in the world, but in 2007, it was also the birthplace of the first rhino born from artificial insemination. No wonder Hungary would be represented when Prince William came to visit our zoo!

Excited by this new information, I decided that in addition to the zoo pages, I would design a page featuring Budapest, our Sister City. I cut out strips of red, white, and green, so that croppers could use the colors in that order to recreate the Hungarian flag. A small map of the country added a fun touch as well. As an afterthought, a gold star was included in the page kits to make it easy for people to mark the country's capital.

I was totally absorbed in what I was doing. So much so that I didn't notice that Clancy was standing at my elbow until she spoke up. "Cute, but if we don't put together a description of the event, all your hard work will be wasted. No one will know about it, and no one will come." She picked up the tiny map of Hungary, just as we heard a knock on the back door. She carried the map along with her as she let Curtis in.

"Hungary!" His face brightened when he noticed what she was holding.

Gracie got up from her dog bed and wandered over to sniff the newcomer. Fortunately, Curtis wasn't scared by big pooches. In fact, he loved up Gracie as if she were his own stuffed dog. She wagged that huge tail of hers hard enough to beat a cadence against the drywall. After letting her indulge her love of affection, I put Gracie back in her doggy playpen, and Curtis went to work.

On that happy note, Clancy and I came up with descriptions and prices for the page kits.

"I still need a mega-cute project for the event." We're known far and wide for the diverse papercrafting ideas I've produced. No fun crop would be a success without one. I put on my metaphorical "thinking cap" and went to my work table to get down to the nitty-gritty of crafting.

Although the tabletop wasn't too wet to use, it was definitely damp. Curtis helped me spread a thick layer of oilcloth on the surface. With my self-healing craft mats, that would be enough for me to use while spreading out my papers and supplies. Now all I lacked was inspiration.

Because Will and Kate were coming to town, and because they were bringing their two young children, I decided the focus should be on kids and animals. After all, that was a natural pairing.

"Sorry to interrupt, but what should I do with these?" Curtis held up a large yellow plastic container. Inside were toys we kept here at the store for the express purpose of keeping children busy while their mothers shopped. A doll's arm stuck out as did a molded plastic dinosaur. Clancy could easily wash and sanitize both, a chore we did weekly, although we sprayed the contents of the box with a sanitized spray at the beginning of each business day. While Curtis patiently held the tub, I rustled around in it, doing a touch-test to see how wet the toys were. My fingers found a thick board book, and I pulled it out.

"Would you mind taking the rest of this stuff to Clancy in the back?"

"Not at all." The lilt in his voice suggested he had a tiny crush on my pal.

Good, I thought. A bit of positive attention would be perfect for Clancy's ego right now. Although I hadn't asked, I was fairly certain she hadn't heard from her kids. If she had, she would have told me.

I set the board book on the oil cloth. It had to have been the ugliest, dumbest board book I've ever seen. Clancy had found it at a garage sale. I've often said, "I've never seen a book I didn't like!" But I had to make an exception for this one.

The pictures were poorly drawn. There was no story line. The colors were ugly. Our young visitors ignored the book, and who could blame them? Actually, of all the stuff that was worthy of tossing out after our fire, this travesty rose to the top of the list.

Or did it?

Only one corner of the last page was damp. The other sturdy cardboard pages were fine. The book measured six by five inches. There were eight pages internally, plus a front and back cover. Ten surfaces that I could transform into a zoo-themed album. Yes, this was an ugly book, but it wasn't the only ugly book in the world. There were probably more like it. I could send Clancy to Goodwill and thrift shops for the purpose of buying more of these hard-cover children's board books. If we could get them cheaply enough, they could form the basis of a terrific project, a zoo book.

With that in mind, I dove into my project. A couple of hours later, I had an adorable finished album. One crop down, one to go. If I could come up with another great idea, that would encourage people to attend both crops, instead of just one.

Thinking, thinking, thinking...

I needed a bathroom break.

"Did you hear the latest?" Clancy came into the back room. She held her phone in one hand. "I get these news alerts, and one just came through. They're going to issue tickets to control the flow of visitors to the zoo on Sunday when Will and Kate are there."

"Makes sense. I presume they'll vet the visitors, too."

"Yes," Clancy said as she scrolled down the screen. "To apply for a ticket, you have to send in your driver's license number, passport number, and other personal information. Once they decide if you've passed the vetting test, they'll put all interested parties into a hopper and draw names. Sounds fair enough."

"I guess it does." With that, I ducked into the john.

After doing my business and washing my hands, I changed out the toilet paper because the roll was down to its two last squares. Holding the paper tube in my hand, I had a brainstorm. Why not turn empty tubes like this into animals? By flattening the tube, you would make an envelope, a sleeve. Into that you could put a narrow album. How cute would that be? Super-cute!

An hour later, back at my worktable, I fairly shouted, *"Voila!"* One of the few words I've retained from four years of French, but useful nonetheless.

Clancy took one look at my prototypes and said, "You amaze me." Once we'd hashed out the costs, I sent photos and descriptions to Lee. She called me a few minutes later.

"Kiki, I am so pleased. These projects should fill up seats quickly, don't you think? I imagine that you already have people signed up for Friday night, because that's your regular crop night. Once I send out emails to our list, we should be able to fill up seats on Saturday, too."

"I sure hope so." I explained about the page kits I intended to make. "Did you know that the Budapest zoo was the first to have a successful birth from the artificial insemination of a rhino?"

Lee hadn't known that, but the fact impressed her. "That's fascinating. I figured the ambassador from Hungary was coming because of the Sister City program. I had no idea that rhinos were the string that tied everything together. Good for you! You really are a talented sleuth!"

I ended the call feeling better than I had in a couple of days.

Later that afternoon, I phoned Brawny to check on the boys. She reported that they were cranky but better.

That night Gracie and I walked into a dark house. The tantalizing fragrances of garlic and oregano drew me into the kitchen where I discovered that Brawny had made spaghetti and garlic bread. Erik was sitting proudly at the table, waiting for me. He pointed out that Brawny had lit the candles so that he and I could have a dinner just like the one in *Lady and the Tramp*.

That got me giggling. As I sat down, he poured me a glass of "wine," grape juice. We clinked our glasses together and made silly toasts.

Detweiler called to say he was working late. Again. I assumed it was in preparation for the visit by the young royals. I did my best to compartmentalize. Anya continued to ignore my text-messages. She stayed at the Moores' house, breaking my heart with each passing minute. I locked my misery into a box and stored it, only to have it pop out and overwhelm me at the most inconvenient times. How could my daughter stay away this long?

I really began to doubt my daughter's love for me. By Thursday morning, I was on the verge of tears every minute. Brawny tiptoed around me, understanding that she was a part of the problem. Detweiler was busy, packing in the hours at work, which meant he had no time to listen to me while I fretted over ever seeing Anya again. I swallowed my sadness, going through the motions of being my normal self. Often I turn to Gracie as a welcome distraction, but Erik had been sitting next to the big dog on the floor and I didn't have the heart to make him give up his pal. Instead, I told myself to toughen up, even as I climbed into my empty car and drove to the store.

Curtis showed up every day at store opening and worked methodically. Part of his job was to take moisture readings of the drywall. If we couldn't get it to dry out, he would have to tear it out and replace it.

Clancy worked diligently to help me finish inventorying all that had been ruined and to assist me in kitting up all the bits and pieces we would need for the Friday and Saturday crops. Standing at the cash register, she reviewed the clipboard where she'd written down reservations. "The calls are coming in at a brisk pace. In fact, we're almost full to capacity both days," she said. "Won't Lee be thrilled?"

As if she'd been summoned out of thin air, the front door flew open. Lee staggered in. Her skin was paler than a sheet of copier paper. I shoved a chair under her because she looked like she might faint.

Clancy ran to the back to get a cup of strong coffee.

"Lee? Put your head between your knees," I suggested.

She did, sitting up only when Clancy nudged her to indicate she'd provided Lee with fortification. "You'll never believe what just happened to me. The police took me in for questioning! I think they are trying to link me to Nancy's death!"

"We'd better go into the back. I'd hate to have a customer walk in on us." Clancy picked up the coffee and led the way.

My first question was, "Does Jeff know?"

"Not yet. He's out of town. In New York City for a board of

directors meeting," Lee said, settling into one of the kitchen chairs that sits around our break table. "Clancy? Thanks for the coffee. I'm not even sure I want to tell him."

"Jeff is going to have a cow," I said, pushing sugar Lee's way. Clancy got up and grabbed the carton of cream we keep in the refrigerator. Then, thinking better of what I'd said, I amended my comment. "Jeff wouldn't have a cow. He'd have a racehorse. A Triple-Crown winner. Jeff wouldn't be caught dead with a cow, would he?"

"No." Lee shook her head. A sad little smile indicated she understood I was joking around. "Not hardly. I don't want him to have to deal with this. He's working on a big project in the UK. When he hears about this, it'll be a distraction for sure."

"Any word on the cashier's check?" I asked.

"Not a peep. They've sent bulletins to banks all over the world. Fareed is pulling his hair out. He's decided he'll have to tell the prince what happened in advance and give him a fake check at the event. Then we'll fulfill our obligation later."

Clancy sat down, and I put on a new pot of coffee because Lee might need more than one jolt of caffeine. Even though it was sub-zero outside, I grabbed a Diet Dr Pepper for myself.

Once I popped the top and sat down, Clancy jumped to her feet. It might have been comical to an onlooker, because neither of us could sit still.

"All this fuss just because you wanted to track down a missing check. This is just crazy," I said.

Clancy reached into the refrigerator and brought out a loaf sealed in plastic wrap. "Chocolate Chip and Walnut Banana Bread. I baked it last night. Seems like a good time to offer both of you a slice."

My mouth watered at the thought of the Chocolate Chip and Walnut Banana bread. Any crisis is a terrific excuse for a sweet treat to eat, and this certainly qualified as a crisis. I watched eagerly as Clancy unwrapped and cut pieces.

"The detective seemed sure that all of this is linked. Somehow."

"What was the detective's name?" I wondered if it was anyone that Detweiler knew.

"Detective Blanco Albertez. Two guys in uniform took me to Ferguson Police Department. Albertez interviewed me in a conference room."

"At least they didn't put you in jail. That's something to be thankful for!" I'd been wrongfully accused and taken to the county jail. It was not an experience I cared to remember.

"Right. There's that to be thankful for." Lee detailed what had happened while she was in police custody. "The detective kept asking me questions about Nancy screaming at me in the parking lot. The spat that everyone saw after our board meeting. Albertez keeps hinting that there must be more to the situation, like perhaps I'd accused Nancy outright when we were in the ladies' room. Just to set the record straight, I never, ever accused her of theft or malfeasance."

I took one bite from my piece and pronounced it "heavenly."

After nibbling at her slice, Lee continued, "I have no idea what came over Nancy. She seemed nervous, but otherwise she seemed fine in the board meeting. I thought she was just excited about giving that much money to the Tusk Trust. I went into the stall, did my thing, and when I came out, she started screaming at me!"

"I've been wondering about something. Is it possible that the missing money market check was a trial run? I can't work out the details, but it just seems so odd that first one check would go missing and then another."

"I certainly didn't understand how cashier's checks worked. Did either of you?" Clancy asked.

"It's not like the three of us just fell off the turnip truck," I said, more to myself than anyone else. "Is it possible that the person who's behind this doesn't realize the cashier's check can't be cashed? Could the person who has the cashier's check be the same person who originally took the money market check?"

"If that's the case, it would have to be someone in Nancy's household." Clancy used a fork to delicately cut off pieces of her bread. I, on the other hand, picked mine up with my fingers.

"I think you're right, Clancy. We know there's Nancy's husband Bert and her stepdaughter Rochelle." With that in mind, I told them what I'd learned from Nancy about her rocky relationship with Rochelle.

"Wait a minute. You're suggesting that a teenager is behind all this?"

"Not possible," Lee said. "I happen to know that Rochelle and her father were up in Chicago at the time that Nancy was killed. They were in O'Hare, waiting for their flight. Fareed told me."

"Okay, so neither Bert nor his daughter had opportunity. Did they have motive?"

Lee shook her head. "No. Not that I'm aware of. I'd heard that Rochelle hated Nancy, but that's an angry teen for you."

"Is it? Clancy, you've taught angry teens. Does Rochelle's behavior sound normal to you? It sure doesn't to me. Rochelle hated Nancy. She could have paid someone to steal that check out of spite."

"I can't see that, but I could see an animal activist group being involved." Lee folded her hands in her lap. She stared down at her interlaced fingers. I had this sense that she was at war with herself. Whatever she was thinking, she was unsure whether she should share it with us.

"What do you mean?" I asked.

"Throughout our history of existence, Zoo Keepers has been

targeted by animal rights activists who don't believe in keeping animals in zoos. Lately those people have ramped up their complaints. We've been getting threatening letters from them almost daily. We have a lot of detractors. People who feel that keeping animals in zoos is criminal."

"Surely they don't object to zoos like ours. May I?"

Clancy nodded. "Of course, help yourself."

I got up and cut myself a second slice of the Chocolate Chip and Walnut Banana bread. Boy, was it ever good.

"Actually, they do," Lee said. "Animal rights activists feel the money and attention could be better spent by improving the natural conditions for animals. The most radical among them think that no animal should be caged or kept in captivity by humans. That includes our domestic pets like dogs and cats."

"Not surprising." Clancy clucked her tongue. "Fanatics never see the world in all its complexity. They thrive on black-and-white, good-versus-evil, and rigid stands. Often such groups go off half-cocked because they don't care about the facts. They have convinced themselves they know all they need to know."

"Give me an example." I picked up my plate and carried it to the sink so I wouldn't be tempted to eat more of the sweet bread.

"Here's one off the top of my head," Lee answered. "An animal rights group headquartered in Connecticut went to court when seventeen elephants were flown here from Swaziland in Africa. The elephants were destined for zoos around the country, and the president of the group protested that confinement bores and stresses the animals."

"Sounds like a reasonable argument to me," Clancy admitted. "Being cooped up would drive me nuts."

I thought about Gracie spending hours here in her doggy play pen. Typically she slept all day, but if she had the choice would she have preferred roaming around? She seemed happy enough, but was she? Maybe she was thrilled to stay home rather than come to work with me.

"We agree that animals that are in captivity *can* get bored and stressed," Lee said, nodding her head vigorously, "but in this case, the elephants in question were scheduled to be killed, in order to make room for more rhinos at a reserve in a drought-stricken country. So you see, the truth was more complicated than the animal rights people thought."

"Isn't that the way of life?" Clancy mused. "Everything seems simple until you peep under the covers. That's when you discover the knots and tangles."

"Who is the 'we' who's been getting these threats?" I finished my Diet Dr Pepper and walked the can to the recycling bin.

"All the board members. Past and present. This has been going on for a long time, but it really ramped up this last month. Fareed suspects that they got wind of the fact we were planning to hand Prince William a check for a million dollars."

"Is it remotely possible that the animal rights activists are behind Nancy's murder and the theft of the check?" I wondered out loud.

Lee thought that over. "I guess."

"A million dollars is certainly a good motive for murder." Clancy stated the obvious. "Lee? If I were you, I'd hire an attorney."

"I did."

In chorus, Clancy and I chimed, "Jim Hagg."

"How'd you guess?" Lee looked genuinely puzzled.

Hagg was the go-to guy for anyone who had money or good sense. He was also the man people hired when they were guilty. The cops all hated Hagg, because he threw up one roadblock after another when defending a client. That said, Detweiler and I had often joked that if either of us were ever accused of a wrongdoing here in the metropolitan St. Louis area, we would call Hagg.

I told Lee how we were able to guess that Hagg would serve as her representation.

"He certainly seems to know his job. The very mention of his name put a scare into the detective. In fact, I called, Hagg came, and I walked out." She stumbled a little over that last word. "I still can't believe I was even questioned!"

"They certainly have nothing to go on except the fact that Nancy attacked you, right?" My question was rhetorical.

"Well," Lee drew the word out. "There is one thing. Hagg was pretty upset about it, too. Albertez told me that somebody texted Nancy right before the Zoo Keepers' board meeting ended. That message is the reason she drove to Ferguson. Albertez says he can prove the text came from my phone!"

I did my best to hide my surprise. I could see Clancy's eyes grow wide, too. It *was* possible that Albertez was lying to Lee, but on the other hand...maybe not. I had to ask. "I assume you didn't send the text. Is there any way that someone could have used your phone? Without you knowing it?"

That brought tears to her eyes. "Yes. I feel so silly about it. Someone swiped my phone. I didn't notice it until after the Zoo Keepers' meeting. I thought I'd left it at home by mistake. After the meeting, I went back to the house and turned it upside down. No luck. I tried calling my number from our landline. No luck with that either. I knew that I had my phone in my purse earlier in the day. I used it while I was grocery shopping. After the board meeting, I got in my car and drove off, but I was still upset about Nancy screaming at me. I pulled off of 40 and stopped for an iced tea at a Wendy's. I wanted to talk to Jeff. He would calm me down. That's when I realized my phone was missing. I figured it would turn up sooner or later, and I didn't want Jeff to fuss at me for being careless."

"That explains why I couldn't get you on your phone the day I called about helping with inventory. I wound up calling your landline."

"It's impossible that somebody took my phone. I always keep it in my purse inside a zippered pocket." Lee colored and averted her eyes. "Jeff's been warning me that I don't watch it carefully enough. Sometimes I carry too much inside my purse and the zipper doesn't want to work right. That's one reason I didn't tell him right away that it was missing."

Our conversation was interrupted by the back door swinging open. Of course, Rebekkah knew Lee, and we could certainly talk in front of Dodie's daughter. Dodie had drummed into all of us the importance of keeping our customers' secrets, so keeping mum about a friend's secrets was second nature. After Rebekkah hung up her coat and poured herself a cup of coffee, Clancy got Rebekkah up to speed about what needed to be done with the soggy paper we'd dumped into one big plastic bin.

"Lee?" I put a hand on her arm. "If I had a dollar for every woman who's lost a phone in this store, I could personally write you a check to cover that missing million. It's so easy to do. The smaller the phones get, the harder it is to keep track of them."

"Albertez implied that the text message sent from my phone proves that I set Nancy up." Lee's voice had a hitch in it. "He says that Nancy drove to Ferguson in response to my text message. That's impossible." Lee lifted her chin defiantly. "I didn't do that. I just flat out didn't."

"Doesn't make any sense, does it?" Clancy mused. "Why would you text someone when you were with them at a meeting? Perhaps Detective Albertez lied to you about having evidence of a text message?"

"Hagg said that's possible. He's going to find out."

"Who else was in the building the day that Nancy died? Besides the Zoo Keepers board members?"

"There's always a janitor who unlocks the Meyer Building for us and locks up after we leave. That week it was a substitute."

"Maybe the janitor or somebody 'borrowed' your phone and made that text message," I said.

"Impossible. How would he get my passcode?"

Clancy shook her head. "Remember that old saying from Sherlock Holmes? He was talking to Watson and he said, 'How often have I said to you that when you have eliminated the impossible, whatever remains, however improbable, must be the truth?'"

Rebekkah looked up from her counting. Her dark curls framed her face. "*The Sign of the Four.* That's the name of the story where Sherlock said that. But later Mr. Spock repeated it on *Star Trek*."

"But how would anyone have gotten my passcode?" Lee asked.

"I'm betting there's CCTV in that room. If so, the janitor could have watched what you punch in, written it down, and then used it later."

"Wow." Clancy pulled out a chair and sank down. "None of this could have been done spontaneously. There are so many moving pieces. This must have been a well-orchestrated plan. Whoever did this is pretty sharp. There aren't many exits from 270 into Ferguson. Once Nancy left the beltway, she would more than likely stay on a main artery. Someone could have easily tailed her car."

I was curious if Lee was being singled out, so I asked her, "Do you know whether or not the cops questioned every member of the Zoo Keepers board?"

Lee thought that over. "I have no idea. They did ask me a lot of questions about where everyone was and what they were doing. I told them that I walked in, set my purse on a chair, and looked over my notes before the board meeting."

"You never left your seat?" I asked.

"Well...I did go back into the kitchenette to help Annie Patel make herself a cup of coffee. The Meyer Building just bought one of those fancy Nespresso machines. She didn't know how to use it, so I helped her."

"Who was in the board room when you left your purse behind?"

"No one. Annie and I were the first people there. Vicky Dillon and Peggy Rankin came in just as Annie and I walked back into the conference room."

"We need a way to get those four women to talk to us," I said. "They might have useful information. Is it possible one of them fiddled with your phone, Lee?"

"Not likely," she started to say, but then she stopped. "Oh, no! I just thought of something. In the January board meeting, I used my phone to show off photos from my daughter Taylor's wedding. Vicky, Peggy, Rook, and Annie were all crowded around me when I keyed in my access number!"

Rebekkah spoke up. "Then any one of them could have remembered that code. They could have slipped your phone out of your purse, used your passcode and sent a text to Nancy."

"All four of those women from the Zoo Keepers board knew that Nancy left the Meyer Building with a cashier's check for a million dollars. So did every member of that board. Maybe someone took the check, not realizing they wouldn't be able to cash it."

"What do I do?" Lee sounded shocked, scared, and stunned. "Nothing? Do I just wait and hope that Jim Hagg is as good as they say he is? Should I call Detective Albertez and tell him all this?"

"I certainly wouldn't call Albertez." I felt totally defeated and probably sounded that way, too. "I wish Detweiler could help us, but he can't. At least, I don't think he can. After all the problems they've had up in Ferguson, the cops up there are not interested in talking to outsiders. That includes members of any other police department. Period. And who can blame them?"

"Then there's just one thing to do." Clancy snapped her fingers. "We need to make sure those four board members come to one of our crops here at the store. If they're here, we can pump them for more information."

That sounded to me like a very, very good plan.

17

Lee left shortly thereafter with a promise to come the next night for the crop. Clancy went through the registrations. Zoo Keepers board members Vicky and Annie were scheduled to come tonight. We hadn't heard from Peggy. I sent Lee an email, explaining that Peggy wasn't signed up to attend. She called me on the phone to say that she would make sure that Peggy came, even if she had to drag her along. "I'll remind her that she's a board member and that this is to help us raise money."

"If she doesn't come, that's another reason to be suspicious of her," I added.

I went home at five thirty.

Several times I picked up my phone out of habit and started to call Anya. Then I'd remember that I couldn't.

I distracted myself by turning on the radio. The news was all abuzz in preparation for the visit from the young royals. I listened until I pulled into my garage and turned off the engine of the BMW.

Only then did my phone ring. It was Jennifer. "Anya wants to come home, but she's too stubborn to call you."

"Really?"

"Yes, she keeps mentioning how much she misses Seymour, but she's also missing her family."

"What is she thinking about Brawny?"

"Nothing inappropriate happened. Anya asked her about tampons and how they work. How you use them. She feels stupid now. Plus, she asked Brawny a few questions about sex, and that's bothering her."

I hadn't realized I'd been holding my breath, but I had. "Thank goodness. I understand that she's embarrassed, but if it had been more than that we would have let Brawny go."

"Of course you would have. I told Anya that you would be picking her up after school tomorrow. I explained that Nicci and I needed a little mother-daughter time."

"She didn't fuss?"

"She pouted for half a second. That's all. She thanked me for being so kind to her. I told her she was always welcome at our house. Actually, I think Anya was relieved. She could go home with her head held high because she didn't cave in. But she'd definitely made her point."

"She sure did. Jennifer, I can't thank you enough for all you've done."

"Sure you can. I even have the perfect way for you to show your appreciation."

"Do tell."

"When William and Kate come to town, the Young Women Leaders are organizing the children's activities."

"Sounds like fun. I mean, how can you go wrong with adorable kids and exotic animals? How can I help?"

"As you know, I'm the president this year, and I was hoping you could assist me in entertaining the children. Have you heard about Kali? He's a baby polar bear born at our zoo. Because he's so adorable, we decided that a polar bear theme would be cute. I realize that Will is more concerned about elephants and rhinos, but with the ice cap melting, polar bears are in trouble, too."

The engine of my car *tick-tick-ticked* as it cooled. I hoped Jennifer would get to the point. I was getting cold out here in my garage. "Do you need a fun project for the kids to do? Something for the guests to take home?"

"Not exactly."

Her tone got me worried. "Why am I getting the idea it might be something I'll regret?"

"Would I put you in an awkward situation?"

"Yes, if you couldn't find another patsy to help out."

I could almost hear my friend roll her eyes. I'm fairly positive she learned that from me. It's not the sort of thing a well-brought-up lady like Jennifer would ever do on her own without guidance. "Okay, you're kind of right. But not entirely. See, you and Nancy Owens are nearly the same size. Were nearly the same size. Whatever."

"You want me to pretend to be Nancy?"

"Not exactly. The Young Women Leaders was the first group to celebrate when Kali was born. We thought he was adorable. Maybe we went a bit overboard because our president at the time bought a costume. A polar bear costume."

"If you're asking me to wear a polar bear costume, I have a question. An important question." I paused for effect. "Are you nuts? Polar bears are big! Really, really big. I won't fit in a polar bear costume, will I? In fact, how did Nancy pull that off?"

"Yes, you actually will fit perfectly in the costume, just like Nancy did. See, after the polar bear costume was worn once, our past president put it in her laundry basket. Her cleaning lady thought it was a fake fur rug and washed it. It shrank down to your size."

"Terrific. I always wanted wear a polar bear costume. I especially wanted to wear a fuzzy white suit while meeting Kate

Middleton, the epitome of style and fashion. Thank you, Jennifer, for making my dreams come true. Any photos taken with me in them will be real family keepsakes. I can hand them down to my grandkids. Oh, look, there's grandma somewhere in that big white piece of carpet. Isn't she cute?"

That got Jennifer giggling. "You do owe me."

"Yes, I do, and all teasing aside, I'm happy to help you in any way that I can. If it's wearing a polar bear costume, I'll do it. At least you're asking me to dress in fake fur when it's cold outside. For that I should be grateful."

"You really should. You'll be a very, very cute polar bear. I'm sure of it."

"Thanks," I said. "Thanks a heap. I'll need details."

"And you shall have them. They're on their way to you right now. Check your email, okay? I'll need you to send the forms back to me ASAP so I can get you a security pass."

"While we're on the subject of Nancy Owens, what do you know about her?"

"Not much. She was a good little worker. Always did as asked. In fact, she didn't complain about the polar bear costume."

"Ha, ha, ha."

"Her husband is quiet. Her stepdaughter hates—hated—her. She made fun of everything Nancy did. Stevie told me that. He knows Rochelle from seeing her at football and basketball games. In fact, they're the same age. Stevie and Rochelle. I think he took SAT prep classes with her."

"Look, I'm sitting in my car in my garage, freezing my back-side off. I better get inside or Ty will have a frozen milkshake for dinner."

Jennifer laughed, and I found myself smiling. My daughter was coming home!

18

Rebekkah came in early Friday. That was unusual for her. Even when she's scheduled to work early, she's typically a bit late. Today she was there before Clancy. I was freezing as I opened the back door and greeted her. The air outside was like an assault. Luckily for Rebekkah, she was entirely bundled up.

"Where's Gracie?" Rebekkah craned her neck to look around as she tugged off her crocheted muffler.

"She's home with the little boys. They're both sick with a tummy bug."

"Ah. Makes sense. Who wouldn't love a big, furry cuddle-bug like Gracie? Especially when you aren't feeling well."

Rebekkah stepped away from the coat rack and I got a good look at her. Laurel has influenced Rebekkah to pay more attention to what she wears, and the results have been outstanding. Today she had on a red crew neck sweater and jeans. The cuffs on her pants were turned up to reveal a jaunty red-and-dark green plaid flannel lining.

"Are those warm?" I asked.

"Best thing ever. These and silk pant liners. You ought to try them."

"Maybe I will. How's your dad?"

"They're releasing *Abba* at eleven, but I thought I'd drop by here first and see if there's any more work to do."

"You could help re-stock the wire racks," I said. "That would be super."

She took the new packages of paper from me. We walked out onto the sales floor together, but Rebekkah seemed to be dragging her feet. "Kiki? Anya called me last night."

I stopped in my tracks. "She did? What did she say?"

"She feels betrayed by you and Detweiler. She's really embarrassed about things she said to Brawny. She thinks you two might have known, but kept Brawny's gender issues a secret."

"We did not." I heard the desperation in my voice. "I promise you. We did not."

"I know. That's not like you. I told her I thought she was conflating two emotions. She asked what 'conflating' meant, and I told her to look it up. I explained that it can be really easy to feel emotional, but not so easy to sort out the exact reasons."

I thanked Rebekkah for taking our side.

"No thanks are necessary. I told her the truth, that's all. I don't think that was really what bothered her."

I froze. "Then what was it?"

"I think she's jealous of her little brothers. She suspects that you weren't worried about her, but you were worried about Erik. While she didn't come out and say it, I got the impression she thinks you were so concerned about his safety that you didn't bother to give a second thought to how she, Anya, might feel about Brawny."

"Oh." I sank down into one of the kitchen chairs. "That's a

surprise. It never dawned on me that she'd think I'd put his safety over her feelings."

"I realize you wouldn't. I think she knows that in her heart-of-hearts, but she's coming to grips with everything." Rebekkah lifted a wayward strand of hair out of her eyes. "Please don't tell her I shared this. I think she's having a hard time being honest with herself. I figured that if I said something, it might make it easier for you to get her to open up."

With that, she got to work. Clancy phoned to say she was running behind. She'd stood in line a long time to buy treats for this evening's crop. Because it was a special order—four dozen iced sugar cookies in the shape of various animals—she had to grit her teeth and bear the wait.

Curtis arrived at ten. He told me that things were progressing nicely. Although I didn't really have the time for it, I agreed to let him walk me around the store so I could see his progress. Some of the walls were still damp, according to a meter he used. Most of the store was fine. He felt he had no choice but to rip up a small area of the floor where water had seeped down. "If it got in the struts, you could have a problem. Not today or tomorrow, but down the line."

Rebekkah left at eleven. Clancy showed up a few minutes later.

At noon, Laurel came into the store. Her skinny jeans were tucked into a cute pair of brown booties with tassel trim. Her sheepskin coat came off to reveal a black turtle neck sweater. Maybe it was the color, but she sure seemed pale to me. From a plaid bag over her arm, she removed two stacks of paper, clipped together at the top. One held our original inventories. The other consisted of duplicated copies. She'd gone through every charge on the second copy and highlighted ruined merchandise. First I would double-check her work and then Clancy would run an accounting tape to come up with a total dollar amount of our losses.

"How did you do all this from home?" I asked Laurel as I realized she had marked page after page of useless merchandise.

"Clancy texted me as she went along. She also text-messaged me items as you marked them ruined."

Clancy gave me a sheepish shrug. "It seemed like the fastest way to get everything done."

I nodded gratefully. "Ladies, you two are lifesavers."

"Excuse me." Curtis slipped behind Clancy and helped himself to a fresh cup of coffee. As it poured, the rich aroma of hazelnut and coffee beans filled the air. I found it heavenly, but Laurel turned green and raced into the bathroom. Although we were twelve feet away and the door was shut, we could hear her being violently sick. Repeatedly. When the door finally opened, Laurel wobbled out, barely able to keep her balance. I put an arm around her and noticed how prominent her shoulder blades were.

Have you lost weight?" I asked, knowing the answer.

"Yes. Five pounds."

Clancy and I exchanged looks. Five pounds? Laurel is always thin, and five pounds on her was a lot of weight.

"You're sick often?" Clancy asked.

"Almost all the time. I'm sick more than I'm well. Even the Saltines don't seem to help me now." She propped her head up on her hands. "I just feel a little dizzy, that's all."

I pulled my phone out of my purse and dialed Laurel's fiancé, Joe. He picked up on the first ring. "Joe? This is Kiki."

"Don't!" Laurel tried to snatch the phone out of my hands. I danced away, keeping out of her reach. After Joe said hello, I barreled on ahead. "I think you need to go with Laurel to the doctor, and I think you need to go sooner rather than later."

"Kiki!" Laurel batted at me. "No, I'm fine."

"No, she's not, Joe. She's lost five pounds, she's pale, and can't keep anything down. You need to be very specific with the doctor. How many times a day is Laurel vomiting? Does she ever keep anything down? I have a hunch she's dehydrated. I'm worried about her blood sugar. If she's throwing up after taking her insulin, her numbers could be off."

"That never even occurred to me. I'll be right there to pick her up. I'll take her to an urgent care facility."

"Good idea," I said, still backing away from my friend while Laurel half-heartedly swatted at my hands. Her lack of spunk confirmed I'd done the right thing, whether she was happy about it or not. I ended the conversation with Joe and took the seat across from Laurel's.

"I don't know whether to thank you or be put out," she said, brushing aside a stray lock of her blond hair.

"You don't have to decide right now. In fact, I don't care how you feel about the call I just made. Here's the deal: If you get to Urgent Care and you're fine, no biggie. If you're dehydrated, then it's good you went. If you aren't dehydrated, you can still tell them how often you've been sick. That should spur your ob/gyn into action. There are things he can prescribe."

She bowed her head to hide her expression. "I hate bothering Joe with this. He's busy. His parishioners need him. One of the vestry members is dying, and his wife is distraught. Joe's been spending hours in the hospital, holding her hand."

"I get that. Really I do. However, he has a lot of parishioners and only one of you. If he takes time off work now, he can go back to the dying church-goer with the confidence that you are okay. Can you imagine how he'd feel if you collapsed?" I had to edit my words because I nearly said, "Can you imagine how he'd feel if you lost the baby?" That might have scared the pee-wadding out of her.

Curtis walked past us a couple of times as he dragged equipment to the sales floor. The roar of the wet vac provided white noise. Not too bad of a sound. Enough to be a dull hum in the background. Just as Joe arrived, Curtis came back through to dump water he'd collected.

To my surprise, the two men did a double-take, and Curtis set down his bucket to give Joe a bro-hug. Obviously, they knew each other.

"Curt, this is Laurel," Joe said. Although his voice gleamed with pride, there was also a cautious tone as he looked Laurel over.

"We've met in passing," Curtis said. "Sorry that you're feeling poorly. Can I do anything to help?"

"Actually, you can," and Joe handed Curtis his keys. "Could you pull my car up closer to the back door? It's that gray Honda."

"Of course."

Curtis raced out the back door. Working together, Joe and Clancy managed to get Laurel into her coat and on her feet. In tandem, they moved her to the back door. When Curtis put the Honda in park, he jumped out and came to their aid. Laurel was weaker than a kitten. I suspected she'd been pretending to be fine for as long as she could, and she'd run out of steam. Joe had wrapped his left arm around her waist and was holding her right arm over his shoulder, keeping her upright.

Curtis took one look at her and swept her off her feet, literally. Laurel's knees were a split-second from buckling. That smart intervention allowed Joe to run around the car and open the passenger side door.

In short order, Laurel was on her way to Urgent Care. Clancy and I stood in the doorway, watching them drive away. Curtis waved to his friend from the bottom step of our stoop. Even though the temperatures were frigid, the three of us stood sentinel, staring after the Honda as it pulled into traffic.

Curtis spoke first. "That girl was skin and bones. I have a hunch she's going to be spending a couple of days in the hospital."

"I think you're right," Clancy said with a sigh.

19

My cell phone rang a short time later. I recognized Jennifer Moore's number, and my heart skipped a beat. Did this mean Anya had decided not to come home? Swallowing hard, I answered.

"I'm on my way with lunch for you."

"Have you picked up the food yet? Would you mind grabbing lunch for Clancy and our cleaner, too?"

Of course she didn't mind. I texted her our orders. In record time, Jennifer came through our front door. She carried a brown paper shopping bag from St. Louis Bread Co. Her elegant dark-wash jeans were tucked into tall designer boots, and her long leather coat fluttered as she hurried into the warmth. Even though she was dressed casually, for Jennifer at least, she looked put together in an effortless sort of way. In full makeup, she looked stunning with smoky eyes that matched her gray wool sweater and a gray and blue scarf wrapped around her neck. I helped her set up napkins and drinks on our table in the back before inviting Clancy and Curtis to join us.

"Is Anya okay?" Clancy asked, before I could.

"Yes," said Jennifer in a voice that didn't invite further discussion. I could tell by the brusque way she had answered that she had a lot on her mind.

Clancy picked up on Jennifer's mood, too. "Good. Glad to hear Anya is all right."

"What do I owe you?" I asked Jennifer.

"Nothing. I have a favor to ask that'll more than cover the cost of the meals."

"Let's go eat in my office." The door had scarcely closed when I asked, "How's Anya really?" I set my green tea on the desktop and ignored the streak of condensation that puddled around the plastic cup's base.

"Like I said, she's fine. I actually came by to talk with you about the royals' visit."

"Okay. Let me guess. Now you want me to wear that polar bear costume and dive into a pool of sub-zero water. Is that it?"

"Not hardly. I was wondering if you had any cute items we could have the kids make. Or any ideas of what the kids could do while waiting for the royal family to show up."

This must be the favor I was trading for our lunches. I eagerly agreed to help. "That should be easy enough. How many kids?"

"Eight. All age five and under."

"Sure, I can put together a project." I had more of the toilet paper roll animals in mind. I could make up extras on Saturday when the croppers were making theirs.

But then I got this mental picture of me in a polar bear costume. How could I help the kids with their projects if I was wearing a huge, fuzzy pair of white mittens? I said as much to Jennifer.

"Oh. I forgot to tell you. You've cleared security, and the polar bear costume is out. It's a non-starter."

"The costume is out? Did it get washed again and shrink some more?"

She turned pink with embarrassment. "Um, something like that. I happened to mention the costume to the person at the zoo who's coordinating the whole event. Animal costumes are not allowed at the zoo."

"Really? You're kidding, right?"

"Nope. There are too many predators. Just the sight of an animal costume like our polar bear would get them riled up. Someone might get hurt."

"Uh-huh." I nodded at her. "Hurt? As in eaten? That someone would have been little old me."

She turned redder than a clown's rubber nose. "Uh, yes. It could have been you."

20

After Jennifer left, the rest of the day seemed to drag. I counted the minutes until I could pick up Anya. My mouth was dry and my heart thumped in my chest as I took my spot in the carpool lane. When I rolled to a stop, she didn't glance up from her iPhone. Instead, she kept her head down as she hurried to the passenger side of my old BMW. First she threw in her backpack. Next her purse. Finally she plopped down in the passenger side seat. The leather under her crackled in the cold.

"Hi, honey. I'm glad to see you. Did you have a good day?" I aimed for a mid-point between cheerful and serious. I didn't want to sound too yippee-skippee.

"It was all right."

"Would you like to go to Bread Co.?" Even though it would be my second Bread Co. meal of the day that was fine by me. This was the huge carrot I could dangle in front of my child. She loves eating Bread Co. food, and she's usually hungry right after school. Going there would be a treat.

Instead of answering, she let one shoulder lift and drop in a noncommittal way.

"I'll take that as a yes," I said. Making a sharp turn out of the parking lot, I headed south to the closest restaurant, a location without a drive-thru window. I had calculated that going inside would force Anya to speak to me. At the very least, she would need to order her food and sit with me.

Fortunately my plan worked. Once we took our places in line, Anya's posture loosened up considerably. She placed a huge order, a turkey sandwich with two pieces of cheddar cheese, a side salad, an iced green tea, a bowl of vegetable soup, and two muffies. One was pumpkin and the other chocolate chip.

I ordered half a turkey sandwich and a bowl of the vegetable soup along with another iced green tea. As an afterthought, I added six muffies of my own.

"You choose where we sit." I grabbed an identification number for the table and waited.

Anya scanned the place. She noticed two schoolmates sitting in a booth, huddled over their iPhones. Immediately across from them was an occupied booth. Its inhabitants were clearing their own table to leave.

"That one." Anya jerked her chin toward the group that was departing. Without waiting for someone to wipe it down, we claimed it. Opening my purse, I found a wipe and ran it over the table top.

"You're big on protecting me from germs, but you didn't protect me from a freak." Anya's eyes were as cold as her grand-mother's had been. The venom in my child's voice took me aback.

"Did Brawny ever act inappropriately with you?"

"That's hardly the question."

I shook my head as the waiter delivered soup for Anya and me. After he left, I leaned closer to Anya. "Yes, indeed it is the question, and it's a very important one."

"No. *It* didn't act inappropriately with me."

Okay, that was off the table. Although I had trusted Jennifer Moore to ask that all important question, it was my duty to follow up. Studying Anya, I remembered pledges I'd made to myself when she was born. I would not lie to my child. I would respect her feelings and emotions. I wouldn't try to change her mind just because her stance was inconvenient to me.

"Actually, you're more right than you know. Brawny is an 'it.' She was born intersex, a mix of both sexes. In some ways, her condition is like having a birth defect." There. I had said it. Although it sounded crude and harsh, I'd told my child the truth. I knew that I had Anya's full attention because she said nothing. Suddenly her soup fascinated her. I knew why. Anya has always been curious by nature, and she's always been interested in biology. This whole intersex thing was right up her alley.

"Are you joking?" she squeaked. "I read about that! Stevie sent me all kinds of links."

"I'm totally serious. You can ask her about it. I did a little research, too. It's not that uncommon. Back in the old days, doctors would take it upon themselves to 'correct' kids born this way. As you could imagine, it was often disastrous. They treated the combination of sex organs by chopping off what they didn't think fit."

Anya blushed and then turned pale. "That's horrible. What if you were really a boy and then...?"

Now I had Anya's attention. "Right. Or in Brawny's case, she was really a girl at heart. She never felt comfortable as a man. Of course, boy babies were more desirable than girls, so the doctor made a socially biased choice."

I paused, "None of this gets to the root of your discomfort or mine. Or Detweiler's. We felt like she tricked us."

Again my daughter's mobile face changed yet again. She

went from fascinated to angry. "That's right. You should have told me."

"I couldn't tell you what I didn't know."

"She should have told us."

"I agree. I also thought maybe Lorraine should have told us. I think she'd argue that she was protecting Erik, and there's a bit of truth to that."

"But they both lied to us. Lies of omission is what that's called."

I nodded. "Yes."

We ate quietly, each consumed by our own thoughts. Finally, I reached out and took her hand. "I've missed you terribly. I understand that you needed time, and that you were—are— angry. Detweiler and I were angry, too. I am glad that the Moores are such good friends to us. Having a place to go when you're feeling upset is important, and I respect you for realizing you needed space."

She shrugged that off.

"Erik has been missing you. Seymour has walked around looking for you. Gracie is depressed. We'll all be happy to have you back."

"Yeah." Anya sighed. "I'll be happy to be back, too." A tear rolled down her face. "You really did miss me?"

"Of course I did. I felt like my heart was breaking. It was like getting the flu. I hurt all over. I thought of you all the time. I wanted to cry."

She moved to my side of the booth and hugged me. "I'm not sure how I feel. I'm sad and angry, and it's not like I'm all right with what Brawny did."

"That's fair enough," I said, hugging her and thanking God that she was in my arms. "You have a right to your feelings. All I ask is that you are polite to her. She is sorry that she wasn't forthcoming with us, and she is willing to talk with you, but she knows enough to give you space."

Anya moved to her side of the bench. I toyed with a piece of lettuce. "Anya, Detweiler and I really went back and forth over whether to keep her or not. In the end, we decided that she really does have our best interests at heart. She would do anything, even lay down her life, to protect our family. We also decided that she's a good, decent person who was dealt an unlucky break from birth. I've tried to imagine how I would have reacted if one of my children was born with the sort of confusing signals that Brawny's body had. That couldn't have been an easy choice for her parents. And it sure couldn't have been easy for her."

"Maybe." Anya gave a little "eh" motion of her head.

I clamped my mouth shut rather than to rush in and defend Brawny. Anya would come around in her own time...or not.

"Of course you couldn't fire her. She's too important. What would poor little Erik do?" Anya's voice dripped with sarcasm.

"Is that what you think? That we'd put Erik's welfare first? Above yours?"

Looking down, she drew a word on the tabletop with the tip of a finger. "Maybe." After what seemed like forever, she stared up at me. This time, she didn't make any attempt to hide her tears. "You love him a lot don't you? And Ty, too? I'm the odd kid out. The one without a dad."

If my heart hurt before, it exploded into a zillion pieces right now. "You have two fathers. George Lowenstein and Chad Detweiler. Do you honestly think I could love you less than the others? When you were my first child? When I fought so hard to keep you after George died? When I've known you the longest? Honey, I have two sisters. I understand how it can seem that the other kids get more love. With the boys being little, they have different needs. More on-the-spot needs. But you'll always be the darling child who made me a mother. I can't imagine my life without you!"

"Really? Truly? Honestly?"

"Really, truly, honestly." I grabbed two of the coarse napkins and wiped my face. She did the same.

"But Brawny didn't have any right to fool us. To make us think she was something she isn't."

I thought about correcting Anya. Brawny was a woman at heart. Sure, she didn't have all the right equipment, but you could say the same of any woman who had a hysterectomy, couldn't you? What made a woman a woman? Or a man a man? That was the question at the root of all this.

And it was a question far too complicated for me to answer.

21

On the way home, Anya told me about the project she was doing at school, a research paper on an animal at the St. Louis Zoo. She had chosen to learn more about Emperor Penguins. She didn't have a particular reason why they appealed to her, they just did.

"I totally love penguins. Isn't it cool I get to write a report on them?"

"How is your research coming?"

"It's been hard. Did you know there aren't many books out there about penguins? I was surprised because they are fascinating. I found a book on Amazon, but it only has one page on Emperor Penguins. Is that sad or what?"

I reached over and took her hand as I drove. "Really? Only one page? That's the pits. Tell me about penguins."

"My favorite, absolutely, are the Emperor Penguins. They are the largest bird, but they are flightless. They average 45" tall and can weigh as much as 100 pounds. They live in the harshest conditions ever, out on the open ice in Antarctica. In fact, they don't have any shelter but each other. The temperatures can drop to 40° below zero. To stay warm and to warn off predators, they huddle together."

"I wonder how they decide who's on the outside and who's warm and toasty inside?" I had been on the outside, and I knew what a cold, unforgiving place that could be.

"Beats me. The mother lays one egg, and then she takes off for two months. Can you believe that? Two whole months the dad sits on the egg. While he's incubating the egg, she travels to the sea, often a trek of more than 50 miles. Once she's in the water, she feeds on fish, squid, and krill, a type of crustacean. When she comes back, she relieves her mate, who may have lost as much as 25 pounds, because he doesn't eat the whole time she's gone. While she feeds the baby, he goes off and eats. Even though they aren't marsupials, like possums, the females do have a breeding pouch. The little one is tucked inside for a while, but mainly, the parents take turns feeding and caring for the baby."

"That's all very interesting, Anya."

"They aren't scared of people because they rarely come in contact with us. There was one incident where six men were trying to capture one male penguin. Guess what happened?"

"I couldn't hazard a guess. You tell me." I turned off of 40 onto the artery that would take us into Webster Groves. My daughter's excitement mingled with my joy at having her back. I felt my spirits soar.

"The penguin knocked the men over and tossed them around. Do you remember those toys I had that couldn't be knocked down? Weebles? Penguins are shaped like Weebles. They're hard to knock down, and they are very strong. They can dive 900 feet, swim 25 miles per hour, and stay under water for 20 minutes."

"Did they ever capture the penguin?"

She nodded. "Eventually all six of the men brought that one penguin down, but they had to tackle it as a team."

"That is pretty amusing, isn't it? Sounds to me like you need to write a comprehensive book about penguins."

"Maybe." She regarded me with those denim blue eyes so much like Sheila and George's. "I would need to do more research."

"Do you have a plan?"

"Yes, I do." She lifted her chin. "I want to shadow a zookeeper."

"All right, and how will you get to do that?"

"I don't know. Do you have any ideas?" Her eyes narrowed speculatively, as if judging my worth.

"You might start by phoning the zoo and telling them about your project. Tell them that you'd like to do more research. Ask if you can come and shadow a zookeeper. Provide references before they ask. Our vet might be a good place to start."

"You're pretty smart, Mom," she said this as we pulled into the garage.

After turning off the car, I reached over and grabbed her in a hug. Her stiff body relaxed as she accepted and returned the affection. "So are you, sweetheart. So are you."

We barely made it into the house when Erik squealed, "Annie!" He threw himself into her arms.

"Anya! So good to see you." Brawny's smile was genuine and her eyes were moist.

In return, Anya said a tentative, "Hello," to Brawny. I considered whether to ask Anya to apologize for her bad behavior, but a tiny shake of the nanny's head stopped me. Perhaps Brawny was right. Perhaps it was better to let things take their natural course.

Gracie trotted around the corner. The big dog actually nudged Erik to one side so she could plant her paws on Anya's shoulders and lick my daughter's face.

After all the greetings, Anya raced upstairs with her backpack over her shoulder.

Would she stay in her room? Avoid Brawny? I hoped not.

After I'd fed Ty, I'd dragged out two board games and ordered a sausage and mushroom pizza, Anya's favorite. That brought her downstairs in a hurry, although Erik whined, "I want fish sticks." Brawny had already heated up the oven. She whispered in my ear, "The wee tyke has taken quite a fancy to them. Kraft Macaroni and Cheese, too. I don't know why."

"Anya went through a mac and cheese stage, as I recall. Oh, well."

I had to be back at the store by six thirty for the crop. When I left the house, Anya was using her Kindle Fire to show Erik the book on penguins. The atmosphere between her and Brawny had been tense but civil.

Detweiler was working late again. If I hadn't known about the visit from the young royals, I would have suspected him of staying away on purpose.

"Hello, Sunshine!" Clancy greeted me as I walked through the back door. She was using the nickname I'd been given by Dodie.

"Back at you," I said as I joined her in the back room of Time in a Bottle.

"I can see from your face that Anya's back home and doing okay."

"Yes," I said. "Thanks so much for asking."

"Anya is giving Brawny a wide berth, but so far she's been polite. Brawny has assured me that she's fine and that she doesn't need Anya to apologize. I must say that Brawny's taking this..." I stopped myself.

"Taking it like a man?" Clancy asked. She was wearing what she called her "work clothes." After a series of disasters with people spilling glue and paint on her, she'd bowed to practicality. Her new uniform consisted of a crisp pair of jeans, an older Oxford cloth button-down shirt in light blue, and a pair of low boots. Over the ensemble was a neat black apron with pockets on the front. "That is what you intended to say, isn't it?"

"Guilty as charged." I had on a pair of jeans, too. Mine were left-over maternity jeans with an elastic panel across the tummy. Over them, I'd thrown a cute plaid sweatshirt I'd picked up from the bargain racks at Target. The length of the top disguised the fact I was still wearing mom-to-be togs.

Clancy had started a pot of hot water. I heard the bubbling and took the opportunity to brew myself a cup of peppermint tea.

"How are the little boys?" Clancy checked the expiration date on a carton of almond milk. For some odd reason, she actually likes cleaning out the refrigerator. I think it appeals to her sense of order. Every Saturday, she starts at the top and works her way down, wiping the surfaces as she goes. It's a job I'm happy to hand over to her. When she visits my house, she usually busies herself organizing and alphabetizing the food in my pantry.

Hey, whatever floats your boat.

"Much better. Thanks. Although Erik is on a mac and cheese and fish sticks only diet. He refuses to eat anything else."

Clancy laughed. "That sounds age-appropriate to me. I remember when my son ate mac and cheese three times a day. Shortly after I bought a case of it, he decided he hated mac and cheese. I gave all the boxes to a food bank."

I thought about asking her if she'd heard from her kids, but I figured she'd let me know if she had. Instead, I turned to the topic at hand. "Are we ready for tonight's crop? Are we getting any traction with the Zoo Keepers' folks? Anyone signed up from their mailing list?"

"You'll be happy to know that we have a full house tonight. Standing room only tomorrow, if we would allow people to line the walls. Instead, I put together a stand-by list."

"Could we haul out those two card tables? We've used them in the past."

"Already planned on doing that."

"You mean we've filled both crop tables and both card tables?"

"Yes, ma'am. Thirty people are scheduled to arrive and do their thing. Including all four of our suspects. Vicky Dillon and Peggy Rankin will be here tonight. Lee is coming tonight and tomorrow. Tonight she's bringing Annie Patel. Tomorrow she'll have Rook Smith with her." After closing the refrigerator door, she spritzed it with car wax spray. This she rubbed into the surface vigorously. When she'd given it the sort of shine you'd typically see on a new car, Clancy stepped back to admire her work.

"Good job," I said.

"Same back at you. Looks like you've got a hit on your hands."

"Right. But I wasn't concerned about filling seats. I had hoped to learn more about Nancy Owens."

Clancy put the cleanser back in the cabinet under the sink. The rag was dropped into the bag of dirty things to be washed. Satisfied that she'd done everything she could to organize and sanitize our refrigerator, she crossed her arms over her chest and stared at me.

"Good job," I said as I patted her on the shoulder. "Clancy, what would I ever do without you?"

"It's show time," I said, picking up my folder. In my head, a brass marching band struck up a spirited tune. Every crop thrills me. I hope that if I live to be a hundred I won't lose this enthusiasm for my job. Maybe this is all ego, because seeing the reactions to my newest projects always gives my self-esteem a boost. But I also suspect it has to do with how much I enjoy seeing other people enjoying themselves. Woman's work is undervalued and underappreciated. Even worse, our effects are quickly undone, erased, or consumed. But when a woman commits her memories to a scrapbook, she hands to the next generation a tangible work of art. I am so blessed to be a part of that process.

Of course, this crop served many purposes. In addition to our usual goals, we would be supporting the zoo, attracting new potential customers, and finding out more about Nancy Owens. We usually let our customers sit where they want, but this time, Lee and I needed access to the Zoo Keepers' board members. As always, I stood at the head of the work table. To my left sat Vicky Dillion and Peggy Rankin. To my right sat Lee Alderton and Annie Patel.

After my welcome, I held up the adorable board books we would be making. The "oooohsss" and "aaaahhs" of excitement put a big smile on my face. Once I explained how the book was recycled, I stepped back from my role as instructor.

One person isn't really enough to run a big crop. Two can barely keep up with a huge crop like this, especially when we have a crowd of first-timers who might or might not have much experience with papercrafts. I'd phoned Rebekkah and asked if she could come and help. However, she was running late. The women had already begun working on their projects when Rebekkah burst in through the front door. Standing over the welcome mat, she shook her hair to dislodge snowflakes.

"Is it sticking?" I asked.

"No. Not yet. Might be later."

As soon as she pulled off her pea coat, Rebekkah got right down to the business of helping our guests. I liked that. Her helpful presence gave me the time to chat up guests with the hope I'd learn more about Nancy Owens' death.

I focused on Vicky Dillon. Her look is singular and unusual. In a daring move, she wears a burr haircut that is striking, especially when paired with her designer glasses. To add to her femininity, she always wears a pair of interesting earrings. My immediate impression of Vicky was a woman who knew her own mind.

At first, Vicky had trouble getting her new backgrounds to stick to the pages of her board book. I showed her how she could scrub the slick cardstock with a bit of sandpaper to give the old board pages more "tooth," a word that means a surface with fissures and holes. Surfaces with "tooth" do better at grabbing onto anything applied to them.

"I like the colors you chose for your backgrounds," I said as I looked at her choices.

"Yes," she said, adjusting her purple-rimmed specs. "Aqua and lavender are my favorites."

"I can see that! So cute. May I?" I glanced through her stack of photos, stopping when I found one of Nancy Owens. "By the way, I'm sorry for your loss."

Vicky took the photo out of my hand. "Poor Nancy."

"I don't know how well you knew her, other than as a board member, I mean."

"I brought her onto the board."

"Really?" I stood up and said, "Hey, everybody. There's a lot of food on the tables. Please get up and fill a plate. We have sandwich makings, potato salad, fruit, and cupcakes."

When most of the croppers got up to get food, I pulled my chair closer to Vicky. "How did you meet Nancy?"

"She and I met as volunteers at the library. We used to shelve books. Both of us had just gotten married for the second time, so we had a lot to share. She inherited an angry stepdaughter, and I got an angry stepson. Let me tell you, Kiki, a step-kid who hates you is like living with a blister on your soul. I think that Derrick spends his entire day thinking up new ways to make my life miserable. If he put nearly that much time into his schoolwork, he would be on the Dean's List."

I couldn't imagine trying to parent a child who hated me. Erik, perhaps because he was young, hadn't resented me. It had taken him a while to warm up, but that was because he was grieving for his mother, and because he'd moved across the country into a new family.

Vicky sniffled. "If I had known how miserable Derrick would make me, I would never have married Richard. I swear. Sometimes I find myself looking for reasons to stay away from home, just so I don't have to interact with him. I always thought that love conquered all, but it doesn't. Not really. Or maybe that should be amended to, 'Love conquers all but a determined teenager.'"

Our conversation was interrupted by Annie Patel. Her dark brown eyes were warm, and the severe way she wore her jet black hair set them off, making them huge in her gentle face. "Kiki? May I borrow Vicky?"

"Sure. Annie, do we have enough to eat for you? You're vegan, aren't you?"

"Yes, but so is Peggy. We always bring snacks for each other."

At the mention of her name, Peggy joined us. "I'm having so much fun. I saw the other project you've planned for us. Where do you get your ideas?"

While Annie and Vicky wandered off, I talked with Peggy about my "process," although I still feel a little awkward calling my brainstorming activities, as disorganized as they are, by such a highfalutin name.

"I wanted to offer my sympathies," I said at an appropriate point in our conversation. "It can't be easy to cope with Nancy Owens' death."

"Y-y-yes," Peggy admitted. "I'd known Nancy for years."

To underscore what she said, she pushed an 8-by-8 inch scrapbook toward me. "There I am with my daughters. The girl to the far right is Rochelle. She's the same age as my child, Erin."

I stared down at a sullen-looking pre-teen standing so far right that she was nearly out of the picture.

"Here's a more recent photo." Peggy flipped pages until she found a better shot, a close-up, of Rochelle and Nancy.

"That's probably the only good photo I have of the two of them together. They didn't get along. Bert and I were neighbors before his divorce. My girls played with Rochelle, as you've seen. After Bert and Nancy started dating, we went out several times as couples. Nancy was well-liked, although she did have a temper. She had a bit of a victim mentality because her parents had it so hard when they moved here from Hungary. Her dad worked in the steel mills, which is pretty rough and tumble. Her mom never did learn English."

"What do you think happened to the missing check? The one gone from the Zoo Keepers' money market account" I asked. Immediately I regretted opening my mouth because I'd clearly shocked Peggy.

She stiffened and drew back from me.

Rats. Sometimes I spoke without thinking, and this was definitely one of those times. I would have tried to smooth over my faux pas, but I didn't get the chance. Lee and Vicky joined us. I could tell by the way Lee smiled at Peggy that she'd overheard what just happened.

"It's okay, Peggy. Don't worry about it. Kiki's a dear friend. Vicky? I told Kiki about the missing check that Nancy said had been voided. She knows about the police interviewing me. I thought maybe Kiki could help. She's good at getting to the bottom of things."

Slowly Peggy dropped her defensive stance. "I've heard about your, um, exploits."

That brought a chuckle from Lee. "More than just exploits, Peggy. But honestly, you can trust Kiki. I sure do."

I thanked Lee. "Ladies, it seems to me like Lee got tangled up in this when she discovered that a money market check disappeared on Nancy's watch. Is that what you think, too?"

With a jerk of her head, Peggy signaled for us to move away from the others. Even though the rest of our guests were too busy eating to care about our conversation, I knew that was a wise idea. "Let's go back into the back room. Rebekkah? Clancy? I'm heading into the back for a few minutes, can you take over? Thanks."

"Have a seat". I pointed to the break table as the women followed me to the stock room. But on her way, Peggy paused and stuck her head inside my office. My eyes followed hers and came to light on the framed photo of Dodie on the wall.

"That's right," Peggy said. "I'd forgotten. Dodie Goldfader is the one who originally hired you, didn't she?"

"Yes, that's her daughter Rebekkah who is helping me out there."

"I thought she looked familiar! She's grown up to be a pretty young lady, hasn't she? Dear, dear Dodie. She and I were Boy Scout troop leaders. I remember when her son Nathan died. Poor Dodie and Horace. I can't imagine losing a child, can you?"

We all agreed that would be the worst thing ever to happen to anyone. If Peggy had been standoffish before, she was now in a more conciliatory mood. As for Vicky, I couldn't read her. I trusted that if she wasn't happy, we'd soon know it. The women pulled up chairs. I opened the refrigerator and offered them a selection of beverages. Not surprisingly, their choice was a round of Diet Coke.

"Peggy, do you know what happened to that missing check?" Lee turned to her friend. "I never could get a straight answer. Not from Nancy and not from Fareed."

Peggy and Vicky exchanged looks that suggested they both knew the answer, but neither wanted to say. I caught their silent message. So did Lee, and she wasn't happy with it, because it meant they were privy to information but didn't want to share.

Lee frowned. "Look, ladies. I've been questioned by the police. I think I have a right to know what the truth is."

Peggy gave a tiny nod and Vicky seemed to agree with her. "Here's the deal. That original missing check? Rochelle took it."

"Wow," I said.

"The one from our money market account? I didn't know it had turned up!" Lee's hands gripped the edge of her chair. I could imagine that she was resisting the urge to throttle some-one, and I couldn't blame her. Obviously, she wasn't in the information loop. That wasn't fair, especially since she was carrying a lot of responsibility for the group's funds.

"Fareed asked us to keep it quiet," Peggy said in a mollifying tone. "I only know because I'm the secretary. You see, I wondered if I should mention what happened in our minutes. Vicky only found out because she was standing beside me when I asked Fareed. We were out in the parking lot, getting ready to ride home together. This happened immediately before Nancy came out and started yelling at you, Lee. Fareed said I should let it go, and I trust his judgment. He's known Nancy for ten years, and he's well aware of the problems she's had with Rochelle."

"What did Rochelle plan to do with the check?" I slipped my question in.

Peggy flipped her hands over in a "beats me" sort of gesture. "From what I understand, Rochelle took the check in an attempt to embarrass Nancy. She wanted to ruin Nancy's reputation. You see, Nancy's one of the founding members of Zoo Keepers. I've known—I knew—her for years. Because she doesn't have any children of her own, she thinks—thought—of Zoo Keepers as her legacy. Rochelle wanted to really, really hurt Nancy. She knew Nancy really cared about taking care of animals, and she figured that embarrassing Nancy in front of the Zoo Keepers organization was the best way to accomplish her goal. That child has hated Nancy from the moment they met. I've never seen such a spiteful kid."

"But in a way, Rochelle did Nancy a favor." Vicky crossed her arms over her chest as if to underscore the validity of the statement she'd just made.

"A favor?" Lee sounded incredulous. I, too, was surprised by this twisted logic.

"Absolutely," Vicky said with a nod. "I've known Bert Owens for a long time. I remember how guilty he felt after he divorced his first wife. He swore to Rochelle that he'd never leave her, and she grew up with a sense of entitlement. Bert would never listen when people told him things that Rochelle had said or done. He would laugh them off. To him, Rochelle was his darling baby girl, and he owed her for ruining her life. You're right, Peggy. That kid hated Nancy, but Nancy didn't help herself. She didn't have kids, so she didn't understand why Bert could get so blindsided by his daughter. All that changed when Rochelle took that check, he came around. He was stunned. Totally shocked."

"How did they find out that Rochelle had taken it?" I leaned in to listen carefully. We couldn't stay back here much longer, but I wanted to learn everything I could.

"After Lee brought up the missing check at the board meeting, Nancy went home and told Bert what she suspected," Peggy explained "Together they rummaged through Rochelle's backpack. That's when they found the check. Nancy phoned Fareed right away and told him everything. Fareed's a dad, too, and he's had his share of issues with his kids. He was very understanding. Bert was horrified, but then Rochelle told him it was only a harmless prank. Believe it or not, Bert accepted her explanation."

Lee shook her head sadly. "That's just awful."

"And now Nancy's dead," I said, "and a cashier's check has been written for a million dollars is missing. I wonder if law enforcement officials have questioned Rochelle. If they haven't, they should."

"Why would they?" Peggy shrugged. "She learned her lesson. Now that Nancy's dead, Rochelle has no reason to pull the same stunt again."

I couldn't believe how cavalier Peggy was being. Lee and I looked at each other. I bit my lip. It wasn't my place to set Peggy and Vicky straight, but clearly they had no idea how bad the situation was.

Time for me to act like the gracious hostess. I got to my feet.

"It's been great talking with all of you. Let's get back to the crop before people get suspicious and notice that all three of the Zoo Keepers board members have left."

With that, we all went back to the serious business of cutting, pasting, and creating.

24

U sually I would discuss with Detweiler all that I'd heard about Rochelle Owens. However, his car wasn't in the garage. I hadn't checked my phone while at the crop, so I dug for it now. His message was short: *Working late. Love you. This will ease up after Sunday.*

With the realization that I was flying solo as a parent, I squared my shoulders and went into the house. At first, I didn't hear a peep. That seemed curious because I'd purposely come home quickly after the crop, leaving Clancy and Rebekkah to do the final chores.

Did the silence mean that Brawny and Anya weren't speaking to each other? On tiptoe, I crept down the hallway and into the kitchen. Anya and Brawny were seated side-by-side at the kitchen table. Both stared intently at the screen of Anya's laptop. Brawny was holding Ty in one arm, jiggling him enough to keep him happy.

"Hey, there. What's up?" I asked, holding my crossed fingers behind my back. With any luck, this détente would continue. I hoped my sudden arrival wouldn't encourage Anya to act huffy again.

My worries were quickly put to rest when both faces turned my way. Anya wore the intense sort of concentration that I've come to love. Brawny looked relaxed as well.

"We're researching intersex," Anya explained. "I didn't realize how common it is. In fact, it's almost as common as having red hair. Of course, there are all sorts of variables that combine to make a person, and gender is really, really complicated. Did you know that they used to call intersex people hermaphrodites? That the human embryo actually starts as a female and then, if all goes as usual, it might develop into a male?"

Brawny has certainly mastered the art of keeping her emotions to herself, but in her eyes I detected the distinct warmth of relief.

"Aye. 'Tis much I didna know about intersex either until young miss showed me."

"Anya, I am thrilled to learn more about intersex people. But I'm even more proud that you are educating yourself about this. When I was growing up, we never talked about being intersex. I'm glad you won't be as ignorant as I."

After going back into the hall to hang up my jacket, I puttered around in the kitchen and made myself a cup of hot tea. I quickly found out that Erik was sound asleep upstairs. Because Anya and Brawny were obviously getting along, I felt free to sip my drink before heading up to Ty's room where I would take my accustomed seat in his rocker to nurse him. Brawny carried Ty up to me.

"Ye must be exhausted." She handed him over. The minute he was in my arms, he rooted around like a small pink pig. Once he got situated, he latched on and nursed like a champ.

"I am really tired, but I'm more happy than anything. Thank goodness Anya is okay again."

"She's a wonderful young woman." To emphasize this,

Brawny clutched both hands to her chest and added, "Being a part of her life is a rare privilege for me."

"Brawny, you're a gift. You really are."

Her eyes were wet when she left me.

As I rocked and nursed Ty, I reviewed what I'd learned from the Zoo Keepers. Rochelle had taken the money market check. So was that a dry run for stealing the cashier's check? But how could Rochelle have stolen the cashier's check if she was in Chicago with her dad? No matter how I twisted and turned it around in my head, it didn't make sense.

That led to the other burning question: Who killed Nancy Owens and why? You could argue that Rochelle had motive to kill Nancy, but the girl didn't have means or opportunity.

I went around and around and found myself back at the beginning. Who took the cashier's check and why? Did the police have any leads on who killed her? Or were they content to blame Lee Alderton?

If Detweiler was home, I could ask him.

I couldn't help but think that we had a piece missing from our puzzle. A big piece. Maybe even a corner.

25

The next morning, because Anya wasn't downstairs yet, I asked Brawny how the evening had gone.

"Better than I expected. Thanks for asking. I checked on Erik. He's still asleep. I think he needs the rest."

I fixed myself a cup of tea, while she bounced around the kitchen, checking on supplies of this and that.

"Don't tell me," she muttered as she stared into the freezer. "Ah. Good. More fish sticks. Young sir has taken quite a fancy to them."

Anya came bounding down the stairs. In her jeans and a Cardinals hoodie, she looked adorable.

"Brawny and I are going to the zoo," she announced. Her eyes danced with excitement. "We decided last night. I want to get there first thing so maybe I can talk with a zookeeper. We're going straight to the Puffin Coast where the penguins are."

A mewling cry over the baby monitor interrupted our conversation. Brawny left to run upstairs. While she was gone, Anya chattered happily about her research visit. Brawny returned and handed me a freshly diapered Ty. Then our nanny stood at the foot of the stairs, shifting her weight awkwardly from one leg to the other. "If this isn't convenient, we can change our plans. I warned Anya that you might be bound for the store this morning. With all that's happening, the timing seems right for us to look around."

Although she didn't mention the visit by the young royals, I quickly realized this was an important reason for her to go scout out the zoo. For Brawny to guard the youngest royals, she would need to familiarize herself with the layout.

"Of course, it's okay. I don't need to leave for the store until four thirty. This is perfect weather for visiting the zoo. When it's cold like this, the animals with fur coats are really lively."

"Yes!" Anya did a fist-pump. She fairly danced around the kitchen while Brawny grabbed their coats and gloves.

I carried Ty to the front window where we could watch the car drive away. Taking my baby's hand in mine, I waved at the departing vehicle. I kissed him over and over until he smiled. The baby's fat little cheeks were pink and his smiles were contagious in the very best way.

"Looks like Brawny and Anya have made up," Detweiler said as he galloped down the stairs. He'd been in the shower when I left our bedroom. "I heard the car and happy voices. Did someone say they're going to the zoo?"

"That's the plan." My husband followed me as I carried our son into the kitchen, the hub of our world as a family. A wave of Detweiler's cologne hit me, and I felt as though I'd swoon. There was a part of me that responded to him on the most elemental of levels. I could feel myself getting hot and bothered, yet here we were in our kitchen, doing nothing special. Maybe that was the point. He didn't need to do anything out of the ordinary to make himself appealing to me.

Detweiler tenderly lifted Ty from my arms. Moments like

this I loved Detweiler more and more. He was such a devoted dad. With our son on his lap, Detweiler blew raspberries, kissed Ty, and snuggled with our baby. Throughout all this, Ty watched his father with a mesmerized look on his face, totally fascinated by Detweiler's antics.

"Ty is so bright-eyed. He's taking everything in." Detweiler's voice was husky with emotion as he strapped our son into his bouncy chair.

"Yes, that's his job right now. He's absorbing all sorts of information at an astonishing rate. It's fascinating to think about all that a human has to learn to be functional, isn't it?"

Looking up at me with shining eyes, Detweiler said, "I probably don't say it often enough, but I love you, Kiki. Thank you for being my wife, and for bringing Ty into the world. I love all three of our children. Watching him grow makes me wish I'd been there for Anya and Erik, too."

The lump in my throat kept me from speaking. "Soak up every minute with Ty. He'll change in the wink of an eye."

"If I miss anything, can we have another one? I mean, another baby? I realize this is harder on you than it is on me, but I'm loving every minute of it."

All sorts of emotions battered me. Joy. Exhaustion. Love. Fatigue. Finally, I felt overwhelmed, and my face must have shown it.

"You don't have to decide right this minute." Detweiler pulled me into his arms. "I'm just saying, in a sort of inelegant way, that I love our life together. If you think we can handle another child, I'm totally down for it."

"Down for it?" My turn to giggle. "You've been talking with Anya, haven't you?"

"Yes, I have. In case you haven't noticed, I love all three of our children. I know we're going to have rocky times ahead with a teenager, but she's still a wonderful kid. You've done a fantastic job of raising her."

"Thank you," and I let my head rest against his chest long enough to enjoy the *lub-lub* of this man's big heart. How blessed I was to have found him.

26

I poured Detweiler more coffee and told him what I'd learned about the missing money market check, Lee's interview with Detective Albertez, Rochelle's hatred of her stepmother, and the now missing cashier's check. As always, he listened intently, stopping me only for clarification.

As I talked, he grew more and more concerned. "Of course Albertez had to interview Lee Alderton. He had no choice. Given her conflict with Nancy Owens, Lee would be near the top of his 'persons of interest' list. As for that text from her phone, I don't know if that's true or not. Lee's in good hands with Jim Hagg, as long as she does what he asks of her."

I rinsed out the dishes from our breakfast. I like to check things before I put them in the dishwasher, because with a little extra attention they always seem to come out cleaner. As I swished glasses around in the sink, I felt the need to lighten Detweiler's mood. So I told him that I was planning to help Jennifer entertain the children who would be mingling with the youngest royals.

"I wish you weren't."

His gruff tone took me by surprise. I whirled around to face him.

"I'm sorry, Kiki. I can't help worrying about this visit. Each time I turn around, there are new complications. First Brawny gets dragged into this. Then Nancy Owens gets shot. Then a cashier's check goes missing. Now Fareed Farkada seems to be dodging our calls. The royals are bringing their children. Last night we heard that the Hungarian Ambassador has his own driver, someone local. Each time I check with Jennifer's group, their plans get more and more elaborate. Now I hear you're involved, and I can't help this creeping sense of panic."

"Panic. That describes the look on Brawny's face this morning when she thought we were out of fish sticks. Erik has become a fanatic about eating them. He also likes macaroni and cheese. Anya went through a fish sticks and mac and cheese stage, too. I wonder if Ty will."

While I scrubbed at a cookie pan, I told him about the polar bear costume that I would *not* be wearing. Although I thought it was hilarious, he was not amused.

"See? A mix-up like that about the costume is exactly the sort of complication I'm talking about. Each time I nail down a variable, two more spring up. I hate the fact that my wife and our nanny will be involved in this visit, although you two might be the only two people I trust one hundred percent."

His vehemence surprised me.

"You'll have FBI agents, DSS agents, and local police as well as undercover cops who regularly patrol the zoo. Why are you so worried?"

"It's complicated." Running a hand through his hair, he took his time responding. "I got a summons to appear in Prescott Gallaway's office."

Hearing that name made me cringe. Prescott is the acting Chief of Police. He's filling in for Robbie Holmes while he's out west with Sheila as she goes through rehab. Prescott is a real loser. A total creep.

"Prescott said?"

"He says there's been chatter suggesting something is going to happen when the royals visit. Prescott was vague, but he assured me that he has everything under control."

"I just bet he does." I was wringing out the dishtowel with such force that my knuckles had turned white. "But how about the federal agents? What do they say?"

"They say this is normal. Welcome to the world we live in."

I took the chair next to Detweiler and told him about the animal rights activists who had threatened Zoo Keepers.

"We know about them. They're the same people who've thrown buckets of blood on women wearing fur coats. They've chained themselves to livestock trucks. They've picketed zoos. Disrupted circuses. Broken into laboratories. I respect their right to free speech, but once that tips over into hurting other people and ruining property, I draw a line."

"Are you expecting protests?"

"No," Detweiler was quick to say. "Neither is Prescott. The young royals are almost universally well-liked. The problem is that I don't trust Prescott. He doesn't know what he's doing. He doesn't have a steady hand on the rudder. When Robbie Holmes had that job, Robbie moved forward with a calm that permeated the whole department. Prescott, on the other hand, resents the time I'm spending with the federal agents. He questioned why they need my help! He's positive there's no danger to anyone from Young Women Leaders or to the kids. But when I pressed him for details, he told me that the visit is a 'fluid' situation. I think that's why he had a flunky call Jennifer and ask her to keep eight children occupied until the young royals arrive. And in turn, that's how you got dragged into this."

"I see why it has you worried. A lot of last minute changes

will make it harder for you and the other law enforcement agents to vet all the parties and keep track of everyone. Now you've got me concerned, too."

"That's the point of terrorism. To scare us. That's why Prescott should have kept his mouth shut. He isn't helping the situation; he's just giving the terrorists what they want."

AT THREE THIRTY, Brawny and Anya came home. My daughter fairly skipped into the house. She couldn't wait to show me the book she'd bought, *Animals Always: 100 Years at the Saint Louis Zoo,* by Mary Delach Leonard.

"I want to see," Erik whined. He was sitting beside me on the sofa. Anya gave him the book and sat down on the other side of me so she could share the map of the zoo grounds with me. "See? The Puffin Coast is the first exhibition you see when you turn left after you go through the North Entrance. It's one of the most popular. Did you know that the penguins recognize their keepers? They do. I met one of the keepers. She was about Rebekkah's age. She told me that when someone shows up in khaki like her zookeeper uniform, the penguins get all excited. Did you know that in the winter they take the penguins on a morning parade? That's to give them exercise. Brawny and I watched it. In the penguin area there are actually three different parts, an outdoor penguin exhibit for those in temperate climates, and two sub-Antarctic climates, one for cold-weather birds and one for the puffins."

Anya prattled on and on and on. Erik was absorbed with the pictures of animals. Meanwhile, Brawny moved in and out of the family room. She answered Ty's whimper and brought him downstairs before getting dinner started in the kitchen.

Although I only glimpsed our nanny's face as she moved about, I could see the joy shining from her eyes.

At four, Anya and Erik went upstairs. I nursed Ty in the family room. Brawny came in to see if I needed anything. It was the first chance I'd had to talk to our nanny in private. "Looks to me like your relationship with Anya is better than ever."

"Aye. She's a canny lassie, she is. Fascinated by the world around her, and thank heavens, I think she sees me as a biology project!"

That caused us both to laugh.

27

"Gee, why do I feel like I was just here?" I asked as I walked onto the sales floor of Time in a Bottle.

Rebekkah and Clancy were huddled over an article of interest at the front counter. With my arrival, they looked up.

"Ah, our fearless leader," Clancy said as she gave me a mock salute.

"Here's the scoop. Yesterday we concentrated on board books. Tonight we're turning TP rolls into treasure. Too bad Cara Mia Delgatto isn't here. She would love this project."

"Too bad we aren't there in Florida with Cara Mia," Clancy added. "I would love warmer weather."

"True." I leaned across my worktable to pick up a sample animal. "We need to make an additional ten of these. Jennifer wants to use them when the young royals come to the zoo on Sunday."

"No problem." Rebekkah shuffled over. "I can get them started and bag them up."

"Good deal. Anyone heard from Laurel?"

Clancy nodded. "I talked to Joe earlier. He says she was dehydrated. She's coming home tomorrow. They're giving her fluids and running tests. Her blood sugar was totally out of whack."

I sniffed the air appreciatively. "What're we having to eat tonight? Something smells wonderful in the back room. Onions, green peppers, garlic, and tomatoes, I'd guess."

"Chicken Cacciatore in the two slow cookers. I made it myself." Clancy looked very proud of herself.

"Ha! All she did was dump the ingredients into the pots. I watched." Rebekkah grinned at Clancy.

"How's your dad?" I asked.

"*Abba* is a lot better. The doctor is going to put him on anti-depressants. He didn't really want to take drugs, but I insisted." Rebekkah cocked her head and gave me an intense look. "Something good must have happened at your house. This is the happiest I've seen you in a week or two."

I explained to her and to Clancy that Anya and Brawny were back on good terms. Clancy thought that Rebekkah hadn't been told about Brawny's problem with gender dimorphism. "I wanted to respect Brawny's privacy and yours," Clancy explained. "So I didn't say anything."

"I appreciate that, but Rebekkah knows. Anya phoned her to talk."

Rebekkah nodded. "Anya called me today, too. It's kind of cool that we're so close. Anya seems to think of me as an older sister. In fact, she said as much. I'm one sister and Laurel is the other."

With all those cheery notes, we shifted into high gear, getting the place ready for the crop. As predicted, the Chicken Cacciatore was a huge hit. Clancy had also gotten muffins, donuts, and cookies from the Muffin Man, a bakery she passes on her way to work.

"I have a check here for almost three hundred bucks." Clancy handed me the piece of paper made out to Zoo Keepers. "I wish we could give them a million, but this is all our profit from the two crops we've held on their behalf."

"I'm sure they'll be glad to have it."

THE CROP WAS FUN, but taxing. This group of croppers was not as skilled as those who had signed up the night before. That shouldn't have surprised me. After all, last night's group was primarily composed of our long-time customers. This group came directly from our email to the people on the Zoo Keepers' list.

I'm happy to teach people new skills, but wowzer, it sure can wear you out to say, "A little glue is better than a lot" twenty times to the same person. Rook Smith was demanding but she wasn't a good listener, and she took directions as suggestions to be cheerfully ignored. She seemed to think I should stand over her and be her personal assistant. A couple of times, I caught Lee covering her mouth rather than burst out laughing at Rook's ongoing complaints, such as, "How on earth am I going to get all this glue out of my clothes? I think you should have provided us with protective garments." I thought about going into the back room, grabbing a black garbage bag, cutting a hole for her head, and handing it to Rook. I mentioned as much to Clancy who said, "Don't you dare!"

We'd told participants to bring their own short-bladed scissors. Rook brought a pair of sewing sheers with blades nearly a foot long. Totally useless for "fussy cutting," which is the industry term for small, intricate cutting.

By the end of the evening, I had to restrain myself lest I

snatch the project out of Rook's hands and scream, "This is obviously too complicated for you, you ninny!"

Rook's incessant demands meant I didn't get the chance to talk much to Lee Alderton. As the crop wound down, I seized the opportunity to squat next to Lee's chair and hand her the envelope. "This is for Zoo Keepers. There's a check for a little less than three hundred dollars inside."

"Kiki, you are so kind. Thank you very, very much."

"I'm glad we could help. How's everything going?"

Lee scanned the area and made sure that no one was paying attention to us. We could talk privately because everyone was crowded around the other worktable, admiring each other's zoo critters.

"Still no word on the missing cashier's check," Lee said. "Fareed has contacted a private investigator. The police have alerted all the local banks to be on the lookout for someone trying to cash it. We filled out the paperwork for the indemnity bond."

"I'm so sorry, Lee."

"I am, too. But I also have a bit of good news to report. Someone heard about our problem and contacted Fareed. This anonymous person has offered to give us fifty thousand dollars in exchange for the honor of personally handing a check over to the prince when he arrives at the zoo. Fareed talked to Prescott Gallaway, and Prescott is having the person vetted. It's not the large amount we hoped to give Prince William, but it's more than we had. I've been told he's been incredibly gracious about the fact we'll be giving him a fake check while we go through the process of replacing the original cashier's check. Maybe our patrons won't need to know what a mess this was."

"Keep the faith," I said, as I gave her a hug.

"Before you go," she said, grabbing my elbow, "I want you to know that your crops have been a lot of fun. People have mentioned they've learned a lot about Zoo Keepers from them. I also learned a thing or two about Hungary. Who would have guessed that the first rhino born by artificial insemination happened there?"

Tiring or not, the evening proved to be a smashing success.

28

I expected the house to be quiet when I got home. However, when I turned onto our street, I realized two extra cars were parked in our circular drive, and all the lights were on in the house. As I walked through the hall that leads from our garage to the kitchen, I recognized familiar voices. Agents Sanders and Montana were sitting at our kitchen table across from Hadcho and Detweiler with Gracie at his feet. Brawny stood at the sink, rinsing out dishes and listening in.

"What's up?" I tried to sound cheery, but I was tired and not particularly happy to see that an impromptu meeting of law enforcement officials had taken over my home.

The men all stood to acknowledge me. Before they had the chance to say anything, I asked, "How are my kids?"

Brawny dried her hands on a towel. "Anya is upstairs in her bedroom working on her penguin report. Erik is in bed. Ty should sleep for another hour or so. I gave him a bottle."

I immediately turned to Detweiler. "All right. To what do I owe this dubious pleasure?" I admit I sounded a bit angry, because at that moment I resented that when I'd had a long day,

I had to deal with more problems. Problems right here in my kitchen! Argh. Since when do problems follow people home like stray dogs?

"There's been a development," Detweiler said, getting up to yield his chair to me. "Have a seat, honey. Are you hungry?"

"Do we have any brownies?" Okay, I'd already eaten cookies and other junk at the store, but faced with these gun-toting home invaders, I needed a treat.

"Coming right up." Brawny scurried around. By now she knew that I consider brownies inedible without a big glass of milk. As she set the plate down in front of me, the two federal agents tried not to look interested, but they failed, and soon all of us were tucking into a plate of fudge brownies. Boy, do I love chocolate.

"There's been a development," Detweiler repeated himself. He'd grabbed a stool from under our kitchen counter and perched on it. "That tummy bug that our kids had last week has infected five of the eight children who were supposed to greet Prince George and Princess Charlotte. The three children that are healthy are all girls. That's not going to look good when they all get together to play. From what we've been told, George is a sweet little guy, but like most boys his age, he's into trucks and cars and..." Detweiler gave up. "Can you see where this is heading?"

"Sort of. You need to find another boy or two close to Prince George's age, right?"

"Exactly." Sanders jumped in. "That's why we came to you. Agent Montana remembered that your son looked to be around five."

"He is."

"Then we'd like to enlist his help." Agent Montana had the gall to look very proud of himself.

Fortified with the brownie, I was one tough cookie. "Since Erik is only five, you can't possibly enlist his help. Certainly legally you can't. You can only ask sweetly if we'll help out. I assume you came here to beg?"

Both agents turned deep crimson.

"I guess you better fill me in on the details."

Agent Montana sat up in his chair. If there ever was a man with a corncob stuck up his butt, it had to be Montana. In his haughty voice, he said, "This is highly classified information that we only distribute on a need-to-know basis, and you haven't been cleared to hear this portion of our plan."

"Guess what? You haven't been cleared to borrow my son. How do you like them apples? You and all the other little girls will have so much fun tomorrow. Enjoy!" And I jumped to my feet.

"Please!" Sanders almost shouted. "Please wait, Mrs. Detweiler. I think what Agent Montana means is that we're worried about your welfare. If we share too much information with you, you could become a target. If we tell you absolutely everything, in a moment of stress you might look over at someone for help and blow his or her cover. That would be dangerous for everyone. Of course you need to know more about our strategy. It's only fair."

Okay, that explanation made a bit more sense to me. I sank back down in my chair. "I'm not saying yes, but I'm willing to listen."

"We're only asking that your child be involved at the point that the young prince and princess are brought into the party room." Sanders was smart enough to look sheepish at this point.

"I need you to be honest with me. What sort of danger are you anticipating?"

"We have credible information that animal activists plan to make a statement. They'll be carrying signage. They want to block the entrance to the zoo, and maybe even disrupt the royals' visit. Our worst fear is that they'll incite violence. For that reason, we're using metal detectors and sniffer dogs. No one with any sort of baton or rod can enter the zoo. We'll be searching every backpack and handbag. We've even gone so far as issuing tickets for guests."

"Yes, I know." I crossed my arms over my chest. "I've already passed your security screening. So, the animal activists are your biggest concern? You don't think they'll try to kidnap Prince George or Princess Charlotte?"

"That's always a concern when we're guarding high-value individuals. We haven't heard any suggestions anyone is planning a kidnapping, but we have to cover all our bases. The royals will be protected by bodyguards, by security en route and onsite, misdirection, and by decoys. Detective Detweiler and Corporal Macavity will be two of our ad hoc bodyguards. Once the royals arrive, they will be escorted through the North Entrance gate of the zoological park and get immediately on the train. You're familiar with the small train that circles the zoo, correct?"

Of course, I was. For years, I rode that train around and around the zoo with Anya. We never, ever saw a single animal, because she was so enthralled by the train that she wouldn't get off long enough to walk over to an exhibit.

"Good. We have surveilled the route. We will secure it, make it hard to target, and protect our visitors. They'll make two stops, one at the rhino exhibit and the other at the gatehouse."

"What happened to the party room?"

"We've decided that's too vulnerable. The zoo president and the on-site coordinator will be notified of the change later tonight. Once the children are inside the gatehouse, they'll all be presented with stuffed animals and have a moment to interact with local children. That's where we'd like to include your son."

"Whoa." I held up a hand. "Our son? You mean Erik?"

"That's right."

"Not just our son. Erik *and* our daughter Anya will be there to greet the royals or neither of our children will be in attendance. Anya is not going to be left out. That would cause all sorts of hard feelings."

"We thought you'd be happy to keep her home. That's one fewer child in a hazardous position!" Montana threw up his hands with the sort of exasperation that generally happens with toddlers.

Sanders cleared his throat. "I'm terribly sorry, Mrs. Detweiler, but we can't adjust our plans just because of a little sibling rivalry."

I smiled at him. "Then you can adjust your plans to exclude the Detweiler family in total."

"Mrs. Detweiler, you are being unreasonable." Montana glared at me. His eyes were small and bright, like those of a fox, and his pointed chin added to the illusion that he was more feral than human.

"You're asking me to sacrifice my family's safety, to put my young son in danger, to loan you our nanny, to give up my free time, to provide you with hospitality while you hatch plots in my home, and I'm being unreasonable? Hmmm. Perhaps you should take a minute and think over my request. Detweiler? Brawny? Meeting in the Detweiler's office."

Gracie hoisted herself to a standing position right alongside of me as I took two steps away from my chair. Bless their hearts, both Detweiler and Brawny stood up, too. I felt like a drum major at the head of a very solemn parade as I marched out of my kitchen. We made it as far as the hallway when Sanders said, "Wait. Please wait."

He walked over and stared down at me. I expected to see an angry look on his face. Instead, I saw a smile that included a twinkle in his eyes. "I have four kids of my own. I can see where you're going with this. Believe me, being a parent is every bit as hard or harder than working as an FBI agent. If you're positive that you are willing to expose another one of your children to this situation, then we'll find a way. Anya is thirteen, right?"

Just then we heard a soft cry come through the baby monitor. "I'll go get young sir," Brawny volunteered.

"Yes, she is thirteen, and she's been working on a school project that involves penguins, so there's a logical way to get her involved. Anya has wanted to learn more by helping out a zookeeper. She knows that zoo like she knows her way around her school, and she's terrific with younger kids."

"We might need the help," Sanders admitted. "Prince George is quite the character. Adventurous. Curious. He'll have been cooped up most of the day. I remember my son's first birthday party. My wife invited twenty kids. Twenty toddlers cruising around, pulling on furniture, dropping food, falling, crying, fighting over toys, and terrorizing the dog. What a mess."

I was beginning to like this guy. "Yup. I don't know how many adults you planned for, but for six kids, I'd count on at least three grownup handlers."

"True." Sanders laughed out loud this time. "You've made your point, Mrs. Detweiler. Anya might be a helpful addition. Consider it done."

His partner sulked, but that didn't matter. I'd gotten what I wanted. Anya would be included. I led the way as we paraded back to the kitchen. That gave me an idea.

"It's a tradition at the St. Louis Zoo and others around the country to lead the penguins in a parade. That gives the animals exercise, and it stimulates their minds. Most children love penguins. Why not schedule a penguin parade for when the royals stand at the North Entrance?"

Sanders stroked his chin. "That would provide an interesting distraction. I'll look into whether that's feasible or not."

Brawny was carrying Ty, cradling him against one shoulder when she rejoined us. Her face was suffused with a soft radiance that was rare for her. "Anya and Erik fell asleep on her bed. Seymour is lying right next to them with his head on Erik's shoulder, and he's purring like a car motor. The three of them are a jumble. I think it's best to let them be."

She hesitated. "By the way, I talked with your sister Catherine last night. She's home from her visit with your Aunt Penny. I warned her that we might need her help babysitting with Ty tomorrow. She assured me that she would keep her calendar clear."

I mentally shook my head. I'd forgotten my sister would be back from her travels. Trust Brawny to know where my family was even though I'd totally forgotten.

Detweiler stepped between Brawny and me and lifted our son from the nanny's arms. When he settled back on the stool, he angled himself slightly away from me. It wasn't much, not to the casual observer, but I saw it. With a jolt, I realized my husband had subtly moved away from *me*. Usually Detweiler sits with one knee touching mine. Or he takes my hand when we're seated. Then it came to me that ever since I demanded that Anya be included, Detweiler had been silent. Right now, he was holding Ty as though the baby was a wall, separating me from my husband.

A little pang stabbed me in the heart. I adjusted my position in my chair, hoping to catch his eye, but Detweiler didn't look my way. My hand reached for his knee, but he didn't acknowledge the caress. One of the many things I loved about Detweiler was the way he showed his affection. Not in big showy ways, but with warm glances and gentle touches that said, "I love you." Where was that affection now?

Something was wrong. Really wrong. But what?

Then it hit me: I had acted like Anya was *my* daughter, not our daughter. To add insult to injury, I'd made decisions about Erik and his involvement without consulting Detweiler. Was my husband in favor of involving Anya? Did Detweiler want Erik to be involved? I hadn't given him the chance to voice his concerns. I had shut him out.

29

The rest of the meeting went by quickly, for me at least. Sanders explained that there wasn't much for me to know. "We'll guide you from place to place. Tomorrow morning, I'll supply you with a 'tick-tock,' an overview that's heavy on chronology. You'll have a schedule and a list of the moving parts."

He unfolded a map with a highlighted route that ran around the perimeter of the zoo. "I'll review our protective detail placement with you two later," he said with a nod to Detweiler and Brawny.

"We'll need somebody to drive you to the zoo. Preferably somebody with a panel van so you can slip out the side door. We want limited visibility of your arrival." Sanders was thinking out loud.

"Maybe Curtis Priva could help. He's the owner of Speedy Service Cleaners, and I know he's been vetted to attend. He told me he has a ticket."

"Look him up," Sanders told Montana.

While Montana did exactly that, Sanders continued, "The zoo has given us access to all their floorplans and resources.

Local law enforcement will be on hand in various capacities, undercover and in uniform. Federal agents will be there as well. Of course, the Secret Service will be involved because the Hungarian ambassador will be on hand to represent Budapest, which is a sister city to St. Louis."

"That's a lot of agencies," Brawny said with a solemn nod of her head.

"Priva's a go," Montana interrupted. "In fact, he's a great choice. Naturalized citizen. Came here from Hungary as a young teen. He has a distinguished military service record. Former Marine. I'll send an agent to talk with him."

That seemed like a fast fix to me, and I must have betrayed my thinking because Sanders said, "Fortunately, St. Louis is well-prepared for visitors who are high-profile. We have a good handle on people who know the drill. I suspect that Priva was okayed back then." Sanders did this little shrug of explanation. "That's one reason we suggested the prince come here, to St. Louis. Most of your various law enforcement bodies have had a dry run at a visit like this."

Detweiler agreed. "We've also had a lot of political visitors. Just before Robbie Holmes took his leave of absence, we did a mock drill, taking us through various training scenarios. Robbie has been careful to keep all our certifications up-to-date."

"But it's always harder when kids are involved. Let's face it, little ones are unpredictable," Brawny said "I know Anya and Erik, and they know me. They're accustomed to paying attention to what I say, but what about the other children?"

"We can only rely on what we've been told. I've stressed to their families that their children have to be able to pay attention. I realize we're talking kids here, but some are more compliant than others." Montana sighed.

"Will there be media?" I asked.

"Of course. We're in the process of vetting and credentialing members of the press."

"There will be some sort of ceremony, I would guess. Otherwise there will be nothing for the media to record." Brawny's eyes narrowed as she imagined the scene.

"Of course. After we have all our players in place, we'll load up the royals at their hotel. The ambassador has his own driver. We've designated that the cars will pull up under canopies and awnings that we're having erected."

I must have seemed puzzled because Brawny turned to me with an explanation. "It's a best practice to erect a curtain around the routes in and out of the final destination to make the movements of the protectees more difficult to track."

"That's right," Sanders said. "There will be cars, escorts, and decoys in the mix of vehicles. Once we arrive at the North Entrance to the zoo, we'll whisk the dignitaries out of the vehicles. It's customary for a child to present the duchess with a bouquet. The granddaughter of the zoo president will do that at the Welcome Desk inside the Living World. The royals will walk through the Living World under an awning and board the train. The train will take the prince, the duchess, and their children to a covered stop near the rhino enclosure. Prince William will make a short presentation there, mainly a photo op, explaining his efforts to keep these animals from extinction. Then he, his wife, his children, and the ambassador will climb back on the train. They'll go back to the Living World. The president of the board of directors for the zoo will give Will a signed book about the zoo as a keepsake. Ditto the Hungarian ambassador. The prince will likely say a few words. We'll also arrange for each of the children to receive a stuffed toy. *All* the children. We don't want a tussle to break out over sharing. The kiddies will play for a few minutes, and then we will whisk the royals out the way they came, relying on subterfuge and decoy vehicles."

"Explain, please," I said.

"Without going into too much detail, a limo will pull up. Decoys dressed like the royals will hop in. The motorcade will drive away. A few minutes later, a secure vehicle will arrive and the real royals will get inside that car. After that, the Hungarian ambassador will leave in a second car."

After studying the map, Brawny asked, "Counter-snipers will be stationed around the area, I presume?"

"Of course."

A chill ran through me. *Snipers? Counter-snipers?* What had I committed to? I opened my mouth to voice a protest, but the words stuck in my throat. After choking on them, I decided to wait and ask Brawny for details about the snipers. The thought of men training guns on my children made tiny stars dance at the edges of my vision.

"Snipers? How do these people cope with this? The royals, I mean? What would it be like to be a target, day in and day out? To know your children are constantly at risk? No amount of money or power on earth could be worth this sort of stress and danger. Not to me."

Sanders gave me a sad, small smile. "Not to most of us."

Brawny jumped in. "Remember the prince didn't ask for this type of notoriety. He was born into it. His mum, Diana, tried to protect him from the hoopla. She raised him to be as normal as she possibly could. Under the circumstances, that is. As for Kate? She's a rare jewel. Seems to be able to keep her head on straight. One can only presume that her relationship with her husband makes all this hassle worthwhile. From afar, it might seem like a fairytale. Up close, I suspect it's more like a nightmare. Especially when you consider bringing wee little ones into the mix."

Wee little ones. Anya and Erik. My babies.

Was I out of my mind?

30

A fter I heard all I had been cleared to hear, I took Ty upstairs for a diaper change and a nighttime snack. My tiny fellow looked more and more like his father every day. As I admired him, I wondered what would happen when Erik realized he didn't look like Detweiler or me. How did other families cope with a child with different ethnic roots? That worry could be tucked aside until later, I decided.

Lifting Ty to my shoulder, I paused to enjoy the décor in his room. Over the expanse of three walls, I'd painted a mural of animals marching two by two onto an ark. It wasn't perfect, but it turned out better than I had thought it would. The paired creatures crossed a pastoral background and a daisy-covered field, past giant oak trees, and going up and down over rolling hills of grass.

I picked up the white, green, and yellow colors in a trio of fabrics that Brawny had pieced into a quilt perfectly sized for Ty's crib. Next she used the same fabrics to make a quilt for a twin-sized bed, a place that came in handy when Ty was up and down all night. She'd also used white dotted Swiss to make crisp curtains and tied those back with yellow and green sashes. A comfy pillow rested on a white rocking chair. All in all, this had become one of my favorite rooms in the house. No matter how gray the day, the cheerful colors lifted my spirits.

Noises drifted up from downstairs. The slap of leather soles against the marble foyer. The creak of a door opening. The slamming of that same door. The FBI agents and their demands were leaving. Good riddance, I thought. Take your predictions of violence and get out of my house, I silently warned them. You're making a mess of my life.

This nursery was a happy place. A room full of light and love and joy. However, as I rocked Ty, I had to be honest with myself. The longer I rocked, the more I had to admit that I was using the room to avoid my husband. That caused my stomach to knot up.

As I heard him trudge up the stairs, I could tell he was unhappy. Each footstep echoed with sadness. Usually he races up and down the steps like a cartoon of a mountain goat. Not today.

In self-defense, I wiggled the rocker around so I faced the window. I didn't want to face my husband, even though I realized how cowardly I was being.

The door opened with a metallic protest. I made a mental note to oil it.

"Kiki?"

"Uh-huh?"

"How's Ty?"

"He's fine."

"Catherine agreed to come over tomorrow and watch him while we're at the zoo."

"Good." But I didn't look directly at him. Instead, I saw him in my peripheral vision as I stared out the window at the naked branch of the big maple tree.

He stood in the doorway with his arms crossed over his chest —and he did not look happy.

"You need to make a decision, babe. A tough choice. Either Anya is our daughter or she's your daughter. You can't have it both ways." His voice was totally reasonable, and anyone else would have thought he was fine, but I could pick out the rasp that suggested he was hurt.

"I know her better than you do."

"Yes, you do. I can't argue that." He inhaled deeply. I could hear the air being draw into his lungs. "I know law enforcement and the dangers of an operation like this better than you do. That's why we should act like a team. To make important decisions about *our* children *together*."

"She's *my* daughter." I have no idea why I blurted that out. Maybe the whole stress of our commitment to this endeavor was tugging at me like a loose thread that had been caught on a twig. I had the sense of coming unraveled. Frayed at the edges. Worst of all, I knew I was being hurtful to the man I married. Detweiler had always treated Anya as his own. He'd adopted her legally. In some ways, he'd been more of a dad to her than George had, although my late husband had been there for the first eleven years of Anya's life, George had been distracted to say the least. Detweiler, despite the demands of his job, gave Anya his total attention. He was transparent, without any hidden agendas.

Detweiler called my bluff. "You don't mean that. I know that you don't. If you do really think that, then you're fooling yourself. I'll agree that you know Anya best. Maybe you do know what's best for her, but you can't let the stress of this drive a wedge between us. Please don't ever question my love for Anya. That's not fair to me, and you know it."

I swallowed hard and kept staring out the window. My pride got in the way of the words I should have said.

"There are details I need to nail down for tomorrow," he said.

But I didn't respond.

After a few minutes, he turned around and left.

31

When I crawled into bed, Detweiler was still downstairs. I pulled up the covers, feeling miserable and scared. For the first time in a long time since meeting Detweiler, I felt alone in the world. I had made a terrible mistake in how I handled our meeting with the FBI. On the surface, an outsider might not have noticed the seismic shift, the way our world had tip-tilted. Try as I might, I couldn't get comfortable.

Later I felt Detweiler join me. I inhaled his familiar smell, the scent of Safeguard soap and a touch of patchouli. He didn't reach for me as he usually did. At first, he rested with his back to me. Then he rolled over. This he repeated several times. Finally I couldn't take it anymore. I pulled my arm out from under the covers.

"Sorry," I whispered as I tried to caress his face. Instead, I poked him in the eye.

"Ouch!" He sat bolt upright.

"Sorry, sorry, sorry. Are you okay? Can you see?" I sat up, too.

His shoulders heaved. "No. I'm blinded. Permanently. That means my career in law enforcement is over."

"Oh, no. Oh, no." I covered my face with my hands. "Let's get you to the ER."

He burst into laughter. "Can I drive?"

That got me laughing, too. Soon we were holding each other and trying not to make too much noise. We snickered and chortled and giggled until we were exhausted.

"I really am sorry," I said, when I could at last get enough air to breathe properly.

"I know you are. You wouldn't have tried to take my eye out if you were angry. Right?"

"You sure you're okay?"

His laugh was soft. "As long as I have you in my arms, babe, I am okay. Definitely okay."

ANYA AND ERIK were grumpy about getting up early on a Sunday, but they changed their tune when we explained we were going to the zoo. They grew even more excited when Detweiler explained we would be meeting Prince William and his wife Kate, the Duchess of Cambridge.

Anya could barely sit still. "I think I'll faint," she said.

"Don't you dare. That'll cause a huge problem."

"I was just teasing, Mom!"

Brawny gave us a quick tutorial in manners. "Royal protocol says that you call them, 'Your Royal Highness,' when you first meet. After that, you call them 'sir' and 'ma'am.' You don't touch them. They can touch you. They're pretty relaxed about all this, but you do want to make a good impression."

A knock on the door signaled that Catherine had arrived.

"Auntie Catty," Erik yodeled with delight. Anya threw herself into Catherine's arms. When she let go and moved away, it was my turn to give my sister a hug. "Thanks for helping out with this."

"I've missed my nephew. This is a great chance to have a little bonding time." So saying, she walked over to Ty's bouncy chair and lifted him out.

Detweiler walked in. "Hey, Catherine. Good to see you, but I've got to go." After brushing black dog hairs off the leg of his khaki pants, he addressed the children. "Please notice I'm dressed as a 'civilian,' not as a cop. That's on purpose. I will blend in with the crowd. Pretend you don't know me, okay? Listen to Brawny and your mother. I'm there to help protect everybody in case of bad guys, so I'll be keeping an eye on all of you. I'll never be far away."

After hugs all around, he left.

Brawny had suggested that both our kids wear navy and white. That put Anya in a navy skirt, a white blouse, and a navy cardigan sweater with pockets at the hem. Erik wore the same combination, except that he had on pants instead of a skirt. That left me to run upstairs and dig through my closet. Hanging in the very back was a navy blue wrap dress. Totally simple, perfectly plain. Although I hadn't lost my post-baby poundage, I miraculously managed to tie it around me. As an after-thought, I found an old navy sweater at the bottom of my dresser. It had been George's, and I'd forgotten it was there. When I buttoned the sweater over my wrap dress, it disguised the extra flab around my waist. The loose fit and deep pockets seemed useful. After a quick confab, Brawny and I decided that I would bring along the animal kits that Rebekkah had put together. Along with a handful of glue sticks, these would keep the children busy if need be.

Rather than give me a copy of the schedule, we agreed that Brawny would direct our actions. A quick breakfast was in order. I sniffed the air curiously. "Fish sticks?"

"Young sir demanded them. I felt it was better to do as he wished and be sure he had a full tummy than to argue."

Anya wanted pancakes, of course. She talked non-stop with Catherine, telling her about her project on penguins.

A rap on the front door sent us all into a mad scramble. Brawny answered it and came back with Curtis. I introduced him to everyone. Curtis was wearing nice khaki pants, a white button-down shirt, and a navy blazer. On the lapel was an enamel pin.

"That's the Hungarian flag!" I was pleased that I recognized the banner.

"Yes, ma'am. It is indeed."

We had coats on and were ready to hit the trail when Brawny's phone rang. She stepped into Detweiler's office to take the call. When she came back, her face had shut down. She didn't look like "our Brawny." There was a severity, bordering on anger. With a nod of her head, she signaled that Curtis and I should step away from the kids.

"Chatter has escalated. The only thing they know is that there's to be an exchange. We're to keep our eyes open, but not to interfere unless it puts one of the children in harm's way."

"That's what sniffer dogs are for." Curtis sounded loose and relaxed, but I noticed a twitch in the muscle that ran along his jaw.

Anya poked her head around the corner. "Can we go? I can't wait!"

32

Hurry up and wait. Hurry up and wait. That seemed to be the order of the day. Curtis drove us to the North Entrance of the zoo, as per his instructions. We came to a barricade where guards were standing. Curtis flashed an ID. Walkie-talkies crackled. A valet ran over to open our doors. Once we were out, he drove the van away. It was cold outside, but we were all so keyed up that we barely noticed the temperature.

"This awning wasn't here when Brawny and I visited." Anya pointed at the white canopy overhanging a red carpet that marked an obvious pathway. Two uniformed cops bookended the red carpet. At the far end of the path was a longish table with a metal detector and body scanner. Two more men in uniforms stood on either side of the x-ray machine. A third man with a dog stood at parade rest, blocking the pathway.

"Very observant about the canopy," Brawny said to Anya, while avoiding my eyes. "This is common when a dignitary arrives. Wouldn't want our beautiful Kate to get rained on, would we?"

I bit my bottom lip. So Brawny'd decided not to mention

snipers in front of my child. *Good.* Her explanation had been helpful but not alarming.

Our nanny flashed her ID at one of the uniformed men and explained who we were.

"You're expected. Adults? I need to see all of your IDs please."

We handed over identification. After the guard inspected them, he made a call on his walkie-talkie.

Brawny held Erik's hand, and I held onto Anya. We were processed through the metal detector and came up clean. A uniformed female officer led us into the Living World building. Jennifer Moore was waiting for me, as was Lee Alderton. Both gave me a hug and welcomed the children as well. I introduced Lee to Curtis. Of course, Jennifer already knew him. She'd recommended him to me.

The area around the Welcome Desk had been decorated with flowers. Velvet ropes marked off the area where the royals would be walking. A low table was set off to one side. Around it were eight kid-sized chairs.

The kids were invited to sit down. Another family joined us. They had three little girls. They looked to be ten, seven, and six. I was too nervous to pay attention to their names. Jennifer gave each child a coloring book and crayons. Anya decided to sit with the younger kids. She encouraged everyone to color. We adults stepped to one side and waited. All of us had our cell phones out, but a professional photographer appeared with a huge Nikon. Jennifer nudged me. "That's the official photographer. She'll take photos, post them online, and share an access code with you."

Walkie-talkies crackled. The royals were on the move! A general flurry of excitement bubbled up around us. Although I tried to be "cool," I felt anything but. Like my daughter, I'm a confirmed Anglophile. This was a big moment for me. It occurred to me that Nicci Moore was going to be really jealous of Anya, and that would be kind of, sort of, cool.

The royals were escorted past us. There were so many other bodyguards and officials that we couldn't see much. Just Prince William's receding hairline and Kate's shiny mane of auburn hair. I also caught one quick glimpse of Detweiler as he brought up the rear. His sandy hair caught my eye because he was one of the tallest men in the group. As the knot of people moved on, the train blew its whistle. The *chug-chug-chug* of its engine alternated with the hissing of steam. The train would run only while the royals and the dignitaries were on board. Since Detweiler had disappeared, I figured he was either on the train or guarding our area.

What followed was a very, very long 45 minutes. Not only were Erik and the three little girls excited, but they were quickly getting hungry, too. There was candy, but the other mother and I didn't want to pass it out. The last thing we needed was a bunch of kids hyped up on sugar.

"How about if we do crafts?" I asked. The ten-year-old girl pouted in an "I'm too old and too cool" sort of way, but soon boredom won out. Anya started assembling an animal. Miss I'm Too Cool quickly realized that doing crafts *might* be more fun than just sitting around.

"Mom? Did you bring any glitter?"

"As a matter of fact I think Rebekkah might have put some in the bag with the kits." Sure enough, she had.

As I leaned down to hand Anya the glitter, she wrinkled her nose. "What's that smell?"

"I don't know. Where's it coming from?"

"From you, Mom." Surreptitiously, she inhaled deeply, moving her head down the length of my body. "It's coming from your pockets."

I reached inside and pulled out a mashed up fish stick.

"Yuck. Erik must have crammed a fish stick into my pocket while I wasn't looking."

Anya covered her mouth to smother a laugh. "He tried to put one in my pockets, but I caught him. I didn't realize he'd put it in yours!"

I was on my way to the restroom to dump the fish stick when the walkie-talkies came alive. The royals' visit to the rhinos was over. Over the static, we heard the train whistle blowing. "Quick, everyone! Take your places. They're coming!"

Rather than sneak off to the john, I found myself pressed into service. One of the little girls had dumped glue all over. Anya and I grabbed baby wipes and began wiping up the mess. There was a lot to mop up—and very little time to get it done.

According to the plan, the train would return here, the North Entrance, and the VIPs would get out.

Reading the schedule to us, Curtis said, "There will be a wrapped book given to the royals, a wrapped book given to the Hungarian ambassador, and Jennifer's group will be introduced. Fareed Farkada will make a quick statement of welcome from Zoo Keepers. A penguin parade will follow the gift giving."

"Hurrah!" Anya bounced to her feet. "The penguins are coming! Hip-hip-hooray!"

In the distance, the train whistle tooted loudly. The royals were just moments away.

Curtis continued, "After the penguins pass by, stuffed T-O-Y-S will be distributed. The young royals will come in here to play, leaving the adults to get their photos taken with our special guests. Then the children will have their pictures taken, and the event will be officially concluded."

Catching Anya's excitement, Erik raced over to my side. "Mama Kiki! Dey is pen-gins, and I is going to feed them!" With that, he reached into his pocket. In his clenched fist he held something important.

Could it be?

"Erik? What do you have?"

"Pen-gin food."

Gently I pried open his fingers. Smashed in the palm of his hand were two more fish sticks.

"What on earth?"

That little booger had stashed fish sticks all over the place!

"Honey, I'm not sure if penguins eat this kind of fish sticks. I think they eat special fish sticks just for penguins. These are for little boys."

"Oh." His lower lip trembled as I picked the mashed fish out of his hand.

"Wait right here."

I looked around for a trash can. Whoever set up the "play area" had done a fine job, but there were no trash cans. "Do you see a trash can?" I asked Brawny.

"No trash bins. They've all been removed. 'Tis too easy to hide a bomb in a trash bin."

"Great," I mumbled to myself. "Erik, honey? Come stand by me."

There was nothing I could do but tuck the fish sticks back into my pocket. I was about to meet Kate Middleton, one of the most stylish women in the world. She, undoubtedly, would be wearing White Gardenia Petals, her favorite scent. I, on the other hand, would stink of fish sticks.

But I didn't have much time to fret because the train whistled to a stop. All of us in the Welcome Center crowded around the velvet ropes, hoping to catch a glimpse of our guests. I caught quick snapshots of two fair-haired children. A shiny mass of bouncy auburn curls. The top of a balding head. A small raised platform had been moved to the far end of the Welcome Center. I saw Prince William take the microphone. In his deep voice, he thanked the city, thanked the zoo, and talked about the importance of conservation. When he finished, Mayor White joined him for a grip and grin. We all applauded, and that gave me the chance to look around.

That's when I saw Rochelle Owens. She was standing to one side of the podium. I recognized her from the photos in Peggy Rankin's album.

But why was Rochelle here? Okay, the uncomplicated answer might be that like Nancy, she loved animals. But that didn't seem to fit. This girl had stolen a money market check from a group dedicated to helping endangered species. That didn't sound like an animal lover to me. Not at all.

Why was she here? Had Rochelle had a sudden change of heart? After Nancy's death, had she found solace in supporting Nancy's cause?

The Ambassador from Hungary climbed the steps to join Prince William and Mayor White. Something was wrong about the enamel pin on his lapel. I did a double-take. The stripes were green, white, and red, but wasn't right. I couldn't explain why, but I knew it wasn't.

"Psst. Curtis!" I pulled him close so I could whisper in his ear. "Look at the ambassador's pin."

After shooting me an annoyed gaze, Curtis did as I asked. I watched him look, squint, and look so hard that his neck jutted out like a turtle's sticking out of its shell. "The pin..."

"It's not right!" I whispered.

"Mooo-oomm! You're going to ruin everything!" Anya whined quietly.

Erik leaned against my leg. I reached down and took his hand.

"You do know about diplomatic immunity, don't you?" Curtis winked at me.

"Point being?"

"Our law officials will give that guy a wide berth. They can't really hold him or convict him, so why arrest him?"

Brawny noticed us talking. I explained my misgivings. "You would think that the ambassador to a country would be very, very particular about how he wears the emblem of his country."

"You would think." Brawny frowned.

Walkie-talkies crackled. A cymbal crashed. The marching band was coming our way. The penguins and their handlers would bring up the rear.

"We can't do anything about the ambassador," I said, "except keep an eye on him, right? If he is a foreign diplomat, it would be a big *faux pas* to accuse him. Especially right now when he's surrounded by onlookers."

"But we do need to keep eyes on the target." Brawny lifted her walkie-talkie and briefly explained the anomaly.

Now Kate joined her husband. She really was lovely. Mayor White urged a small girl forward. The tiny tot was holding a bouquet as big as her head so she probably couldn't see her feet. She was hesitant, even as he pressed his left palm up against her back.

The Hungarian ambassador moved to the rear of the podium. His eyes searched the crowd. He turned left and then right. Rochelle Owens gave him the tiniest of waves. He lifted his chin in acknowledgement.

Something was about to happen. Something. Something big. But what?

"Psst." I grabbed Brawny and pointed to Rochelle. "That's Nancy Owens' stepdaughter. Nancy who was shot in the head."

Rochelle edged her way through the crowd, walking behind people who were crowded around the platform. In response, the Hungarian ambassador was slowly moving closer to Rochelle.

"Look! In her hand!"

Rochelle was holding a business envelope. The ambassador

had stepped down from the platform. He was trying to maneuver around a large woman. She didn't want to move. Rochelle flapped the envelope at the ambassador, waving, signaling, offering up the piece of stationery.

"That's it," I said to Brawny. "That's the hand-off. That envelope has a cashier's check for one million dollars! We have to grab it!"

I didn't yell, but the stress gave my voice a desperate screech. Brawny and Curtis were on full alert.

"What?" Anya asked.

"See that girl? The one in the black coat? See the envelope in her hand? There's a check in there for a million dollars."

The marching band had moved off to one side.

"The penguins!" Anya said. "I see them!"

"I want to see!" Erik stood on this tiptoes.

"I'll tackle the ambassador," Curtis said. "I have dual citizenship. If we're making a mistake, it won't matter so much."

"I can grab Rochelle," I said. "She's right there, in front of where the penguins are heading."

"No, you don't. What about Erik?" Brawny had a strong grip on my shoulder.

"He's safer with you than with me!" I complained.

"You stay right here and make sure Erik is okay."

Just then I felt something burrowing down inside my sweater pocket.

"Trust me!" Anya said as she pulled out the fish sticks. "I've got this, Mom!"

Pushing me aside, she sprinted toward Rochelle.

"That's my cue." Curtis followed on her heels.

"We have a situation, 10-67," Brawny said into her walkie-talkie. "Suspect is transferring what looks to be an envelope. Our million-dollar check might be inside. Ten-39 to take down and capture."

33

Everything happened so quickly. Using their bodies as shields, federal agents hustled the royal family past us and into a waiting vehicle. In less time that you can spell, "zoology," the prince, his duchess, and their two little ones were whisked away.

Pandemonium ensued. Sort of. A girl's voice shrieked, "Let go of me!"

I held Erik's hand tightly. Brawny told me to stay with him, which I really didn't appreciate. Not when my daughter's life was on the line. In a matter of seconds, the law enforcement officials had everyone herded into a tightly knit group.

Everyone, that is, except my Anya.

Later, when we were back in the safety of my kitchen, I would hear how she snatched the envelope out of Rochelle's hand. With that precious piece of paper in her firm grip, Anya waded right into the midst of the colony of penguins.

"Waddle," Anya informed me. "Not a colony. The correct name for a group of penguins is a 'waddle.'"

Once surrounded by the bottom-heavy birds, Anya played keep-away. She held onto the envelope despite the best efforts of the fake Hungarian ambassador. Using Erik's fish sticks as bait, she encouraged the penguins to swarm around her.

The fake ambassador screamed with rage. He kept trying to get past the penguins. He demanded that Anya hand over the envelope. But she was too smart for him. She used those big birds like a mobile, bottom-heavy barricade.

Meanwhile, Curtis bounded over people. He managed to tackle the fake dignitary and knock him to the ground.

Uniformed police officers quickly handcuffed the culprit. Detweiler barreled his way through the penguins. While I was holding on to Erik, Detweiler hoisted Anya over his shoulder and carried her to safety.

34

"But why did Nancy Owens have to die?" I asked. Erik and Anya had gone to bed. Finally, we adults could talk freely. To make sure the kids couldn't overhear us, we crowded into Detweiler's office.

"It was a devilishly complicated plot," Sanders said as he leaned over the back of a kitchen chair he'd dragged in. "It all started with Rochelle's hatred of her stepmother. She knew that Nancy's love of Zoo Keepers was her soft spot, and she'd overheard Nancy talking to Bert about the big check they were giving Prince William. Realizing this would be the highlight of Nancy's life, Rochelle decided then and there to thwart her stepmother."

Montana nodded. He was seated on a folding chair. "Rochelle went online and quickly connected with a terrorism group posing as an anti-zoo protest group. These terrorists are way ahead of us in recruiting and manipulating disenchanted people. Especially young people who are naïve about their true intentions."

"The terrorists guided and shaped Rochelle's next steps," Sanders continued. "They talked her into getting a check for them, hoping they could somehow use their banking connections to get it cashed. Rochelle did as told, ripping a check from the money market bank book. When Lee Alderton discovered the missing check and told Nancy, Nancy immediately suspected Rochelle. Bert didn't believe it, of course, but Nancy was adamant. She'd caught Rochelle going through her things before. Finally Bert agreed to look in Rochelle's backpack while Nancy watched. Sure enough, they found the money market check."

Montana shook his head. "Rochelle had her daddy twisted around her finger. She cried and told him it was just a joke. Of course, he believed her. She said she'd learned her lesson. As far as Bert was concerned, that was that."

"But Lee had talked to Fareed, right? He must have spoken with Nancy about the check," I said from the comfort of one of Leighton's wonderful club chairs.

"He did," Sanders agreed. "Because they were old friends and because Mr. Farkada knew how much it meant to Mrs. Owens that she be the one to present the check to Prince William, he let it slide. He'd had problems with his own son, so he understood how difficult things could be. As a sign of good faith, he actually let Mrs. Owens continue to hold onto the cashier's check for a million dollars after it was written. Of course, Rochelle knew all this. Her father told her everything. That was another reason she hated her stepmother. Before Mrs. Owens came along, Rochelle was her father's only confidant."

"The terrorists hadn't given up," Montana picked up the narrative, "the minute they heard about the cashier's check, they put plans in place to grab it. They instructed Rochelle to get her father out of town. She begged Mr. Owens to take her to Chicago for an exhibition at the Museum of Science and Industry. He agreed, not knowing he was a pawn in a deadly chess game."

"Nancy was particularly easy to manipulate," Detweiler said. He'd claimed his office chair. From behind his desk, his eyes were sad. I could tell he was thinking about the terrible position she had been in. "She only cared about two things: Zoo Keepers and Bert. With Bert out of town, it was easy to move Nancy around. Rochelle got her hands on her father's phone. She texted Nancy saying that he'd forgotten something important having to do with his business. Rochelle, pretending to be her father, instructed Nancy to drive to Ferguson were she'd be met by a courier. That's one of the text messages Nancy got during that last Zoo Keepers' meeting."

"The other text was from Mrs. Alderton's phone." Sanders gave a little snort of anger. "This is where you really have to wonder if some people are born mean or just plain irresponsible. The terrorists got to the janitor at the Meyer Building. They bribed him to take the day off. Can you believe it? How irresponsible is that? He hands his keys to one of the terrorists and spends the day at home watching TV. When Mrs. Alderton had stepped out of the board room to help Annie Patel with the coffee machine, the fake janitor grabbed her phone. Then he sent Mrs. Owens a text message from Mrs. Alderton's phone accusing her of being a thief and a liar. Nancy Owens read it during the board meeting, and she was steaming mad."

Montana chimed in. "You have to put yourself in Mrs. Owens' place. She's sitting in a board meeting, across from a woman who discovered a missing check, and now that same woman is calling her a thief and a liar."

"Of course, this whole time, Lee is acting perfectly pleasant. Why wouldn't she? She has no idea what's going on or that her phone was missing," Detweiler said, filling in the blanks.

I understood what happened next. "When Nancy bumps into Lee in the restroom, Nancy goes ballistic."

"That's right," Sanders said, nodding his agreement. "That

little spat in the bathroom and the text from Mrs. Alderton's phone threw suspicion on her. It was flimsy stuff, but the terrorists knew it would give them a head start."

"But who actually shot Nancy Owens?" Brawny asked. She was in the other club chair. "I heard she was sitting in her car with the engine running and the windows down when it happened."

"On the face of it, her behavior did sound reckless," Sanders said. "But you have to remember, she'd gotten a message from Bert, or so she thought. He asked her to meet a courier in the parking lot up in Ferguson. She expected to be handed a package. Of course, the fake courier knew she had the envelope with the cashier's check. He'd watched her put it in her purse."

I put the pieces together in a flash. "Then then shooter had to be the janitor, right? He was able to keep tabs on Nancy through the CCTV in the Meyer Building. He locked up after her and followed her to Ferguson. When he approached Nancy in her car, she thought he looked familiar. That's why he was able to walk right up to her and shoot her point blank."

"That's right." Sanders heaved a big sigh. "We asked local law enforcement to keep it quiet that the check had been stolen from Nancy Owens' car. That wasn't entirely true. The cashier's check was taken. Of course, we couldn't keep it a secret for long. Fareed Farkada found out, and he had to tell the board. Otherwise he would have taken the blame. Besides, the board all knew that Nancy Owens was dead, and she'd wanted to hand Prince William the check. For that reason alone, they had to change their plans. Naturally, they'd ask where the check was."

Montana chimed in. "With all the anti-Muslim sentiment in this country, setting up Mr. Farkada to possibly take the blame for the missing money was a stroke of genius—and another red herring that sent local law enforcement sniffing down the wrong foxholes."

I still didn't understand one crucial point in this whole scheme. "Why did Nancy Owens have to die? Because she recognized the janitor?"

"No." Detweiler spoke softly. I could tell this was the part of his job that wore him down. "If you recall, Mrs. Owens was Hungarian. It was because of her efforts that St. Louis joined with Budapest in the Sister City program. The real Hungarian ambassador was actually an old classmate of hers. That was yet another reason she'd been so thrilled to be handing over a big check to Prince William. Like most of us, she was happy to be able to show an old friend how well her life had turned out.

"But Rochelle knew about her stepmother's friendship with the ambassador. In fact, Bert and Nancy had even invited the ambassador to have dinner with them after the event at the zoo. So Rochelle passed along that information to the terrorists as well. When they heard that Nancy knew the ambassador, they panicked. You see, they'd planned all along to swap out a fake ambassador for the real one. It was their Plan B if they couldn't steal the cashier's check before the ceremony. Plan A called for the fake to muddle his way through the event and then run off with the check. His job was to get it to their bank in Chicago. The fake diplomat knew just enough Hungarian to fake his part, but he wasn't careful about his pin."

Sanders slapped his knee. "That dope actually borrowed a flag of Italy! That's why it caught your eye, Mrs. Detweiler."

"But to answer your question, honey," Detweiler continued, "Nancy Owens had to die because otherwise she would have recognized that the Hungarian ambassador was a fake. The terrorists thought that shooting Nancy would solve all their problems. And it very nearly did."

"Okay," I said, "but why didn't the janitor try to deposit the cashier's check for a million dollars immediately after he killed Nancy? Why did he wait?"

"He waited because his instructions were to hand the check over to Rochelle. She would pass it to the fake ambassador, and he would take it to Chicago. We've had our eyes on a bank up there that the terrorists have done business with in the past. In fact, we haven't shut down their operation because it's been useful to track money as the terrorists move it around. If they tried to present the check down here, someone would have surely asked questions. But up there, they had a good shot at getting the funds."

I still didn't understand. "Why hand it to Rochelle? Wasn't she superfluous at that point?"

"Yes, she was," Sanders agreed. "You are right. They had two choices, kill her or blackmail her. They decided she might be useful in the future. By asking her to hand the check to the ambassador, they protected the identity of the fake janitor, and they got her so deeply involved that they knew they could control her from then on out."

"What happens to Rochelle now?" I wondered.

"She'll face charges," Sanders said. "It is my intent to see that she is charged with everything we can. Then we'll stand back and see what sticks. Providing material support and resources to terrorists will just be the start. Frankly, the law is overly broad and non-specific, but in light of this case, it's just the ticket. Rochelle's also an accessory to murder. Although a good attorney will argue that she didn't know her stepmother would get killed, she did knowingly put Mrs. Owens in grave danger. After Mrs. Owens died, Rochelle was less than candid. She covered up the crime. She also knew that the money was going to support terrorism. Granted, she can argue that she thought it was going to stop animal cruelty, but I bet when we crack open her social media, we'll be able to prove she knew all along that the goal wasn't to set the penguins free."

He grinned. "By the way, please tell your daughter that was

one impressive escape plan. Who would have guessed that penguins could be so uncooperative? And those fish sticks? Brilliant. Absolutely brilliant. Your Anya has a fabulous career ahead of her if she decides to go into law enforcement. We can always use bright agents who think outside of the box."

EPILOGUE

"I'm sorry you didn't get to speak directly to Prince William or the Duchess of Cambridge. I know that's a big disappointment, honey." I hugged my daughter when she finally got out of bed and wandered into the kitchen. She must have been exhausted because she didn't wake up until one.

"It's okay. Brawny taught me a line from a poem by Robert Burns. It says things *gang aft agley*, and that means stuff happens. But *gang aft agley* sounds a lot cooler, doesn't it?"

"It sure does." I passed along the compliment she'd been paid by Special Agent in Charge Sanders. Anya beamed with pride.

"Wow. Do you think he'd write me a recommendation?"

"I think if you stay in touch with him, he would. After all, he probably doesn't solve a lot of cases that involve penguin parades at a zoo. I have a hunch you'll be easy to remember. That said, Anya, you scared the dickens out of me. What possessed you to head straight for the penguins?"

"That story I told you about the one man who got knocked around by those Emperor penguins. Remember? There was another story, too. I stumbled over it while I was doing my research. Did you know that when Newt Gingrich was running for president, he visited our zoo? Yes, it's true. And guess what? He got bitten by a penguin. The bird tried to chomp off his finger. How funny is that? I guess he has this habit of posing with animals, but—" and she shrugged "—I bet next time he'll skip posing with the penguins."

"How bad was the bite?"

"Bad enough that he had to wear a bandage." Anya laughed. "Want to hear what makes it even funnier? He was here for a meeting of the NRA, the National Rifle Association. I bet he never expected an attack by an unarmed bird. Get it? Penguins don't have arms!"

"I got it." I pulled her close and kissed the top of her head. "It's so good to have you home again and to hear you laugh."

"Yeah, I don't like being upset. At first, it's sort of thrilling, but it gets old fast. I'm glad to be home."

I spoke to her scalp. "Everything okay between you and Brawny?"

"Better than okay. She didn't tell you?"

"Tell me what?"

"I'm in charge of getting speakers for our student government meetings. I asked our sponsor, Mrs. Phelps, if I could ask Brawny. She said sure, and then when she heard all about Brawny's background, she went to the headmaster and asked if he'd hold a special convocation in the chapel. Brawny is going to come and talk to the whole school, all of CALA, about growing up with gender confusion and how she served her country anyway. She's going to talk about listening to yourself, knowing who you are, and not burning your bridges with other people who have trouble accepting you. I've already told a few of my friends at school about her, and they think she's absolutely awesome!"

"I think *you* are absolutely awesome, young lady." I kissed her on the cheek. For a while, we just sat there. I held her and she let me, even though we both knew that one day soon she would be too big for this.

"Fish sticks," I said. "Honestly. Who would guess that terrorist would get brought down by a couple of fish sticks."

"It worked, didn't it? I knew the penguins would go for it." Anya paused and pressed her hand to her tummy. "By the way, Mom, what's for dinner? And please, please, please, don't say fish sticks."

—THE END—

KIKI'S STORY CONTINUES...

Fatal, Family, Album is part of a series of books and short stories that continue with *Grand, Death, Auto: Book #14 in the Kiki Lowenstein Mystery Series.* Get your copy today by going to https://amzn.to/2oB6uLC

OUR FREE GIFT FOR YOU

Kiki and I have a Free Bonus Gift for you. It's a digital book with craft ideas and recipes. Just go to
https://dl.bookfunnel.com/fsu24mc5qi
All best from your friend,
Joanna

P.S. If you enjoyed this book, I hope you'll consider writing a review and posting it on Amazon or Goodreads. In today's crowded marketplace, more and more of us turn to reviews to make purchasing decisions. (I always read all the reviews before I buy. Even the bad ones, because they are enlightening.) Your opinion matters. In addition, I read reviews to get a better understanding of what you, my readers, like and enjoy. So...thanks in advance.

THE KIKI LOWENSTEIN MYSTERY SERIES

BY JOANNA CAMPBELL SLAN

Every scrapbook tells a story. Memories of friends, family and ... murder? You'll want to read the Kiki Lowenstein books in order:

Love, Die, Neighbor (The Prequel) —

*

Paper, Scissors, Death
(Book #1 — Agatha Award Finalist)

*

Bad, Memory, Album
(Exclusive Full-Length Book that's a gift for Newsletter
Subscribers. Get your copy here
https://dl.bookfunnel.com/cy5ba6qiqs

*

Cut, Crop & Die (Book #2)

*

Ink, Red, Dead (Book #3)

*

Photo, Snap, Shot (Book #4)

*

Make, Take, Murder (Book #5)

*

Ready, Scrap, Shoot (Book #6)

*

Picture, Perfect, Corpse (Book #7)

*

Group, Photo, Grave (Book #8)

*

Killer, Paper, Cut (Book #9)

*

Handmade, Holiday, Homicide (Book #10)

*

Shotgun, Wedding, Bells (Book #11)

*

Glue, Baby, Gone (Book #12)

*

Fatal, Family, Album (Book #13)

*

Grand, Death, Auto (Book #14)

*

Law, Fully, Dead (Book #15 — 2020 release)

THE BACKSTORY: BLENDED FAMILIES

A blended family occurs when parents who have children from other relationships form a new family unit. At least half of the children in the United States live with a biological parent and a step-parent. When the bliss of a new relationship between consenting adults wears off, they might well find themselves in the midst of a pitched battle as they try to merge two families.

Dr. Phil McGraw is fond of saying that if a person didn't raise a child before the age of four, that person will never be truly considered a parental figure. It is wise to remember that although a parent may choose another partner, the child hasn't made (and might never make) the choice to accept the newcomer. Of course, beyond the particular problems inherent in every family, a blended family has specific and unique concerns.

1. Discipline. Often parents feel a tremendous amount of guilt after a divorce. To ease that emotional burden, they might not discipline their children as they should. One sociologist calls this the Disneyland Dad (or Mom) syndrome. The absent parent swoops

in, showers a child with gifts and privileges, and leaves. That forces the custodial parent to be the "bad" parent.

2. Sibling rivalry. A child might go from being an only child to another spot in the birth order ladder. An older child might go from being a parent's confidante to a child again. Children near the same age may feel intense competition with each other. Whatever the change is, someone is likely to feel left out or hurt. It's important to keep the lines of communication open. Do not have unrealistic expectations! Finding a new place in the family tree will take time.

3. The other spouse. On occasion, a former spouse will try to sabotage a new marriage by using a child as a wedge. This can be disastrous for all involved. The child can become a pawn and actually have his/her needs ignored while the parents act out a power struggle.

4. Turning two into one. There are a myriad of problems to be solved as every family has its unique culture, traditions, and habits. Whether it's how to celebrate the holidays or what brand of toilet paper to buy, someone will need to make an adjustment.

From all I've read and seen, anyone attempting to raise a blended family should first go through couples counseling. The advice of a disinterested professional is critical to making such a huge transition work. After all, if it doesn't work, there's more at stake than a divorce. There are children who will suffer from additional upheaval in their lives.

ACKNOWLEDGMENTS

Many thanks to the wonderful people who've helped me with this book: Allyson Faith McGill, Amy Gill, Amy Goodyear, Dru Ann Love, Lynn Tondro Bisset, Marla Husovsky, Tricia Yifat Cestare, Nena Hanna, Frank Wright, Bronwyn Best, and Frances Walker.

Special thanks to my dear pal and Author Assistant, Sally Lippert, and my Queen of All Proofreading, Wendy Green.

Also I want to express my appreciation to Lee and Jeff Alderton, who are really much, much more terrific than any characters who'll ever appear in my books. Love you, guys!

THE CARA MIA DELGATTO MYSTERY SERIES

BY JOANNA CAMPBELL SLAN

A contemporary spin-off from the Kiki Lowenstein Mystery Series, these romantic mysteries are set on the Treasure Coast of Florida. Cara Mia Delgatto desperately believes in second chances. But when she stumbles over a dead body is it too late for her to start over?

Tear Down and Die (Book #1)

∾

Kicked to the Curb (Book #2)

∾

All Washed Up (Book #3)

∾

Cast Away (Book #4)

Sand Trapped (Book #5) – 2020 release

LET'S STAY IN TOUCH

List of Joanna's Works
http://tinyurl.com/JoannaSlan

∼

Amazon
http://bit.ly/Joannasbooks

∼

Joanna's Website
http://www.JoannaSlan.com

∼

BookBub
http://bit.ly/JCSlanBookBub

∼

Facebook
http://www.Facebook.com/JoannaCampbellSlan

Joanna's Coloring Club
http://www.Facebook.com/groups/1913215222271455/

Joanna's Readers Page (Cool Girls Club)
http://www.Facebook.com/groups/1602372550058785/
http://bit.ly/IamaCoolGirl

Blog
http://www.JoannaSlan.blogspot.com

Twitter
http://www.twitter.com/JoannaSlan

LinkedIn
http://www.LinkedIn.com/in/JoannaSlan

Instagram
http://www.Instagram.com/JCSlan

Goodreads
https://www.goodreads.com/JoannaCampbellSlan
http://bit.ly/JCSGoodRead

Pinterest
https://www.pinterest.com/joannaslan/

ABOUT THE AUTHOR

JOANNA CAMPBELL SLAN

New York Times bestselling, national bestselling, Amazon bestselling, and award-winning author Joanna Campbell Slan has written and/or edited 40 books, both fiction and non-fiction. She was one of early Chicken Soup for the Soul contributors, and her stories appear in five of those *New York Times* bestselling books.

Her first non-fiction book, ***Using Stories and Humor: Grab Your Audience,*** was endorsed by Toastmasters International, and lauded by Benjamin Netanyahu's speechwriter. She's the author of three mystery series. Her first novel — ***Paper, Scissors, Death (Book #1 in the Kiki Lowenstein Mystery Series)*** was shortlisted for the Agatha Award. Her first historical mystery — ***Death of a Schoolgirl: Book #1 in the Jane Eyre Chronicles*** — won the Daphne du Maurier Award of Excellence. Her contemporary series set in Florida continues this year with ***Cast Away (Book #4 in the Cara Mia Delgatto Mystery Series).*** In addition to writing fiction, she edits the Happy Homicides Anthologies and has begun the Dollhouse Décor & More series of "how to" books for dollhouse miniaturists. Recently, one of her short stories was accepted for inclusion in the prestigious ***Chesapeake Crimes: Fur, Feathers, and Felonies*** anthology.

A former talk show host and sought-after motivational speaker, Joanna has spoken to small and large (1000+) groups on four continents. *Sharing Ideas Magazines* named her "one of the top 25 speakers in the world."

When she isn't banging away at the keyboard, Joanna keeps

busy walking her Havanese puppy, Jax. An award-winning miniaturist, Joanna builds dollhouses, dolls, and furniture from scratch. She's also an accredited teacher of Zentangle. Her husband, David, owns Steinway Piano Gallery-DC and five other Steinway piano showrooms. The Slans are the proud parents of one wonderful son, Michael, who is married to a terrific young woman, Chelsea.

Visit Joanna at http://www.JoannaSlan.com

Made in the USA
Las Vegas, NV
30 May 2024

90525979R10164